LIVEON - NO EVIL

STACY EATON

❀ Created with Vellum

OCTOBER - JACQUELYN

here are two things that inevitably happen whenever you are picking someone up at the airport. First, you could be running late—like really late, and when you finally do arrive, you find the person you're meeting standing by the curb tapping their foot with impatience because their plane arrived ten minutes early. Or, you might be extremely early just to find out that the plane is running on its own backward schedule. The latter would be today.

So here I find myself standing in the terminal at the airport looking up at the arrival screen and re-reading that my friend's flight is still thirty minutes out. Wonderful, just freaking wonderful. Like I've got nothing better to do than to sit around and wait for Rebecca to get in.

Oh wait, I didn't have anything better to do. That's right. I had no life other than my extremely busy career and hanging out with a few friends once in a while. I didn't have a family waiting at home for me or any pets that need attention. It's just little ole me, Jacquelyn Liveon.

I glanced around and found a solid white pillar to lean against where people couldn't walk up behind me. I don't like people where I can't see them, especially ones I don't know. As a police officer, it's been ingrained in my brain that you always know what's at your back. No matter where I am, I always prefer to be against a wall or facing the doorway so that I can see what's coming my way. I don't like surprises—ever.

I stood against the cool stone and scanned the area for a few minutes. If I must be in a crowd, I like to people watch. People watching is another thing that police officers like to do, more out of habit than anything else. By watching closely, we can read what's going on. We rely heavily on body actions to tell us when a person is being honest or about to become aggressive.

As I glanced around, I saw a guy trying to pick his right nostril without being seen; he wasn't doing a very good job at it and I wrinkled up my nose and continued to observe the crowd. A woman in a tight white pencil skirt—totally inappropriate for flying, in my opinion, was trying to work a wedgie out of her butt crack by walking funny. She was getting quite a bit of attention and not just from me. Several tired looking male businesspersons rolling their briefcases or overnight bags watched her walking wiggle. At this time of night, they were probably just making it home after a long day of work. Sad to think, she was their entertainment.

It wasn't all that busy here since it was nine o'clock at night. The rush was over for the day, but there were still a good number of people wandering and waiting. I looked at my watch, another twenty minutes until Becca's plane landed. Damn, I wish I'd grabbed a cup of coffee before I got here; I passed a popular coffee shop about ten minutes away from the airport, but I was worried I'd be late if I stopped. Being the good friend that I am, I had passed up on my need for caffeine. There weren't any coffee stands on this side of the security gate either, so I had to wait until we left to get my much needed fix.

I pulled out the cellphone that I'd slipped into the side pocket of my cargo pants and browsed through some work emails that I hadn't had a chance to answer. Occasionally, like every ten seconds, I lifted my head and glanced around, keeping my eye out for any trouble. It was a hazard of the job, never fully being able to relax, always waiting for something bad to happen, or for someone to yell for help.

I went back to my emails after watching a family drag four suitcases and two exhausted children past me. I wasn't sure who I felt sorrier for, the parents or the kids. I snickered to myself as I typed a response.

Maybe it was the energy that caught my attention next, or just the fact that there was a lot of movement to my right, but I turned to find an entourage of people coming in from the parking garage. They climbed onto the walking escalator; the one that makes you feel like you're walking three steps for every one you actually take.

I actually really liked walking on those. I wish I had one of those for life, I could zip right past the bullshit. Although with my luck, I'd end up behind the group. There were signs above them that explained how to use it in both words and pictures. One side for walking, one for standing, but obviously, the entourage wasn't paying any attention. They were the type who got under my skin because they stood in a large group and blocked the passing lane.

Everyone in the group appeared happily excited as they were talking over one another. There were six people in the group, two men and four women, all dressed casually but expensively, and they appeared to be traveling light with only one small bag for each of them. I watched as they climbed off the walking platform and looked around, unsure of exactly where they were going.

I figured they were either going to step into the security line or to the ticket counter. They did neither. They continued to mill around and talk, blocking the exit off the moving platform.

I heard giggling to my left and turned my head to see two young girls, probably around seventeen-eighteen, chortling to themselves and staring at the group. They took out their cellphones and started snapping pictures. When I looked back at the group again, I noticed that one of the men was smiling down into a woman's face. She beamed brightly back up at him.

"Wait till everyone sees these pictures of Ryan Palmer!" I heard one of the girls giggle.

"Oh my God, he is so freaking hot," the other one replied.

Ryan Palmer was a film star, I knew that much, but not much else. He's probably in his late twenties, maybe early thirties, and from the few movies I'd seen of his, he was a pretty good actor. As I watched the group, I saw the man start to glare at the young girls and then quickly look away, turning his back on them to shield his face. Huh, it really was him.

"Did you see that? He just looked at us!" I heard the giddy voices of the girls giggling as they spoke back and forth to each other. Man, to be young and silly again. *Yeah, or not.* I rolled my eyes.

Just then, an airport police officer walked up and told the girls if they didn't get outside and move their car right this second, it would be towed. It was my turn to chuckle. I could only imagine how much that towing bill would cost. I watched as the girls followed the police officer, turning to look over their shoulders at Ryan one more time before he was out of their sight.

I glanced back at the group and saw that Ryan was now eyeballing me. I held his stare for a moment and then looked away. He was most likely wondering if I was trying to snap his picture, too. I shook my head. Not likely. I was not a groupie of any sort, and the thought of falling into the hoopla of some mega movie star was not my deal.

I put my cellphone away and crossed my arms over my chest. I looked over the crowd that had gathered in the area, many of them rubber necking to get a peek at the six people congregating as more and more people began to recognize him. I surveyed them as I waited. One man, about thirty, seemed a bit out of place. It was about seventy-five degrees outside —warm for a fall night—but he was wearing a heavy jacket. Immediately, my instincts were on alert.

I observed him as he peered nervously around; he shoved his hands deep into the pockets of his jacket. I could see a slight sheen of sweat on his face. The fine hair on the back of my neck rose rather quickly. I followed his train of sight and found that it led right to Ryan's group. Ryan was inspecting me again, and I considered him for a moment. I could tell his eyes were a bright blue even from the distance between us. I wondered how much brighter they would look up close. I blinked and looked at the floor. *Where did that even come from?*

I turned my attention back to the suspicious guy, taking in every detail about him. From his thinning brown hair to his metal-framed eyeglasses, all the way down to his ratty Nike sneakers. Something was up, and it wasn't going to be good. *Figures.* I left my off-duty weapon at home. I shook my head at my own stupidity; I never leave it at home. It's always the one thing that you need when you don't have it—right now being the perfect example.

The man continued to peer around nervously and always returned his sight to the group who had now moved over near a window. I continued to keep my eye on him, and I found myself standing up straight, no longer leaning against the pole. My arms came down to my sides and I scanned the large area quickly to see if there were any police officers in the area. Nope, none. Great…just great.

As the movie star entourage started to move toward the security line, the strange guy tensed, and I noticed that there was a bulge in his pocket that caused the material to droop. Based on the sag, he appeared to be concealing something heavy. If I took wild guess, I'd say that it was most likely a gun. Little jolts of adrenaline started to spike through me. This could get really ugly—fast.

The man followed the group toward the security checkpoint. He had to walk quickly to catch up, his strides longer than what was reasonable for a man of his size. I kept pace right behind him, ready to move when I saw a chance. The group was so involved in itself; they didn't notice anything happening around them. Normal behavior for most people.

One of the ladies in Ryan's group dropped something on the ground, and two of the other women stopped to wait for her to pick it up. Ryan and the other two people in his traveling group continued on, oblivious to what was going on behind them. They were separated now, easier to pick them off. This was not good, I moved closer to the suspicious man.

When they were about forty feet from the security checkpoint line, the man began to pull out his hand, and in his palm was a semi-automatic pistol. My instincts had been dead on. I stepped into action without a second thought. Why I did what I did, I will never know; but my actions started a uncontrollable ball to start rolling in my life.

Instead of grabbing the guy or going for his gun, I stepped in front of him, blocking his view of Ryan, who apparently was his target. At the same time, I put my hand on Ryan's arm to gain his attention and push him back. He turned to me, but my focus was already on the man holding the gun, my back to Ryan. I felt him stiffen beneath my touch, or maybe that was the wave of fear that flew out of him and slammed against my back.

I looked the guy in the eye, but he didn't see me; his gaze was trained over my head at Ryan. Although his attention was on the man behind me, he pointed the gun directly at my chest. A fierce stab of adrenaline surged through my veins at the sight of the muzzle. I heard a woman scream, but I didn't look to see where it came from. It sounded like it came from a distance, but my tunnel vision had kicked in and the outside world faded as I concentrated on the subject in front of me.

"Whoa! What's going on?" I asked him quietly as I put my hands up to shoulder height, palms toward him.

The man's gaze flicked to me quickly and then moved back to Ryan. "Move!" he yelled.

"Why are you pointing a gun at me?" I asked him, purposely keeping my voice low. Rule number one for any hostage negotiator was to always remain calm and talk softly, to try to get the person to stop and listen.

He regarded me again, glanced at his gun, and then looked back up at Ryan. "I'm pointing it at him, not you. Move!" he said loudly, although not quite shouting this time.

"Why do you want to point a gun at this guy?" I pointed to Ryan over my shoulder. I still stood directly in front of him and his fear continued to roll over me like a stormy night on the beach. Thank God, I didn't normally get seasick.

The gunman directed his attention back to me, this time keeping eye contact as he spoke. "Because I'm going to kill him. Now move, or I'll shoot you, too!" His voice rose with each word.

"Why would you want to kill this guy?" I turned to glance quickly behind me and saw Ryan staring over my head at the man with the gun.

"Because my wife is in love with him!" he shouted. I almost found this funny. *Almost.* Half of the world's population of women was probably in love with the Ryan. He *was* smoking hot, but you wouldn't hear me say that out loud to anyone.

I heard a small grunt behind me, and I wanted to turn around and slug Ryan; instead, I bladed myself so I stood sideways, and inspected him closely, taking Ryan all the way in. Yeah, he was drop dead gorgeous, but I was able to control my drooling. I learned a long time ago that if someone thought they were good looking, they wouldn't get a bit of attention from me. It only made them more conceited, and I didn't feel the need to contribute to that.

Ryan was peering down at me. Our eyes met for a moment, and when I saw the light blue flecks in his dark blue irises, my heart skipped a beat. I forced myself to turn and face my opponent before I could notice anything else about Ryan.

"Your wife is having an affair with *that?*" I made it sound like Ryan was a total loser, but I was purposefully playing on the guy's feelings.

I felt Ryan's body heat against my back as he stepped closer to me—why I didn't know—but I was torn between wanting to lean back into him and turning around to push him away. I did neither as I observed the profusely sweating man holding the gun in his shaky hand.

As the guy gawked at me in surprise, he glanced at Ryan. I broke my tunnel vision enough to glance around and saw that there were quite a few armed officers in the area now, but unfortunately, they were not well placed. If one of them tried to fire a shot and missed, it would sail past us and strike someone on the other side. We were at a T intersection of the terminal and there was a growing crowd of onlookers. I had to get this guy to calm down quickly before it escalated.

"No! She's not having an affair with him; she's just in love with him. Everything is about him!" The gun in his hand wobbled up and down with his words. "She has pictures of him everywhere in our house and she is constantly watching his damn movies and telling me I need to look more like him." He said the last part bitterly; and, if it was because he was being honest with himself, there was no chance in hell he'd ever come anywhere close to looking like Ryan.

"So you want to kill him, *why?*" I asked quietly, as I drug out the last word, trying to keep him calm so that I could continue to talk to him.

He furrowed his forehead, and anger passed over his features. He pointed the shaky gun out further toward us. "If he's dead, then she can't love him anymore," he said sternly. I didn't think his reasoning was very sound, but, hey, whatever; they were his thoughts, not mine.

"I don't think killing him is the answer." I took a slow deep breath and hoped that what I was about to say would get his attention long enough so that I could get the gun away from him. "If you kill him, you will go to jail, and then you won't have your wife at all." I took a very small step toward the man, more of a foot shuffle then a step. "Is that what you want?"

The man scrutinized me, tilting his head to the side, and then glanced over my head at Ryan. He was thinking about what I said. I could almost see the hamster wheel turning in his mind. I took another small shuffle in his direction.

He glanced down at the floor, and for a second, I thought maybe he noticed my foot shuffle, unconsciously he probably did. I took the opportunity to make eye contact with one of the tactical officers. I put my hand out to the side as if I was pushing something away. He seemed to understand, and he murmured into his mic. I watched as he and two others started to move slowly backward, just a few feet.

I nodded as I saw the movement in the corner of my eye stop. Thankfully, the airport police who had just arrived to replace the lower end airport security were good.

"No. Of course I don't want to go to jail. I would rather be dead!" He glared at me, squinting his hazel eyes behind his wire-framed glasses.

He surveyed the onlookers who gathered, and I took the opportunity to take another small step toward him. I was only a couple of feet from him now.

"You don't really want to die. Imagine the pain that would cause your wife." My voice was soft to keep the conversation between us and away from all of the noisy people who were gathering.

"Yeah, I do." He glared hard at me now and a bead of sweat ran down the side of his face.

I maintained eye contact with him, keeping my hands low and in front of me with my palms out to show him I was not a threat. I heard some commotion off to my right, and when I heard the voice, I almost laughed.

"Really, Jack!" a female's voice called out just loudly enough for me to hear. I fought back the laughter when I realized that Becca's plane must have landed, and she was now being held back behind security until we got this issue resolved. If she was able to, she would've walked right into the scene with me.

"I don't think you really do." I cocked my head to the side as I continued to study the man. "Why don't you give me the gun before someone gets hurt?"

He tensed as I spoke, glancing over his shoulders again at the police officers. Two had M-4 rifles trained on him, they could easily take him out at their distance, but there was a chance that the bullet would pierce his body and travel through to strike someone on the opposite side.

"No," he said and stepped back, pointing the gun at my head as he raised it. Well, shit, not a good feeling. My heart sped in my chest as the adrenaline pumped harder. I heard Ryan shift behind me, but I didn't move. I saw the officers on both sides of us tense. I pushed my hands down toward the ground, hoping that the officers might catch it and calm down a moment before they tried to neutralize the threat.

"I know you don't really want to hurt him. If you do that, it will only hurt your wife and your family, and then you'll spend the rest of your life in jail." My voice belied my racing heart and remained calm. I should get an Oscar for my performance here; maybe Ryan could nominate me. That is, if we lived through it.

"But what am I supposed to do?" he asked, and I realized that I had just hit a crucial point. He was responding to me.

"Hand me the gun, and we can figure it out." I took a step closer to him and started to raise my left hand toward the gun, keeping my palm open and low.

I heard gasps and murmurs from the crowd. I could see flashes going off, bouncing off the glass of the terminal walls, and I knew people had cellphones and cameras out snapping away at the dramatic scene in front of them.

I locked my eyes on the gunman's. He glanced jumped around nervously before it returned to me. He now had the gun pointed at my chest again.

"Please," I said, and took one very slow step toward him.

He stared at me for a long moment, and then contemplated his gun. He nodded once, and everything around us got quiet. Like really quiet, like dead silent. Maybe it was just my tunnel vision kicking back in that blocked everything else out, but I think every person watching stopped breathing at the very moment that I took my next step. I was so focused on what I was about to do, that I neither paid attention, nor cared, what anyone else did. It only mattered what happened in the next few seconds.

I slowly reached out with my left hand to take the gun from him. It was still pointed at my chest, but he was lowering it. I searched his face for any adjustments that might mean he was changing his mind. Just as my hand came in contact with the barrel of the gun, everything moved in even slower motion.

I stepped forward with my left foot and planted it solidly on the ground. As my hand wrapped over the top of the gun covering the slide, I pulled up on the gun, and his hand released its grip. As I twisted slightly to the left, I brought my right leg up to hip level and extending it directly into his midsection. It must have been the extra adrenaline that rushed through me, because he flew about eight feet back and slammed into the thick glass observation wall.

With two hands now on the gun I pushed the button on the grip to release the magazine and slid back the top slide. I heard the magazine clank to the ground and watched as the chambered bullet flew out and began to roll away. With the slide now locked back, I flipped the gun upside down to hang on my finger with my arms above my head. I was not a threat, and I wanted everyone to know that.

Four officers jumped on the guy as soon as he landed on the ground. The gunman was too surprised to fight and laid there considering me with hurt in his eyes. I turned away to look at an officer who was approaching me. He reached for the gun from me, and I pulled it back.

"Either put gloves on or give me an evidence bag. You don't want your prints on this." He looked surprised, but nodded and pulled out some nitrile gloves from his belt pouch.

Another officer approached, and I glanced over my shoulder to where Ryan and his group were all huddled around each other. The woman he had been talking to earlier had her arms wrapped tightly around him. His back was to me, which I told myself I was grateful for.

"You might want to get them someplace secure." I smiled at the new officer and tipped my head toward the group.

He spun around to talk to someone and then looked back at me just as Becca walked up. "Jack, I can't take you anywhere, can I?" She laughed.

"It's your fault. Your damn plane was late." I joined in with her laughter. My adrenaline still blazing through my veins and laughing was the easiest way to deal with it. I would crash later and wonder what the hell had possessed me to do what I'd done.

"I assume you're a badge?" A new officer with the sergeant stripes on his arm asked as he watched the banter between Rebecca and me.

I nodded. "Where do you want me to write my statement?" I raised my eyebrows in question as I slipped my shaking hands into the pockets of my cargo pants.

He chuckled and started to walk away as he led us to an unmarked doorway. He put a piece of plastic up to the panel, and the lock released. As I went to step through the frame, I turned one last time and found Ryan watching me with an intense look on his face. It was a look I didn't want to acknowledge, so I stepped through the doorway instead.

"Can you make sure I'm kept separate from that group back there?" I asked the sergeant who was leading us.

He glanced at me. "Sure, you saved me a lot of problems, I'll do anything you ask." Several officers milled around in the offices and hallways we wound through, and I saw a television hanging in the corner above everyone's heads. Seeing the TV reminded me that during the incident, there were numerous flashes. I wondered how bad the fallout was going to be and where my photos were going to show up online. I physically cringed at that thought. I hated attention.

The sergeant walked me back to a sparse interview room and I sat down to fill out the paperwork that the prosecutor would need from me as a witness, while Becca waited in another area. The sergeant read it over and we both signed the form. He asked me a couple more questions and then I was free to go.

As we left the room, I heard Becca laughing in the hallway. I rounded the corner and saw her staring up at the television. "It's all over the news!" She laughed again.

Great! I turned back to the sergeant. "Do you think you could get me out a back way? I really don't want to deal with that circus," I said as I pointed at the television. They were already interviewing witnesses.

"What? You don't want your moment in the spotlight? You just saved that guy's life!" I wasn't sure if he meant Ryan or the man who held the gun, but either way, a life had been saved—maybe two or three if you counted mine.

"Not my idea of a spotlight." I laughed softly. "I would appreciate a bit of professional courtesy. Could you possibly not tell them who I am? The Palmer group that is?"

He considered my words for a moment. "Wow, you really don't like the spotlight, do you?" He grinned. "Sure, if that's what you want."

Becca and I followed him down another hallway. A few minutes later, we were out of the maze of hidden halls and in the parking lot. With no press around, we quickly made it to my SUV without anyone seeing us.

It wasn't until we climbed into my Jeep that Becca spoke. "You do realize that you just saved the hottest man on the planet, don't you?"

"Whatever, Rebecca."

"If I were you, I would have been all over that! How come you didn't want him to know who you were?" I turned to her as I backed out of the parking space.

"Why would I? The last thing I need, or want, is some crazy thank you. They would turn this into a huge publicity stunt." She laughed as I put the vehicle into drive.

"I can't figure you out. You just saved a man's life—not to mention the hottest freaking actor alive—and you don't even want him to know your name. You never know, maybe he might want to give you a personal thank you gift." She nudged my arm with her hand, and when I peered at her, she winked.

"Oh, give me a break, Rebecca. He's not my type," I muttered as I pulled up to the window and paid for my parking.

"Jacquelyn Liveon, you are the strangest person I know. Anyone else would be begging for that guy's attention. You could have it and yet you turn and run away." She was shaking her head at me.

"I'm not running away. I just don't need the attention, Rebecca. Can we drop this now? How was your training?" I pulled away from the toll-booth and we headed for the highway.

OCTOBER – RYAN

"I like the property Ryan," Kayla said grinning up at me. I gave her a terse smile back. "The area is so large, and so country. The horses in the back are the perfect touch."

"I think it will work out pretty well. It's nice and secluded, but not too far from anything," I replied. We were standing outside of the security checkpoint at the airport waiting for the last member of our group to join us before taking a flight to Los Angeles for a last minute change to a production that we'd just wrapped up.

I glanced around like I usually do when I'm out in public. I was wearing jeans and a T-shirt, and while I tried to blend in, I knew I never did. People always looked at me. If it wasn't for the fact that I was splashed over every tabloid in the world and had eight box office hits in the last four years, I might have been able to blend in better. Unfortunately, I could no longer do that. No matter where I went, there were people watching me and snapping pictures.

Just like the two girls standing over by the glass wall. I tried to turn away from them, but I knew they had already gotten a few shots with their cellphones. They would be on Facebook within minutes, they always were. I glanced back over at them as they giggled and noticed a police officer escort them out. As I looked away, I noticed another woman standing against a pillar.

She was smiling as the officer led the girls away. Her cellphone was in her hand. Was she taking pictures of me, too? Somehow, she didn't seem the type, but I could never really tell. I studied her as she turned my way and met my questioning gaze. We only considered each other for a few seconds before she put her phone back in her cargo pants' pocket, shaking her head.

I examined her for a few more seconds; she had a very confident air about her. The tan cargo pants with her un-tucked brown T-shirt made her look rather earthy—natural—fun. She had a physical look about her, as if she liked adventure and I watched as her eyes constantly roved the area.

"So when are we moving in?" Kayla asked. I tore my gaze away from the woman. I wasn't sure why Kayla thought she was moving in with me, we had only been seeing each other for a few months. I was already tired of her constant chatter and endless need to be in the spotlight all the time.

I ignored her question as I spoke with my agent, Beth, for a minute. "How much longer do we have to wait? I should probably get down to the gate. I can't afford to miss this flight."

"Yeah, we should probably head down that way." The answer didn't come from Beth, it came from Troy, my bodyguard. Troy, a longtime friend of mine, was big enough to be opposing and smart enough to know when to use his strength. He was also the one I enjoyed hanging with to hide from the real world, drinking a few beers and watching football or hockey on television.

As we waited for Beth and her two friends to get their identification and tickets out for security, I glanced around again and saw that the woman who was leaning against the pillar earlier was now standing up straight and staring at something, her level of alertness gave me pause. Her arms were at her side, and her chin up as she looked at a group of people. Just as I was about to look away, she eyeballed me again. Our gaze held longer this time, and I waited until she broke the connection. Kayla kept talking beside me as our entire group made its way to security. I was good with selective hearing, so I tuned out her endless chatter.

I walked ahead of my group, and Kayla and Troy quickly caught up to me, but stayed two steps behind. Beth and her friends lagged, but I wasn't worried about it. I could hear Troy and Kayla as they talked about their seating arrangements, and I mulled over how to tell Kayla that she wasn't moving in with me.

Just before we entered the security line, I felt a hand on my arm as it pushed me with enough force to be more than a casual brush. I stopped and turned around to find a man standing in front of me with a gun pointed at me. Shock made me motionless, but I managed to glance down and see that there was someone between us. It was the woman in the tan cargos. How had she gotten next to me, and why the hell was the guy pointing a gun at me?

The woman started talking to the guy quietly. I was glad that someone was thinking, because my brain had gone black blank with one look at the gun.

I tore my eyes from him and took in the woman's blond hair. She was probably around five and a half feet tall and I could see completely over her head.

I heard her ask the man what was going on.

He looked at her quickly and then flicked his eyes back to me. "Move!" he yelled, and I flinched. Why wasn't she moving? If someone was pointing a gun at me and told me to move, I would. I wanted to, but my feet felt glued to the floor.

"Why are you pointing a gun at me?" she asked him, her voice soft and smooth.

He looked at her again, glanced at his gun, and then focused on me. He told her he wasn't pointing it at her; though, actually, he was. I wasn't stupid enough to think her thin frame would stop a bullet if he decided to fire at that close of a range.

"Why do you want to point a gun at this guy?" The woman jabbed her thumb over her shoulder at me.

The guy looked at her hard. "Because I'm going to kill him. Now move, or I'll shoot you, too!" he shouted. His words ran quickly through my mind as nausea grew in the pit of my stomach.

"Why would you want to kill this guy?" I saw her look over her shoulder, but I was staring at the gun. I knew Kayla was behind me and, for once, she wasn't talking. Troy was to her left, and neither of them moved a muscle. It wasn't like he could do much anyway.

The man with the gun shouted that his wife was in love with me and I cringed. I had heard this before, although I had never had a jealous husband threaten to kill me because of it. I made a sound low in my throat. I wanted to speak, but I couldn't get the words out over my dry tongue.

The woman turned sideways, and I met her serious expression. She appeared so calm. How could she be so damn calm? She inspected me from bottom to top, stopping when our eyes meet. Her eyes were heated, intense, and a light clear blue, like the summer sky. I kept staring at her until she turned away.

"Your wife is having an affair with *that?*" The way she said that made it sound like I was a piece of low-life trash, not exactly what I expected after seeing the heat flare in her eyes. Somehow, I wanted to prove that I was more than that, and I took a step closer to her, finally finding the strength to move my feet.

"No! She's not having an affair with him; she's just in love with him. Everything is about him! She has pictures of him everywhere in our house, and she is constantly watching his damn movies and telling me I need to look more like him." *Yuck, that's kind of creepy.*

"So you want to kill him, *why?*" the woman asked. I wanted to know that same thing. Why did he want to kill me if it was his wife with the fatal-attraction problem?

My knees almost buckled when he answered.

"I don't think killing him is the answer," the woman responded.

I couldn't agree more, and I couldn't believe she was able to speak so calmly. I wasn't sure I could have gotten a word out without stuttering. It's amazing how different it feels when you're filming a movie, and someone points a gun at you. You know it's not real. But *this*, this was way to fucking real.

"I don't think killing him is the answer. If you kill him, you will go to jail, and then you won't have your wife at all." *Hell, he's still going to jail even if I'm not dead.* "Is that what you want?" This woman had a death wish, I realized, when I saw her move closer to the gunman.

The crazy man stared her down and then glared at me. As our eyes locked, I could have sworn she took another step closer to him.

It was at the moment when I noticed all of the activity around us. There were people on both sides, most of them at a distance, except for about eight officers all with their guns drawn and aimed in our direction, a couple were long guns. My stomach heaved thinking about being in the center of this three-ring circus. Three of the officers slowly moved back. *Hello! Where are you going?*

The guy said he didn't want to go to jail, but didn't he realize he was either going there or to the morgue? I looked back at the lunatic in front of me as he finally spoke again. My eyes widened when he said he would rather be dead. He might be getting his wish if this went on much longer.

"You don't really want to die. Imagine the pain that would cause your wife." She spoke so softly it was hard for me to hear her clearly with my pulse beating so loudly in my ears. *Who cared about how much pain it caused his wife!*

I watched and listened as she went back and forth with him for a few moments, every once in a while, she took a step closer. She was about a foot and a half in front of me when I noticed the back of her shirt. Written in small grey letters between her wide shoulders were the words, "I Fear No Evil." She fears no evil. So that's why she stepped in front of a gunman? This woman was crazy. Mind you, at the moment, I was happy she was standing between us and was able to communicate with him. Nevertheless, she was still crazy. Beautiful, but crazy.

I lifted my head so that I could stare at the man as he spoke. "But what am I supposed to do?" He was speaking intensely with her.

"Hand me the gun, and we can figure it out." She took another step closer and started to reach out to the guy. It was insane, but I wanted to grab her and pull her back to keep her safe.

Cameras flashed all around us as I heard her say very quietly, "Please." She took another step forward, and I stared again at those four simple words on her back: I Fear No Evil.

Everything around us was silent; there was not a sound as everyone looked on, and he finally nodded at her. She took another step, her hand reaching out to him.

Before I could even comprehend what was happening, the woman was standing in front of me with the gun's slide back, and it hung from her pointer finger. Her hands were above her head, and the guy was against the wall sliding down. That was the best action scene I was ever in, and I didn't remember a bit of it.

Four officers were on the guy in a second and they hauled him up off the ground and started to move him away. Kayla threw her arms around me.

"Oh my God, Ryan! Ryan, are you all right? I was scared to death. Who was that man? That woman must be nuts to get in the middle of it; maybe she was in on it. Maybe, it was all a publicity stunt."

"Kayla, I'm fine. Would you do me a favor and hush for a minute, please." My arms shook. The whole episode had been so quick and surreal. I looked up to find the woman and speak with her, but she had walked toward a door off to the side. She was following an officer and there was another woman with her.

Our eyes locked for just a moment before she nodded once and disappeared behind the white metal door. I wanted to say thank you, but how do you express such gratitude with two simple words? As she left my sight, I vowed I would find her and thank her later.

"Sir, we need to get you and your party into our offices for your statements." An officer stood in front of me while I continued to stare at the place where I had last seen her. Who was that woman who feared no evil?

"Yeah, sure. Who was that woman?" I asked the officer in front of me.

"Don't know, sir. If you will all follow me, we'll get this done as quickly as possible so that you can still make your flight." The officer turned and started walking away. We all followed, although I was surprised that I could walk with how badly my legs were still shaking. The adrenaline of fear was still rushing fiercely through my blood.

He took us to a non-descript set of offices near the security checkpoint, and gave each of us a statement form to fill out. When I finished, an older man walked into the room.

"Mr. Palmer, if you wouldn't mind, I need to speak to you privately for a few minutes." He motioned for me to follow him. I assumed he wanted to ask me some additional questions.

I followed him down a hallway and into a plain white office. A simple metal table with four chairs sat around it; there were no other furnishings except for a camera mounted on the ceiling and a mirrored window.

We sat down on opposite sides of the table, and the man introduced himself as Lieutenant Dorsey. "Mr. Palmer, I want to make sure you have all your questions answered and you understand how this process will work."

"Actually, I do have one question," I said.

"Sure," he answered and leaned back in his chair.

"Who was that woman who stepped in front of me?" I looked him directly in the eyes. "Does she work for you?"

The Lieutenant studied me for a few seconds. "No, she doesn't work for me; and she requested that we not disclose her name." *Well, maybe that was for the press.*

"To you, or to anyone else," he added after a brief pause.

She didn't want me to know who she was? Why?

"Well, can I at least speak with her?" I leaned forward in my seat, the chair creaked under me. I wanted to thank her for what she did; I needed to understand why she had.

"Mr. Palmer, I'm sorry, but she is involved in a detailed interview right now. I'm afraid you won't have a chance to speak with her before your flight." He appeared completely relaxed sitting across from me.

"Then I'll take a later flight. I'd like to speak with her before I leave."

"Sir," he cleared his throat, "she doesn't want to speak with you. She specifically asked that we keep you and your entourage separate from her, and that we keep her identity private. I have to respect her wishes." He looked down at the table for a second and I had the feeling he was about to say something else, so I waited. "I will tell you that she does work in law enforcement, but that is all I can tell you about her." He had lifted his head back up to face me. "Now, Mr. Palmer, you better get going so you can catch your flight, we are currently holding it at the gate for you all." He stood and dismissed me, just like that.

As my friends and I walked out of the offices and made our way toward the boarding gate, I saw that a TV station was already playing a segment about what happened. Someone had taken video of the incident. I stopped dead in my tracks as I watched the way the woman took the gun from the man and then kicked him across the room. Across the bottom of the screen, were the words, "Who is the heroine?"

I was glad to see they didn't know who she was either. For once, I was happy that the media was involved. They would figure out who she was; it would only be a matter of time. Then I could find her and ask her why she had done that and if she really feared no evil.

OCTOBER – JACQUELYN

"*J*ackie, can you come into my office for a minute." My chief spoke to me over the office intercom system on my desk phone.

"I'll be right there, Chief." I closed the case file I was reading and sat back in my chair with a heavy sigh. I hoped he wanted information on a case I was working, but for some reason I didn't think that was it. If it was, he probably would have mentioned which case, so that I could make sure I had all my information on it.

I figured it probably had more to do with all the events that had taken place over the last week. Hundreds of phone calls were flooding the station, the mail was coming in buckets, people stopped by, and there were endless interview requests. Not to mention the flower deliveries. Dozens of flowers arrived every day from Ryan Palmer's fans. The cards on the flowers said everything from a simple "Thank you for doing what you do," to "You are my idol!" I seriously thought it was ridiculous.

I had no interest in them, and even the guys in the department were running out of people to give to the flowers to, although they were enjoying to food baskets that continued to arrive.

I got up from my desk and walked down the hall to my chief's office. I knocked briefly on the doorframe before stepping inside and found him reading something on his computer screen.

"What's up, Chief?" I sat down in one of the beat-up leather chairs in front of his desk, glancing around his office at the photographs and certificates that lined the walls. I waited for him patiently.

He continued to read and then directed his attention at me as he turned the computer screen to face me. I winced, knowing I did not want to see what I was about to see. *She Fears No Evil* was the headline on the screen. A picture of the gunman, me and Ryan. Palmer was staring at my back, his jaw a little slack.

I sighed and looked away. "Chief, I just want this to end. I'm sorry."

"Jack, we all want this to end. This place is a circus. It's making all the guys nervous, and the residents are even getting annoyed." He leaned back and put his arms on the chair's armrests.

"I don't know how to get it to stop. Trust me, if I could come up with a way, I'd do it." I looked at him. I was tired of the endless phones ringing in the station, and the cameras on me as soon as I walked out the door. They were even camped outside my house now. It was beyond ridiculous.

He took a deep breath and then looked at me hard. "There is something you can do, and," he hesitated, "Well—you're going to do it."

I wasn't sure I wanted to hear what he had to say, but I had to ask. "What's that, sir?"

He put his hands behind his head, slightly ruffling his short brown hair. "You're going to give a press conference in about thirty minutes."

"What!" I wasn't asking a question; I was giving an explicit "Why should I even entertain them?"

He sat up to his desk, both arms resting on its top. "Because, hopefully, it will make them go away. We need to get back to work, and we need all of this nonsense to stop."

I put my hands to my face, covering it to keep my composure. I blew air out in a huff and glared at him. "What am I supposed to say?"

"I can't tell you that. You know how to do press conferences, do what you know." He shrugged. He had a lot more faith in me then I had in myself. "Now, go freshen up and think about what you're going to say."

I clenched my jaw, and would have argued if I thought it might do any good, but I knew it wouldn't. Somewhere inside, I knew this was eventually going to happen, and I'd been dreading it every second. I shook my head and stood, returning to my office just as Susan was walking out of it.

"Hey, Susan. Did you bring me something?" She was our administrative assistant, the one who fielded the majority of the phone calls that were coming in about this whole mess. I owed her a couple of drinks, that was for sure.

"Oh, yeah, I brought you something—another hundred pieces of fan mail." She laughed as she walked away.

I turned to my desk and saw the tray of mail. *You have got to be kidding me!* I picked it up and dropped it into the corner of my office with a loud thud. It would all be filed in the trashcan later.

What the hell was I going to say at this press conference? I had no clue. It's not like I could talk about the incident. It was a current investigation that had not gone to court yet, so there was little I could say about it. I sat down in my chair and stared at the swirling colors on my computer's screensaver.

Time went by way too fast, and before I knew it, the chief was standing at my door. "Let's go, Jacquelyn." I stared up at him for three full seconds, sighed heavily, and then stood, snatching my gray blazer off the hook behind my door before I followed him out. The chief might not be happy about what I was going to say, but I was going to say it, no matter what.

We walked down the hallway toward the township meeting room. Several of the guys on duty followed us down. The nerves in my body tingled on edge and I felt like I was going to throw up as we opened the door leading us down another hallway to the front part of the room. As we got closer, I could hear a lot of people talking. *A lot* of people. I clenched my jaw and fisted my hands at my side.

I had not looked outside to see how many people were out there, so when I stepped into the room and saw it packed with television cameras and reporters, I almost spun and high-tailed it right back out. There must have been at least thirty different television cameras in the room. My chief must have read my face because he grabbed my arm and guided me up behind the podium at the front of the room. I stood to the left of him, my knees shaking under my slacks.

Cameras instantly showed red lights blinking on the front, and digital cameras flashed as people started snapping pictures. There must have been at least a hundred people jammed in this little room. My hands were sweating, and my stomach rolled.

The chief actually thanked everyone for coming, and I fought not to roll my eyes. Then he introduced me, and as I stepped up to the microphone, I thought I was going to be sick. Wouldn't that make for some great news? Swallowing the bile that threatened to come up, I scanned the room. So many people were making such a big deal out of such a small thing. I took another deep breath and began.

"I'm Detective Jacquelyn Liveon. I am a twelve-year veteran of the Rosewood Township Police Department. On the fifteenth of October, I was involved in an incident at the Philadelphia International Airport. During that, a man held a gun directed at Mr. Ryan Palmer, a well-known actor. The gunman was taken into custody without further incident." I scanned the crowd, talking much more firmly than I thought possible with how the butterflies were flying around inside my stomach. "This is all part of an ongoing investigation, and I will say nothing further about it.

"I do not know Mr. Palmer. I had never spoken to him before the situation occurred, I did not speak to him during the incident, and I have not spoken with him since. In fact, I have no intention of speaking with the intended victim at all." I was gaining speed now, and my nerves calmed down. The cameras kept flashing, and the reporters examined me closely.

"I am a sworn law enforcement officer. When I took that oath twelve years ago, I swore to protect not only the citizens of my township, but also the citizens of the Commonwealth and those who are passing through our area. On October 15, I did just that. If the roles were reversed, and Mr. Palmer had been the man with the gun, I would have done exactly the same thing." I narrowed my eyes as I made that point.

"My decision to get involved in that scene was due to the fact that a human being was in need of assistance—not to mention all of the other innocent bystanders. The media has turned this into a circus. Every single one of you have put Mr. Palmer up on a pedestal as a movie star god. He's not. He's a human being. What you all seemed to forget is that while Mr. Palmer was a victim that day, there were other people's lives that have been forever altered due to this situation." I stopped for a second to take a calming breath and allow that to sink in.

"Not only has Mr. Palmer's life been affected, but Mr. Patrick's life has forever changed, too, along with the lives of his family members. I am not a hero. I did what I was trained to do, and that is all." I scrutinized the crowd, and the reporters started to raise their hands to ask questions.

"I do not understand how the media can make such a big deal about this one incident when tragedy strikes everyday all over the place, and none of you care to report about it. Just because Mr. Palmer has his name up on the silver screen, you seem to think he is better than others. He's not." I stopped for a second and more hands went up. I had already decided I was not entertaining questions.

"I will not be answering any questions. In fact, after I leave this podium, I will not speak about this incident with reporters again. I would like to request that all of you pack up your things and leave our township in peace. There are residents and other situations that need our undivided attention. There is no further story here. Thank you for your time." I nodded once and turned to walk away from the podium.

As I began to step down the stairs, I heard one question in particular yelled at me. It made me stop, and I considered the crowd for just a moment. I turned and walked back to the podium. "Who just asked if I really did not fear evil?"

A man from the left side of the room raised his hand. I looked squarely at him. "That is the one question I will answer. Yes," I said quietly, "I fear evil every single day. That was ink printed on the back of my T-shirt. It was just ink."

I turned and walked away quickly, shutting out the rest of the questions and not making eye contact with anyone as I exited the room.

"Jack, you did well." My chief put his hand on my shoulder as we made our way down the hallway. "Now, get out of here. I want you to take the day off. Go relax." I was going to say no, but then I thought about the fact that I really did need to get away from here.

"Mind if I take Susan with me?" I asked as I peered up at him.

He laughed. "No, she could probably use the time off, too." He knew where we would end up—a small dive of a bar where we could hide in the corner. I nodded and went to find Susan.

DECEMBER – JACQUELYN

*C*rime never stops, and around the holiday season, it usually picks up. That is why I found myself at the station at ten o'clock at night two days before Christmas.

I put the case file in my stack to work on when I came back in three days. I was actually going to try to take two full days off; try being the operative word. It had been a while since I took a couple of days off. It wasn't like I had much to celebrate, or even anyone special to celebrate the holiday with. I simply needed a few days of peace and quiet.

Things finally calmed down after my press conference, and for that, I was grateful. The flowers continued to come for a few more days, but even they eventually stopped. Mail still arrived, and I looked behind my desk as I stood up; hundreds of letters had been sent to me, and I had never even read one of them.

I reached over and picked up a handful, flipping through the envelopes and taking in the return addresses. They were from all over the world, and I shook my head in amazement. I was about to drop them back in the mail tray when I saw an envelope with the words "PLEASE READ" written boldly on the front. There was no return address on it.

I put down the other envelopes and looked at that one as I held it in my hand. It was a card envelope, and from the weight of it, I could tell it did contain a card. I opened the envelope and found a plain greeting card with just "Thank you" printed in a soft script on its front.

When I opened the cardstock, the simple pre-printed message on the inside said, "You will never know how much you did for me." The card was signed with blue ink and read, "Please call me, Ryan." Under his name was a telephone number. I inspected the card for a few minutes and ran my fingers over the dried ink. I checked the postmark on the envelope and saw it was dated just last week. I wondered how many other cards he might have sent with this same message.

He had called several times over the last couple of months. I knew that he wanted to say thank you, but I didn't feel it was necessary. I had put the incident behind me, and I wanted to move on with my life. He needed to do that too.

I shoved the card back into the envelope and instead of tossing it into the pile; I dropped it into my backpack and walked out of my office, turning the lights out as I went. It was quiet on this side of the station, but I could hear some of the guys on duty talking in the patrol room, so I worked my way over there to say goodnight to them.

When I walked in, they were having a mini party. They were all kicked back in their office chairs drinking eggnog, that I could only assume was not spiked, and nibbling on cookies. I smiled at the warm scene in front of me; these guys were my family.

"You want some 'nog, Jack?" Brad asked as I walked into the squad room. He sat with his feet up on a desk, a Santa cap lopsided on his head.

"No thanks, I'm gonna head out." I smiled at everyone and wished them all a Merry Christmas. Before I left the squad room, I snagged a candy cane from the table.

"Be careful out there; it started snowing, and the roads are getting slick," Mark said as I made my way to the rear door that led to the parking lot.

"Thanks for the heads up. You guys be safe, too," I called out as I opened the back door.

The wind swirled around me while a cold blast of air hit my face making my eyes water. Damn, it was cold for so early in the season. As I climbed into my Jeep, I thought about how it was really just the start of winter, and it already felt as though it was going to be a long, cold one. I pushed the button for the seat warmer after I started up the vehicle. In my opinion, it was the best option you could have in a car. Before I pulled out, I unwrapped the end of the candy cane and put it in my mouth.

I didn't live that far from the station, but with the way the roads looked, it might take me twice as long to get home as normal. Good thing it was late. I didn't see any other cars out on the roadway as I pulled out of the station's parking lot.

About three miles away, I started to round a curve, and felt my tires start to slide. I took my foot off the gas but didn't touch my brake. I didn't need my tires to skid. As I came around the curve, I saw headlights bouncing off the trees at a weird angle. I was able to get control of my vehicle and allowed myself to slow down as I continued around the bend in the road. When I came out of the curve, I found a vehicle lying on its side in the middle of the asphalt.

"Damn." I stopped as quickly and safely as I could and put my car in park. I didn't see anyone outside of the vehicle, and pieces of it were scattered all over the roadway. I dropped my candy cane in the cup holder and climbed out of my Jeep cautiously to make sure my footing was secure before I moved too fast.

I grabbed my cellphone out of my pocket and hit the county dispatcher's phone number. They answered on the first ring. "Emergency Services," an intense male voice said on the other end of the line.

"This is Twenty-Six David Sixty-One. I have an accident with an overturned vehicle in the twenty-one hundred block of Hill View Road. I'm not sure of injuries yet. Advise my officers to respond and tell them to get our road crew out here immediately with salt. They're gonna need to close off this section of the roadway, too."

"Okay, Jackie. Advise on injuries when you can," answered the guy on the other end of the phone.

Since the guy called me by name, I knew it had to be one of the older dispatchers who knew exactly who Twenty-Six David Sixty-One was. It was my radio call sign, and told the dispatchers what department and officer was calling in, either over the radio or by phone.

I walked around to the front of the car and found the windshield almost entirely smashed out. I could see a man inside the vehicle, and my heart started beating faster. He wasn't moving.

"I have someone inside the vehicle; start Medics, EMS, and fire for extrication," I stated quickly into the phone. "I'm hanging up so that I can try to get to this guy. I'll call back if I need anything else." I didn't wait for a response; I pressed the End button and slid the phone into my jacket pocket.

Luckily, I had leather gloves on for the cold, or I would have cut my hands when I grabbed the front windshield and pulled it back. Auto safety glass was great because it usually stayed intact. You could easily pull it out of the way when you needed to, but it could still cut the hell out of you.

I dropped down on my knees and looked into the vehicle. There was only one person that I could see, and it didn't look like there were any car seats in the back to worry about. The driver of the vehicle was a man, and his head was hidden in shadows, so I couldn't see his face. I shimmied into the vehicle through the windshield and felt glass and rocks crunch under my elbows, knees and hips.

I pulled one of my gloves off so that I could reach out and feel for a pulse. As I touched the side of his face, I saw his eyes flutter. "Oh, thank you, God!" I said to myself softly. His eyes didn't open, but they didn't have to. He was alive, and that was all that mattered.

As I wiggled closer, I tried to get a better look at him. I was halfway through the window when the smell of his cologne caught my attention and I inhaled deeper. The random thought of how sexy it smelled crossed my mind, but I brushed it aside immediately. The man's eyes fluttered again, and he tried to move.

"Don't move. Just stay still. We have help coming." As I spoke, the man's eyes opened, and he turned his head the last bit. My eyes had adjusted to the darker lighting inside the car and it was when his eyes found mine, that I froze. It was Ryan Palmer.

"Quen? Is that really you?" he asked groggily. I felt practically paralyzed seeing him there like this, and then I blinked when I realized he had called me Quen, a name I had not gone by in many years. Why did he call me that?

"Ryan, yes, it's Jacquelyn. Ryan, can you hear me?" I lay down on my side, not concerned about the glass or snow or anything else that might be beneath me. I reached over and pulled my other glove off, taking both of my hands and putting them on the sides of his face.

His eyes fluttered again as I touched him. "Can hear you," he said very quietly.

"Ryan, I need you to stay with me I need you to stay awake. Can you do that?" I held his head so that he wouldn't move his neck. There was a laceration along the side of his face; a small stream of blood trickled down. Normally, I would have been concerned, but I didn't have time to worry about having my hands in his blood. I was more worried about him staying conscious until the EMS and Medics arrived.

"Trying," he mumbled, attempting to open his eyes again.

"Ryan, you don't need to open your eyes. Relax, and just stay with me. I'm right here, I'm not going anywhere. I'm going to make sure you get help." My heart was beating hard against my chest, and as I lay there staring at him, I couldn't help but think back to when I had first seen him in October. He was so vibrant looking, tall, smiling, and full of humor—not to mention totally freaking gorgeous.

He managed to open his eyes; I was only about eight inches from his face. It took him a second to focus, and I could see him trying. "I need to see you," he said quietly as his heated breath vaporized in the cold air between us. I felt him start to move.

"Ryan, stay still. I need you to stop moving. Can you tell me what hurts?" I was so afraid that he might have hurt his neck. I already knew he probably had a concussion, but I was praying it wasn't something more serious.

He didn't listen to me, and his arm slowly made its way up along my side. I felt his hand touch my shoulder and then his hand came to my face. He cupped my cheek and looked into my eyes. Even in the dim light, with pain etched across his face, I could see the flecks in his blue eyes. "Jacquelyn," he said softly. "I knew I would see you again."

I heard sirens in the distance, and I knew it would be some of my guys. "Yeah, well I never thought I would see you again." I couldn't tell him that I had dreamed of seeing him, but I never actually thought that I would be face to face with him again, and sure as hell not like this.

The sirens grew closer and cut off. Someone would be here in a minute and the fact that help was on the way soothed me. I was afraid of how Ryan looked. His eyes seemed to be going in and out of focus.

A very small smile was on the edge of his mouth, and then he winced. "Ryan, what hurts? Can you to tell me what hurts?" I was getting more worried about him by the second.

"My head," he said quietly.

"Okay, anything else?" I asked, looking his face over. He closed his eyes and winced. Sometimes pain was easier to deal with when you shut your eyes. I knew that from experience.

"My left shoulder."

He was lying on that shoulder; I wasn't surprised it hurt. I could hear multiple sirens in the background now, and the sound of booted feet moved toward me. I wanted to look to see who it was, but I couldn't tear my gaze from Ryan's face.

"Why didn't you call me?" he asked when he got his eyes open again.

I didn't know how to answer that, so I was glad when I heard Brad behind me.

"Jackie, what do you have?" he said as he bent down behind me tapping my foot.

I glanced over my shoulder to look at Brad; he still wore the Santa cap. "Head injury, possibly neck and shoulder injury. He was unconscious when I arrived." I saw Brad nod. "And Brad," I stopped, not sure how to say this. "It's Ryan Palmer."

His eyes popped wide open. "You're kidding me?"

"No. We need to keep this quiet. Make sure no one snaps any photos or gives anything out over the radio. Tell the Incident Commander for the fire department they are not to take any photos. We can supply them with pictures if they want to put them on their site later. I don't want anything showing Ryan. Got it?"

"Yeah sure, Jack." We both heard car doors closing, and Brad turned from me to go talk to the emergency responders who had finally arrived.

While I was talking to Brad, I noticed Ryan began to shake. Whether it was from the cold or the shock I wasn't sure, but it worried me more.

"Jackie, can you slide just a bit so I can get in there to him." I heard Scott, one of our medics, speaking to me from outside the car. I shifted to move over and felt something jab me under my right shoulder blade. I winced when pain stabbed through my back, but I didn't make a sound. Ryan's eyes were closed, his breathing was steady, but he was shaking violently now.

Scott slithered in beside me with a collar. "Keep his head still while I put this on." I was glad that he was getting the collar on, my arms were starting to get tired from the position I was holding them, and I felt my body shaking, too. I knew mine was from a mixture of adrenaline and the cold.

After the collar was on, I pulled my hands away. Ryan popped his eyes open. "Don't let go," he pleaded.

"I need to move out of the way so that they can help you. I'm not leaving; I'll be right here."

"What's your name?" I heard Scott ask him.

"It's Ryan, Ryan Palmer," I told Scott. He looked at me, eyes opened wide.

"Seriously?" he asked.

I took a deep breath. "Yes, seriously. You need to keep this as quiet as you can, Scott. No one needs to be near him unless it's absolutely necessary."

He glanced at me, then back to Ryan. Ryan's eyes were open, but they didn't look clear. He was staring at me.

I turned back to Scott as he spoke. "Then you need to stay here next to me and help. The less people near him the better; besides, you know what you're doing here, you can help me with this."

I nodded. Scott gave some orders to people behind us, and someone brought a sheet in to cover Ryan up while they cut up the car to remove him safely. As the motor of the Jaws of Life started, Ryan's hand grabbed my arm. I reached over and held his hand tightly. The sheet metal cried out as a firefighter pried it apart. The joints popped as the roof and car body separated. It was almost surreal being here, under a sheet with Ryan, as they cut the car apart around us. I had seen this done two dozen times from the outside, but I'd never experienced it from within the confines of the work area. It was intense.

Ryan crushed my hand in his grip, and his breathing became strained the longer they worked on the car. Once they had it apart enough that they could get access to him, I told them to keep him covered. I already heard some buzz behind me about who this was. Who said something, I don't know; but it wouldn't be long before everyone here knew the guy with me was a movie star. Not that he was with me.

They worked quickly. I stayed as close to Ryan as I could, talking to him to explain every step along the way about what was going to happen next. At some point, Ryan lost consciousness again, and I prayed that he would make it.

As they pushed his stretcher into the ambulance, I heard someone say behind me, "Jackie, did you know you're bleeding?"

I looked over my shoulder and shook my head. "Not mine, it must be his."

"No, it's yours. There's a cut in your jacket and your back is all bloody." Scott went to touch it, and that is when I felt the sting. I winced.

I must have pushed up against something when I was lying on the ground. The cold from the asphalt must have chilled me enough to dull the pain. Of course, the fact that I was so focused on Ryan probably helped me ignore it, too.

"Climb in. I want to look at your back."

I wasn't planning on going to the hospital, so I hoped it was just a small scratch. I climbed into the ambulance behind an EMT while Scott followed behind me shutting the doors to block the whipping wind out. I hadn't realized how cold I was until I got inside the ambulance and felt the heat blasting through the ceiling vents.

"I'm sorry," I heard a soft male voice call out. I looked down at Ryan who was lying on the stretcher.

"Why are you sorry? You didn't do anything," I said as I examined him. Scott lifted up my jacket and shirt to look at my back.

"Scott, I'm fine. You need to work on him." I shifted so that I could move my back away from him.

"You need stitches for that, Jack," Scott said as I moved away.

"You got hurt because of me," Ryan said quietly. His eyes were brighter in the light of the ambulance, and even though pain was written all over his face, I couldn't help but think how incredibly handsome he was.

"It's no big deal." I turned from him, but he reached out his hand for me. "Look, you need to stop moving around. Please relax as much as you can and lay there; they're gonna fix you up." I took his hand in mine and put it on top of his chest. His hand was cold, and his body shook under our connected hands.

The side door next to me opened and Brad stepped in. "You going to the hospital, Jack?" I didn't get a chance to answer before Scott did.

"Yeah, she needs stitches in her back."

I rolled my eyes. "I'm fine," I said to Brad when he looked at me with concern. "It's just a scratch. Can you have someone follow us to the hospital with my Jeep?"

"Yeah, sure. I'll have one of the guys drive it over." Brad nodded and left the ambulance.

It wasn't long before I felt the ambulance move, and Scott went to work on Ryan. There was one other person in the back with us, a young guy who was a new EMT. He did what Scott asked and kept quiet, sneaking looks at Ryan's face and the way Ryan was staring up at me when his eyes were open.

"Ryan, I need a telephone number so that I can call someone and tell them where you are. Who do you want me to call?"

"Troy. Call Troy; my cellphone is in my jacket pocket." I let go of his hand so that I could pat down his coat. I found his iPhone in the inside pocket and pulled it out. No security password was on his phone. I shook my head. That was dumb not to have it password protected, although it did make things easier for me.

I scrolled through the contacts until I found Troy and pressed the Call button. It took three rings before a deep male voice answered. "What's doing, Ry?"

"Is this Troy?" I asked putting on my professional voice. I heard several voices in the background mixed with loud music.

"Who's this?" I wasn't surprised when he didn't answer my question. I did call him after all.

"Troy, this is Detective Liveon. I'm with Ryan Palmer right now. He was in an accident."

"Is he all right?" Troy sounded worried, and the noise I heard behind him started to fade away. He was probably going somewhere quieter so that he could hear me.

"He's being taken to the Pine Temple Trauma Center. He appears to have struck his head and one of his arms hurts, but that's all I can tell you about his injuries."

"Thank you for calling me." I was about to say, *you're welcome* and hang up, when he asked another question.

"Is this really Jacquelyn Liveon? The same Jacquelyn Liveon from the airport?" I wanted to laugh at the way he phrased it, but the gash on my back was starting to throb.

"Ironically, yes. It's one and the same." Before he could say anything else, I continued, "Will you be coming to the hospital?"

"Yeah, I'll head right over. Is he alone?" he asked me.

"No, I'm in the ambulance with him. I tried to keep it as quiet as I could. I don't need a repeat of the media circus." A deep, warm chuckle crossed through the line, and we hung up shortly after that.

The ride to the hospital took longer than normal thanks to the slick roads, but once we got there, things moved fast. They pulled Ryan from the ambulance, and it took some doing to get him to let go of my hand. I had to promise him I wouldn't leave without seeing him again, and then they whisked him away to be worked on. I felt bad for lying; I had no intention of seeing him again before I left.

A nurse came and took me to another area where she had me get dressed in a gown. I told her it wasn't a big deal, but after she took one look at it, she told me I needed at least a dozen stitches. I felt my shoulders deflate, but I changed and sat up on the bed, knowing I had no choice.

While I waited for the nurse to come back in, I thought about what happened tonight. What were the chances of not only seeing Ryan again, but to find him on the road, in the middle of the night, and hurt? Slim to none. Yet it happened, and right after I opened that once piece of mail that was from him. I shuddered to think about what was going to happen with the media now.

The emergency room was busy, and I didn't expect to get treated as fast as I did. Maybe it had something to do with the person I just brought in. No one said anything to me, but I could hear whispers on the other side of the curtain about how I was with him when the emergency personnel arrived. I could already feel the stories building.

After the nurse stitched me up, she came back and handed me a scrub top. My shirt was soaked with blood, and I appreciated the fact that she'd thought about that. I smiled and thanked her as I tossed my other shirt in the biohazard bin and left the treatment area.

As I walked past the nurses' station, one of them glanced up at me. "There is a guy around the corner who wants to talk to you, Detective." She pointed to the left. I nodded and made my way around the corner.

Three people stood in the hallway, one man and two women. I recognized them instantly and fought the urge to groan. I wanted so badly to turn and walk away, but the man saw me and walked over.

"Detective Liveon," he said as he got closer. He was a tall light-skinned black male with bright brown eyes and strong cheekbones.

"Sir," I said and nodded, "I assume you are Troy? I remember you from the airport." I shook the hand he offered, smiling lightly at him.

"Yes, I'm Troy Reynolds, Ryan's friend. How did you find him?" He watched me closely.

"I was on my way home from work. His car appeared to have lost control on the slick road and struck an embankment. It flipped over on its side."

"Of all the cops, it had to be you who found him. I think fate has something to do with this." He stared me down as if he was waiting for me to deny it.

Fate? Who actually believes in fate? Okay, so maybe the fact that I have been around twice when he needed my help and that just tonight, for the first time, I opened one piece of mail out of thousands, and it had been from him; it might mean something, but I wasn't sure I believed in fate. Troy watched me carefully, and I didn't know how the hell I should respond, so I decided to change the subject. "How is he?"

"He seems to be all right, they should be back any minute. They took him for a head CT." I peered around him and saw that the two women he was with watched us as we talked. I nodded to them.

"Okay, good. Hopefully he'll be all right." I didn't know what else to say, and I felt extremely uncomfortable standing there with Troy towering over me while the other two women practically glared holes in my head.

"If you could, please tell him I hope he feels better soon." I started to turn, but Troy grabbed my arm. I snapped my face around to him and tensed. I didn't like to be touched.

"You aren't going to leave, are you?" he said as he loosened his grip but didn't let go.

"That was my plan." I pulled my arm out of his grasp. "It's been a long day, and I'd like to get home."

He studied me, and I saw anger flash over his face. "You might have to charge me with kidnapping then, because if I let you leave before he gets a chance to talk to you, he's going to kill me, Detective. You have no idea how much I had to endure the last time you disappeared after saving his life."

"I was only doing my job. I didn't need any special thank you then, or now, Mr. Reynolds."

"Would you please stay just a few more minutes? Just let him see you and say thank you." He paused, his eyes begging me. I contemplated what to do. As much as I wanted to just disappear and go home to bed, I also wanted one last chance to see Ryan. I finally consented. "Fine, but I can only stay a few more minutes."

He nodded once, looking relieved. He turned back to the two women and gestured as he said, "This is Kayla Rainey and Beth Bradington." I knew who Kayla was. She was not only the woman who was hugging Ryan at the airport, but she was also an actress and had several movies under her belt. I shook hands with both of them out of professionalism.

Kayla didn't seem at all happy to see me. In fact, the look in her eyes specifically said she didn't want me here. For just a feminine moment, I was glad I stayed. A jealous twinge ran through my veins as I thought about her with Ryan.

It looked like she was about to say something to me, but just then, an aide came down the hallway with Ryan lying on the gurney, and I stepped aside to let them pass. His eyes were closed, and as they wheeled him into a room, I saw the neck brace was off and his head had a bandage on it.

I knew from experience that bright fluorescent lights hurt your eyes like hell after a concussion. Troy headed toward the room, but he stopped and turned to me. I realized he was waiting for me, so I reluctantly followed. I heard Kayla mumble something under her breath. Kayla and Beth started to come too, but Troy stopped them.

"You guys wait out here for a few minutes," he told them pointedly as he closed the door after the aide walked out.

I inspected Ryan lying in the bed, his eyes still closed. The lights were so bright in the room, and I looked around to see what I could do to change that. I walked over to a wall and switched on the lights behind the bed. They were pointed up to the ceiling instead of down. I moved over to the main light and flipped it off. It was darker now, and I knew it would be easier for him to open his eyes.

I turned around and saw him blinking. His eyes finally focused on me, and I stopped moving, not only moving but breathing too. The top of the bed was propped up into a sitting position, and he already looked so much better than the last time I saw him. His blond hair was messy, and he had some caked blood on the side of his face, but his color was better, and his eyes looked much brighter.

Time seemed to stand still as we both studied one another. "You really were there. I thought I had dreamed you," Ryan said softly.

DECEMBER – RYAN

"Hey, did you ever hear from her?"

I watched Troy as he spoke. We've been best friends since high school, and he's the only person who knew I still thought about the mysterious fear no evil detective who saved my life at the airport.

I finished the soda I was drinking. "No." I shook my head.

"I can't believe she never called you back." Troy compressed his lips tightly in a frown. "If it had been anyone else, they would have been all over that."

I nodded absently. "I know."

"She's a rare person," Troy said as he slapped me on the back.

I thought about that for a minute. She was a rare person. There were so many women who only wanted to be near me because of who I was, or what I could do for them. Women from all over the world sent me letters or somehow found my email address, some even went so far as to make comments on Twitter about how they were "the one" for me. No matter where I was or what I was doing, I came across women who said they would do anything for me. Would they have put their life on the line for me? I doubted it. But, she had, and that put her in a class above all others.

I remembered seeing the interview she had done. It was a very simple press conference with her only speaking for two minutes. Her body and voice displayed such intense confidence and strength as she gave her speech. Her blond hair hung down in gentle waves around her shoulders. The blue of her eyes seemed dark and stormy with a passion I wish I could have seen in person.

She told the media that they had made me a movie star god. I laughed at her words, but realized that she was right. There was no doubt in my mind that if the roles were reversed that day, and I was the one holding the gun, she would've done exactly the same thing. In her eyes, I was just a human being, not a Hollywood god, but a mere person. I found a great appreciation for that.

That was why I couldn't get her off my mind. It was the fact that this small-town police detective shunned me and refused to allow me to show my gratitude because, to her, she was only doing her job. To me, it was my life.

Some days, I wished I could be that normal person again. As much as I loved acting and giving people something to entertain them, I didn't always want to see my name in lights or have people screaming for my attention and snapping pictures everywhere I went. Some days, I just wanted a quiet, private life that I could share with someone.

Now, more often than not, I found myself coming back to the new house I bought right in the township she worked. I knew I was hoping I would run into her again, or get a chance to see her for just a brief moment. The township she worked in was large, and I hadn't come across a reason to need the services of the police. Maybe someone would try to burglarize my house, and she would come out to investigate it. I had no idea if she knew I even lived out here; very few people did because I had put the house under my parents' names to keep it hidden.

Every week since the press conference, I sent her a simple card hoping that, eventually, she would call me so that I could talk to her. The memory of how calm and intense she had been while standing in front of me with that man holding a gun was ingrained in my memory and came back to me as I slept. The soft sound of her voice as she spoke, and the controlled way she responded to the media at the press conference, echoed through my mind on many occasions. I'd even had visions of her blond hair spread out on a pillow as I leaned over to kiss her.

Troy was watching me when I looked up from my glass. I hadn't even realized I was staring at it. I chuckled softly and shook my head.

"I have to get back to the house. I need to be up early to catch my flight. You coming back with me now, or are you going to stay?" I asked Troy as I stood. We were at a small party with some close friends. I glanced over to where Kayla stood. I wanted to slip out before she saw me leave. Things hadn't been so great since the incident at the airport, and I was trying to put some space between us.

Troy followed my eyes, knowing exactly what I was thinking. "I'm staying here a while longer. I'll keep her busy so that you can get out. Watch the roads, I hear it's getting slippery outside."

"Thanks, man. I owe you." I slapped him on the back and waited until he walked over to where Kayla stood next to the sparkling Christmas tree. Troy had wide enough shoulders that he blocked her view of me, and I quickly took advantage of that and slipped out the front door and into the frosty night.

I almost fell on my ass as I stepped down the first step. Troy was right; it was slick out here. I carefully made it to my car and climbed in without finding out how hard the ground was on my backside. I turned up the heater and put the car in gear heading toward my country home.

No matter where I was coming from, or where I was going, I always ended up driving the long way back to my house. The country roads that wound through Rosewood, the township where she worked, gave me extraordinary views of the beautiful countryside. I'd spent a lot of time gazing out the window as I drove because I never knew when I might get a chance to see her someplace, and I took every opportunity to search her out.

Shortly after I entered her township, I felt the car slide as I began to go around a sharp bend, and the car quickly lost control. I should have been driving slower, but I wasn't. While the car spun on the slick roadway, I prayed it wouldn't hit anything, especially another car. It kept moving, and I lost track of direction before it finally slammed into something with a jolt and bounced off. The pain in my head was immediate and I felt myself losing consciousness.

The first thing I felt as the black fog cleared was a stabbing pain in my shoulder. My head throbbed, and I thought I might be lying on my side, but I wasn't sure. I heard footsteps coming closer, the crunch of glass and plastic under a shoe, and then a woman's voice talking in a rushed, no nonsense tone filtered through the pounding in my ears. She was probably calling 911. At least I hoped she was.

The warm touch of her fingers on the side of my face gave way to the urge to open my eyes, but I found it almost too hard. I heard the woman's soft voice as her sweet peppermint breath washed over my face. Her voice was so warm and sounded vividly concerned. It filled my mind completely, and I tried to open my eyes again, but they still wouldn't budge. When I tried to move my head, she told me not to. That voice—no, it couldn't be. Of all the times I'd driven through here, of all the times that I had searched her out, how could it possibly be her here, once again, while I was in need of help? I had to open my eyes.

I fought this time and finally won against the pain. As I looked at her, I thought maybe I had died and gone to heaven, only she wasn't dead, so that couldn't have happened. Her features were slightly out of focus, but I knew it was her.

Her voice was so soft and full of concern. I wanted to smile, to pull her to me, but my head and shoulder hurt so badly it was hard to think clearly or even talk. I knew she was talking to me, but most of the time I didn't comprehend what she was saying. I tried to focus on her voice. I felt myself falling back into the darkness just as she told me to stay with her. How much I wanted to do just that after all this time.

"Trying," I got out, and thought maybe if I opened my eyes it would help me stay awake. "I need to see you."

I didn't really hear what she said, all I knew was that she was right in front of me, holding my face gently. I needed to touch her, so I slowly moved my arm up to put my hand on her cheek. My arm felt heavy, but I was determined to know that she was real and not just another one of my fantasies.

Our eyes locked as my hand came to her face. Her eyes were so beautiful and so full of concern. I wanted to tell her I was fine and to stop worrying about me, but it was hard to put the words together.

The last time I saw her, she'd been fierce with no fear as she faced down a gunman. Now, as she lay beside me, fear clouded her features just because I had been in an accident. It felt surreal.

She never moved her hands from the side of my face. She held it tightly, and I concentrated on the soft melody of her voice and the feel of her warm palms against my cold skin.

I managed to open my eyes again. "Why didn't you call me?" I asked her. She was so close, and her minty breath washed over me in a quick sigh. I wanted so much to be able to close the space and feel her lips on mine, taste them to see if they were covered in the sweet candy. She stared back at me, never answering.

Her eyes flicked back and forth, and then she looked away for good. When she did, I found I couldn't keep my eyes open so I closed them as she spoke to someone behind her. My mind tried to shut down again, and I fought to keep it in the here and now. She spoke to someone about me, I heard my name, but I wasn't listening to the words; only listening to the cadence of her voice. My body began to shake, although I didn't particularly feel cold, not with her warm hands on my face.

I heard other voices and then felt someone wrapping something around my neck. It was cold and hard, and her hands let go. My eyes opened quickly. "Don't let go," I practically begged as fear stabbed through me. I kept staring at her, so she made sure to keep her hands on me. Although they were no longer holding my neck, she kept one on my face. Her fingers gently brushed my cheekbone while her other hand came down to hold mine. She stayed like that while the unbelievably loud tools ripped the car apart. With each loud creak, my body shook harder, and my head pounded.

They pulled me out of the car, and slid me onto a hard board. The strap was tight over my aching shoulder and Jacquelyn let me go so that they could move me. As soon as I was on the stretcher, she was back at my side and walked with us to the ambulance. I didn't have my eyes open; but I didn't need to, I felt her right there.

I heard someone say something about her being hurt, and I began to panic, thinking she had been hurt because of me. She didn't seem concerned about it, but they made her get inside the ambulance with me, for which I was grateful. I didn't want to be alone.

She told me she needed to call someone to let them know about what happened, so I asked her to call Troy. *Won't he be shocked when he gets this phone call from her?*

I was in and out of consciousness on the way to the hospital, but each time I came around, I listened to her voice as she sat and quietly talked to the other two men in the ambulance with us.

As the paramedics lifted me from the ambulance, panic rose within me. I gripped her hand tighter.

"Ryan, you need to let go of my hand now. They need to take you to get medical attention."

"Stay with me," I pleaded. I couldn't help it. I didn't want her to disappear without seeing her again.

"Ryan, I'll be here. I promise I won't leave without saying goodbye." She squeezed my hand, and I squeezed it back. I let her hand go as they wheeled me away.

They put me through a battery of tests, CT scans, and X-rays. I was so relieved when they took the collar off my neck and told me my spine looked good.

They explained that I had a concussion, and that was why I couldn't open my eyes for very long; it'd be easier if I just kept them shut. I found that if I tried to open them under the florescent lights, I instantly felt sick from the rapid blinking of the lights, so I kept them closed as they wheeled me through the hospital.

The aide told me to relax, and the doctor would be in to see me soon. He moved my bed into a sitting position now that they knew my spine was all right. Troy was talking in the hallway, and then I heard footsteps enter the room.

I was surprised when I noticed the lights dimmed. I gingerly opened my eyes. It took me a few seconds to get them to focus, but when they did, they went right to her.

She stood near the doorway, and we both inspected each other cautiously. She was even more beautiful than I remembered. My breath caught in my chest as I stared into her face and saw the concern.

"You really were there. I thought I dreamed you." I wanted her to come closer, but she stayed where she was. I saw the edge of her lips move up into the semblance of a smile.

"I would think with the way we keep meeting it would be more like a nightmare." She smiled wider after she spoke and shifted her feet.

I patted the bed next to me. "Come here," I said simply. She hesitated, and then glanced at the floor. When she finally lifted her head, she walked to the side of the bed.

"I guess your neck and back are all right if they took the collar off." Her soft voice floated to my ears. I wanted her to sit down, but I was happy enough to have her standing this close.

"Yeah, there is nothing wrong with them. Looks like I have a concussion, but other than that, I think I'm fine." I smiled at her. "How is your back?"

She shrugged. "A couple of stitches, no big deal." I waited to see if she would say more, but she just kept gazing at me.

"You never answered my question," I said and watched confusion cross over her features.

"What question?"

I reached out and took her hand. She let me, and I felt her gently squeeze mine as I pulled her closer to the bed.

"Sit down." She looked at the bed then back up at me. She studied me for a few seconds and then carefully perched on the edge. I kept hold of her hand as she did. Her skin was so soft. I ran my thumb over it before I finally asked her, "Why didn't you call me?"

She swallowed and gave a small shrug, but her eyes never left mine. "There was no reason to, Mr. Palmer." Her words stung as they reached my heart.

"What do you mean there was no reason to?" My head throbbed, and I wished the pain medicine they gave me would work faster.

"Mr. Palmer—" She broke eye contact and glanced down at her lap. I squeezed her hand when she didn't look back up at me. "Look, I know you're thankful. I didn't need to hear you say it, there was no reason to."

"Did you ever think that there might be another reason why I wanted you to call me?" I asked her. Her eyebrows came together in confusion.

"What other reason could there be?"

I explored the soft features of her face and the gentle waves of her hair as it framed her cheeks. I let go of her hand and reached up to touch her cheek. Her eyes widened, she started to pull back.

"Because maybe I wanted to get to know you," I answered honestly.

Her lips parted, and I had the urge to pull her closer to me. I could have easily slipped my hand behind her neck and brought her down to me, but I didn't.

She bit down on her bottom lip and pulled away from me. Standing up, she stepped back out of my reach. "Mr. Palmer, there is nothing to know." She looked over her shoulder at Troy who stood silently near the door. "Look, I'm glad you're all right, but I have to go." She stepped back again.

"Wait, Quen—" I started to say.

"My name is Jacquelyn. Please don't call me Quen." Pain crossed her face, and I wondered why. I knew another woman named Jacquelyn, and she used Quen as a nickname all the time. "I need to go." She turned all the way around and then stopped and looked at me over her shoulder. "I tried very hard to keep your identity as quiet as I could at the accident tonight. I would like to request that you keep the fact that I was there between us. I don't want the media badgering me or my department again." She turned back around and moved to the door.

"Jacquelyn, wait. Please don't go yet. I want to talk to you." She stopped with her hand on the door handle, but didn't turn around.

"Jacquelyn, how can I thank you if you won't let me talk to you?"

"You just did, Mr. Palmer. You're welcome. Now please, leave me alone." She gave Troy a curt nod and walked out of the room.

The door closed slowly; I rested my head back against the pillow. I had a hell of a headache, but the medicine they gave me was finally kicking in. I closed my eyes.

"I said she was rare before, but now I'm thinking she's more than rare. She's one of a kind, man." Troy spoke from where he stood on the other side of the room, leaning against the wall with his arms crossed over his wide chest.

"I'm going to get that woman to talk to me if it's the last thing I do," I said from my bed.

"You better be careful about saying that. You always seem to be in a life or death situation when you run into her." He chuckled.

I couldn't help but laugh with him because his comment was pretty dead on.

APRIL – JACQUELYN

"*H*ey, Brad," I yelled as I walked out of the garage door. "Would you have Matt or Steve go back inside and grab the rest of the evidence bags off the table?"

"Yeah, sure, detective." My hands were full with several evidence bags from our latest homicide. This one should be an easy one. It was actually a murder-suicide, or at least that's what it looked like at the moment. I guess no murder was actually easy. We still had to analyze the evidence and do quite a few interviews before we officially called it that.

I made my way over to my patrol car, an unmarked white Crown Vic. Just as I opened up the back door, my cellphone rang. I put all my bags inside and pulled it out of my pocket seeing my chief's name. He probably wanted an update.

"Chief," I responded as I answered.

"Jack, are you almost done out there? I need you back at the station." While he'd made this statement to me many times over the years, the way he said it raised the fine hairs on the back of my neck.

"What's going on, Chief?" Instinct told me something was up.

It was a few seconds before he answered me back. "Nothing, I need to talk to you."

I could still tell something was up. His voice didn't sound like his normal calm voice; it was overly tense. "I'll be back in about twenty minutes. I'm just loading up the evidence now, and then I'll be clearing the scene." I stood back from the door as Steve walked over with another load of evidence bags and put them in the backseat.

"Fine, come see me as soon as you're back," he replied quickly. I raised my eyebrows when Steve looked over at me.

"Something happen while I was working this? Chief seems pretty intense," I said.

He shook his head. "No, as far as I know, he's been in meetings all morning. I tried to get in to see him earlier, but Susan said he was tied up."

After doing a final walk through of the scene, I cleared it and drove back to the station. I was carrying some of the evidence into the station when the chief walked into the lab.

"Jackie, I told you to come see me as soon as you got back," he practically growled, which was very unusual. *What the hell was going on?*

"Chief, I did just get back, but I need to secure the evidence I gathered. I'll be there in a few minutes." I turned to walk back out the door.

"Jack, in my office. Now." I spun stared at his retreating back. *What the hell was his problem? Did I do something wrong?* I heard him yell down the hall, "Jimmy!"

I was still staring after the chief when Jimmy, our other detective, stuck his head out of his office. "Yeah, Chief?"

"Jimmy, pull the evidence out of Jack's car and secure it. I need to talk to her." He walked away while Jimmy and I shared a confused look, both our eyebrows high with surprise.

"Now, Detective Liveon!" he shouted from down the hallway. Jimmy and I exchanged another look before I headed after the chief.

When I walked in, there was another man seated in the office. I had never seen him before, but I nodded politely and walked to the other chair in front of the chief's desk. I sat down and waited for one of them to speak.

I heard the door close behind us. Susan must have pulled it closed after I walked in. The chief sat down heavily and looked at the man seated next to me.

"Chief, is there a problem?" I didn't like the silence, and every muscle in my body was tense and alert.

"Detective Liveon, this is Robert Smallwood; he's an attorney." *Oh, crap...that's never good.* I glanced sideways at the attorney.

"Am I getting sued for something?" I asked the chief, glancing at the attorney again. I kept my voice level even though my heart was beating rapidly.

He shook his head. "No, you're not getting sued. You're going under-cover on a special assignment." The chief studied me with frustration in his eyes.

My eyebrows shot up. "What special assignment?" I turned to look at the man beside me. He was watching the chief, his hands casually placed in his lap.

"Well, it seems that the township decided to loan you out for a few weeks or months." He sat back in his chair, pushing away from his desk. Chief Wheeler was a strong man in his late forties. To me, he was attractive in that rough, aggressive kind of way. But today, he just looked tired and pissed off.

"Loaned me out? What does that even mean?" I shook my head in confusion. I watched the chief, but I still kept my eyes on the lawyer next to me.

The chief sighed and put his hands behind his head. A body language sign that says, *I know what I'm talking about and don't question me because I am better than you.* Yeah, that's what it really means. Shit.

"You will be working undercover on a very sensitive case. A lot of people are going to know what you do for a living, but they have an alibi for you." He considered the lawyer for a moment, a muscle in his jaw vibrated through his skin.

I shook my head and looked down at his desk. "What am I going to be doing?" I asked him when I finally lifted my head back up.

He glanced to the guy sitting next to me and then made direct eye contact with me. "You're going to be working on a movie production to assist the head of security."

"Excuse me?" My eyebrows went up under my bangs.

"Mr. Smallwood here will take you somewhere to explain all of the details," he told me and lowered his hands to rest them across his stomach as he leaned back in his chair.

I turned to Mr. Smallwood and saw that he was still staring at the chief. He looked uncomfortable, but he didn't say anything and didn't look directly at me.

"With all due respect, Chief, I don't think I'm interested in working as a security guard for a movie." Was he crazy?

"Detective Liveon, you have no choice in this matter." He cleared his throat. "The township has already approved it, and it's done. My hands are tied on this." He sounded angry, and I began to share that emotion with him.

"Why the hell would the township approve this? I've got over forty active cases I'm working on right now. I don't have time to play around on some movie set. Why would they even need someone like me to be a security guard?"

He put his hands on his desk and sat up straight. "It was approved because the movie company donated one million dollars to the township and offered to pay you three times your salary for up to six months."

My jaw dropped. I had just been sold out for a million dollars. "I don't want three times my salary. I want to do my job, Chief," I said when I could finally speak again.

"You will be doing it, just not here. You're to go with Mr. Smallwood now, he'll fill you in on all of the details." He shrugged, "He's taking you someplace so that you can meet the people you will be working for. They will fill you in on anything additional you need to know."

I shook my head. "What the hell is going on? Chief, I've got a murder-suicide case to investigate. I can't just go run off to play on a movie set. You've got to be kidding me!" I was pissed off now. "Why can't they use someone else?"

"Jimmy will take your cases. You can come back later and turn them all over to him," he said as he stared me down, his nostrils flared. "As far as anyone else is concerned, you just went on a leave of absence."

"What! Why the hell do they want me?" I knew I was whining, but this was ridiculous. A freaking movie production? You have got to be kidding me! After everything I'd gone through the last six months, the last thing I wanted to do was be near a movie set.

"Because they want the best," he said simply as he picked up a pen that was lying on this desk and tapped it on the surface.

I grabbed the arms of the chair I was sitting in, gripping it tightly so that I wouldn't lose my composure. "This is all a joke, right?"

"Detective Liveon," the attorney next to me finally spoke. "I can assure you this is no joke. We need your services, but it needs to be a secret. That is why we have hired you under the pretense that you are working security."

I glared at him. His brown eyes looked tired and frustrated. I shook my head and stared up at the ceiling.

"I can't get out of this, can I?" I faced the chief again.

He shook his head. "Sorry, Jackie, but my hands are tied. Go do whatever it is that they need you to do and get back here. They wanted the best; they got the best." He shrugged. I knew that was supposed to be a compliment, but it just didn't feel like it.

I leaned forward and put my elbows on my knees staring at the floor. I sighed. "Fine. What do I have to do?"

The attorney stood and I straightened in my chair. "Detective, you will come with me. I'm going to take you to meet the head of security. You will be working closely with him to deal with a very sensitive matter."

"You're not going to tell me what that matter is, are you?" I questioned as I bent my neck back to look at his face.

"I'm sorry, but no, I am not. You will find out when we arrive." He reached for his briefcase. "We have a car waiting for us."

"I can drive my own car," I said as I stood.

"No, that won't be necessary. As of right now, you are working for us, not your township. So, you need to blend in." He walked to the door before he turned back to the chief.

"Thank you for all your assistance, Chief Wheeler. Detective, I'll be out front waiting for you." He turned to walk out of the office.

I stared daggers into his back until he disappeared around the corner. Then I turned the daggers on the chief. "What the hell is going on?"

"I have no idea, Jackie. They wouldn't tell me anything." He dropped the pen on his desk and leaned forward to put his elbows on it.

I shook my head. "I so don't like this. Something feels wrong."

"Just go do what you need to do, and get back here as soon as you can." He picked up his pen again and sat back in his chair.

"How can the township even do this?"

He sighed. "Look, Jackie, just like every other township out there, it's hurting for money. None of the supervisors want to raise the taxes, but they were going to have to." He hesitated for a moment. "You've seen our budget, and it's getting tighter and tighter. Two of our cars need to be replaced; there is equipment that you and the other guys have been asking for. And, until now, we haven't had the money. All aspects of the township will benefit from this, and we won't have to raise taxes."

I got it. The economy sucked, plain and simple. If this would help the township out, and get us more guys on the street along with the training and equipment we needed, it might be worth it, maybe. I had to look at this in a positive light. If I didn't, it would only make matters worse.

"Hurry up and get this done, Jackie."

"You can bet on it, Chief." I stood and walked to the door.

"Be Safe, Jackie," he called out as I reached the door.

"Always, Chief." I smiled over my shoulder and walked into the lobby where Mr. Smallwood was waiting for me.

He acknowledged me with a quick nod and opened the front door for me to follow him. "What about my car?" I asked him.

"Someone will bring you back later to retrieve your things," he stated briskly and walked over to a limo that was parked in our lot. I had come in from the back lot, so I had not seen the limo out front.

"Nice way to blend in," I mumbled. As I walked to the rear of the car, an older white man was holding the door open.

"Detective," he said and nodded politely to me as I got into the car. I nodded back and slid across the back seat.

I had been in limos before, so I wasn't gawking at the surroundings, but I was still a bit in awe over what was happening. *Three times my salary to work as a security guard? Why would anyone pay that for someone like me?*

The car drove west for a while and neither Mr. Smallwood nor I said anything. He typed something on his cellphone, but I didn't care what he was doing. My mind was a whirlwind while I attempted to figure out what was going on.

About ten minutes later, we pulled up to a large metal gate. A security guard opened it and we drove up a long driveway. There was a large house at the top of a hill. It was a beautiful, sprawling three-story house with lots of windows. The center of the house was almost all glass. You could see all the way through, and even see the balconies on the second and third story that crossed from one side of the house to the other. I had seen this house many times from the road, and always wondered who owned it. I guess I was about to find out.

The limo stopped, I waited for the door to open before I climbed out. I examined the house trying to keep my jaw from dropping. "Who lives here?" I asked Mr. Smallwood as he climbed out.

"Your new boss," he walked past me and toward the front door. Well, that told me a lot. I nodded to no one and followed him.

The door opened before we reached it, and there stood a woman dressed in a maid's uniform. Did people really dress like that?

She smiled at me as we entered. The entrance was part of the glass section of the house, and I lifted my chin to view the floors above me. The rays of sun bounced off the glass enclosure, I immediately loved it.

I followed Mr. Smallwood down a hallway. I could hear voices as we walked, and I was trying to pick up words or recognize the voices that were talking, but they all meant nothing to me.

As we entered, the conversation stopped, and everyone turned to me. I glanced around the large room. It was filled with couches and chairs in different seating arrangements. The back wall was glass, and it looked out over a pool area. Beyond the pool was a pasture where horses grazed.

Three people stood in the room and openly gawked at me: two men and one woman. The woman made a beeline for me with a bright smile on her face.

"Detective, we are so glad you came. I'm Roseanne Samuels. I'll be your assistant." I raised my eyebrows. *I needed an assistant?* I shook her hand. She was only a few inches shorter than I was, but she seemed more petite because of her thin shoulders and the fact that she didn't have an ounce of body fat. I forced a small smile on my face.

I heard two sets of footsteps behind me, and everyone turned to look at the door. Today had been a whirlwind, and I didn't think I could've been any more shocked than I was when I turned around to see Ryan Palmer standing in the doorway. His friend Troy stood beside him, but I barely noticed him.

Ryan's blue eyes sparkled, and his full lips curled up mischievously at me. His short-sleeved blue polo shirt hugged his chest and wide shoulders. The soft blond hair on his arms caught the sunlight as it came in from the window behind me.

I clenched my jaw and closed my eyes. *No freaking way! Why didn't I even consider this? Of freaking course!* I heard him chuckle.

"Please don't tell me you're my new boss," I said when I cracked open my tense jaw.

His smile widened. "See, I knew you were smart." He stepped closer, and I almost backed away; but I held my ground. "Welcome, Detective Liveon." He held his hand out for me to shake.

I looked at his hand for a second before I placed mine into his. The warmth of his hands made my palm burn. He held it longer then was necessary, and I studied his face. His eyes still sparkled as he studied me closely.

"What do you want?" I asked, and it probably wasn't in my nicest voice.

He started to open his mouth but then stopped and grinned. I wondered what he was about to say, but I didn't ask. I kept watching him and realized that everyone was staring at the two of us. I took a step back.

"I need your help," he said. He broke eye contact to walk over to a couch and sit down. "Please, have a seat."

I stood where I was with my feet glued to the ground until I felt someone stand beside me. I turned to see Troy, and he guided me to a chair. It was probably a good thing because my feet weren't working too well at that moment.

I sat down and looked across the sitting area to Ryan. "What help do you need from me?" I was surprised that my voice came out as calmly as it did. Years of practice in stressful situations were paying off.

I squirmed in my seat as his eyes traveled over me; I felt like I was naked as he took me in. His eyes were so bright, even when the sun wasn't shining on them. I felt the intensity of his stare as it traveled over me. Somewhere, I remember reading that he was on a top ten list for having the sexiest eyes. Looking into them now, I believed it.

We sat cautiously studying one another. Finally, Troy cleared his throat and I peeked over to see him next to me smiling. A blush crept up my face, I told myself to stop. *Yeah, like that was going to work.*

"Detective Liveon, may I call you Jacquelyn?" Troy asked me.

"Yes, you may," I answered him quietly.

"Thank you. As you now know, you've been hired to work for Mr. Palmer." I scowled at Ryan and then turned my attention back to Troy. "We need your assistance on a sensitive issue."

I waited to see if he would continue. When he didn't say anything, I spoke. "What issue?"

"Someone has been making death threats against him," he said simply.

After a second, I snorted a quick laugh and focused directly at Ryan. "Why am I not surprised?" He gave me a lopsided grin in return.

APRIL - RYAN

I couldn't stop pacing. I walked circles around the house, unable to sit still for a moment. Would she come? I had my cellphone in my hand, and I waited for the message to come through. Every time my phone made a noise, I jumped and looked at it, but it was not the information I was waiting for.

Finally, the message arrived. "We are on our way." It was from my attorney. The one I had sent to work out the deal with Rosewood Township, the one who was bringing Jacquelyn to me. I grinned like a kid on Christmas morning when I saw the words on my screen and looked out over the third-story balcony and toward the pasture where two horses grazed in the distance. *Finally, I would get my chance to talk to her.*

I knew it wouldn't be long before she arrived, and when the guard-house called to say the limo was here, I moved out of the atrium area so that she wouldn't see me. I wanted to surprise her. I asked Mr. Smallwood not to tell her anything before she arrived. I wanted to see the look on her face when she realized she would be working for me. Would she be surprised, or angry?

I observed the limo from my bedroom window and watched as she climbed out. She wore a tan blazer and brown slacks, and the blazer set off her wide shoulders and highlighted her light blond hair. She looked up at the house and then followed Mr. Smallwood to the front door. I gave her a few minutes to get inside, I actually felt butterflies in my stomach as I walked down the stairs to the room where my security team waited.

I took a deep breath before I turned the corner and entered the room. Troy walked beside me and put his hand on my shoulder. I peered at him, and he grinned at me. He was the only person who knew how much I wanted to see her. As I rounded the corner, everyone turned to look at me. I didn't care about anyone else in that room. My eyes went directly to hers, and I watched her mouth clamp shut.

I knew she probably wasn't used to being surprised, so that made it even better. I laughed quietly and grinned at her.

Her light blue eyes stared intently into mine, and I had the crazy urge to pull her into my arms right there. I let go of her hand after shaking it instead.

"What do you want?" she asked quietly.

I wanted to say, *You*, but I held that back, for now. Maybe she could see in my eyes, because she took a small step away from me.

"I need your help," I walked past her to the couch. Her intense scrutiny and beautiful eyes were making me more nervous than I anticipated. "Please, have a seat." *So you can't see my knees shaking.*

"What help do you need from me?" she asked after she sat down.

I had waited a long time to be able to look at her in person again, and for a few moments, I could do nothing but stare. She was more gorgeous than I remembered. Her light blond hair shone as the sun came in through the window. Her eyes were bright and clear as she scrutinized me. I studied her until Troy cleared his throat. I couldn't help but smile when I saw color start to rise on her cheeks. How cute.

"Detective Liveon, may I call you Jacquelyn?" I couldn't tear my eyes from her as Troy spoke.

"Yes, you may." Her voice was music to my ears.

"Thank you. As you now know, you've been hired to work for Mr. Palmer. We need your assistance on a sensitive issue."

She peeked over at me quickly, but returned her attention to Troy immediately.

"Someone has been making death threats against him," he said simply.

The snort that came out of her mouth was totally unexpected, but her words weren't. "Why am I not surprised?"

There were actually a few chuckles from around the room, but I didn't look at anyone else. "Why aren't you surprised?" I asked.

She examined me as she sat back in her chair and crossed her right leg over her left knee. She rested her hands in her lap. "You seem to have a way with people. Who did you annoy this time?" She was smiling softly.

"Believe it or not, no one," I replied.

"Somehow, I doubt that." She shook her head and turned back to Troy. "But why do you need me? You already have security, and this isn't my job."

I watched as she studied Troy. She was so confident. Now that the surprise was over, she was in control again.

"You're a detective." He shrugged. "We figured you might be able to figure out who is sending the threats."

"That doesn't make sense. If you think the threats are valid, then you should have the State Police or FBI involved in this, not some local small-town detective." While she directed her comment to Troy, I watched lips move with each word and imagined tasting the soft skin.

"We didn't want to make a huge thing of it. That's why we didn't call the FBI." I looked over at Troy as he spoke.

"You mean, I didn't want to make a big deal about it," I said while bringing my attention back to Jacquelyn with a shrug. She cocked her head to the side as I spoke.

"What? You don't take your life seriously?" she asked.

"Of course I do. I just don't think this person is serious." I shrugged once more and scanned the room for a second.

Troy started to talk again. "The thing of it is, we think it's someone who is working the production." Jacquelyn's right eyebrow went up.

"Why do you think that?" She glanced at the three others in the room.

"Some of the notes have shown up while we've been filming and..." Troy stopped talking and looked over at me.

"And what?" Jacquelyn looked between the two of us.

"Someone tried to poison me. They actually told me they were going to do it, and I didn't pay any attention to the threat. But someone spiked one of my water bottles with something. I only had a sip of it and put the bottle down. Someone else picked it up by mistake and drank most of the water. They got rushed to the hospital."

She sat there watching me curiously. "Is that person alive?"

"Oh yeah, he just got really sick for a few days. It was nothing major," I answered.

She shook her head, the waves of her hair gently moving back and forth. "Nothing major? You sure don't hold much value over human life, do you?" She didn't give me a chance to answer before she looked over at Troy. "How is this supposed to work?"

Troy grinned at her, and again, I felt a little twinge of jealousy. "You'll work with me. You will have to move in here for a while, and one of us will be with him at all times. We're hoping that your investigative skills can help us figure this out before the press gets wind of it."

When he mentioned that she was going to move in, I saw her eyes open wider, and she flicked a glance at me.

"Why do I have to move in? I have my own house, and it's not that far away. I don't need to live here." Was that an edge of panic or anger that I detected in her voice?

"All of his personal bodyguards stay at his house. We need it to look like standard practice and not that you are here doing an investigation. Besides, where else would his new girlfriend stay?" His voice lowered as he finished the sentence, I held my breath.

Her mouth dropped. "What?" She gaped at Troy, and I fought back my laughter. "What do you mean girlfriend?"

Troy's eyes flicked over to me once, and I waited to see what he would say. "We figured we would make it look like you and Ryan have been seeing each other secretly for a while. You decided to take some time off from work to spend it with him, and he offered you a job as a bodyguard. The fact that you have saved his life twice now only makes that part more believable."

She leaned forward to put her elbows on her knees and stared at the floor. Her blazer stretched tightly over her back while her hair fell forward and hid her face.

"Please tell me you're joking?" she said without looking up at anyone. It was quiet for about a minute. When she finally lifted her face, she glared at me for a long moment. "Was this your idea?"

I laughed. The look on her face was a cross between anger and shock. "No, actually, it wasn't my idea. You can blame this one on Troy and Roseanne." I pointed casually to each of them as I spoke.

She faced the floor again. "When does all this start?"

Troy cleared his throat. "Now. The limo driver is outside waiting to take you back to your house to get your things. He will bring you back, and we'll get you settled in tonight. Tomorrow, I will go over everything with you."

Jacquelyn sat up straight, her jaw locked. I watched a muscle tick on the right side of her face. "Fine. Your limo driver can take me back to the station. I need to clear up a few loose ends there and then I'll go home to pack my stuff and I will drive back here myself. I would prefer to have my own car."

Troy turned to me and waited to see if I was going to respond. "If you really feel like you need your own car, that's fine. But after you're here, you will be riding with me in the limo when we go places."

Anger flashed in her eyes as she stood. "We'll see about that. Let your guard know I will be coming back in a dark blue Jeep." She turned to walk out the door.

"Jacquelyn," I called before she left the room. She stopped, her shoulders rigid, but she didn't turn around. "You do know that the third time's the charm, right?"

She turned then, squinting her eyes ever so slightly. "Third time for what? You actually getting yourself killed? You seem to have a knack for that kind of thing when I'm around."

I laughed at her. "There's that, or that you will fall madly in love with me," I said with a smirk.

Her eyes went wide. "Start holding your breath. We'll see who wins. My money is on the fact that your lungs won't hold out as long as I will."

She spun quickly, her hair fanning around her back, and she all but ran out the door. Silence filled the room as everyone waited for me to speak. I laughed as I heard the front door close with a bang.

"I think I love that woman."

"Too bad she doesn't feel the same way," Troy chuckled next to me.

"She will," I said as I laid my head back on the cushion. "She will."

"Better start holding your breath," he said, and everyone in the room laughed.

JACQUELYN

$\mathcal{A}$s I walked out of the room, I was in utter shock. I was going to be working for Ryan Palmer. *The* Ryan Palmer. And not only was I going to be working with him, but I had to pretend I was his girlfriend and live in his house! My hair swung around my face as I shook my head at the absurdity of it. The limo driver was waiting, and I climbed into the backseat without a word.

I leaned against the soft black leather seat as we drove away. How the hell had I gotten stuck doing this? I was a small-town girl who just wanted to do her job and have a life of peace and quiet. Now, I was being thrown into a world that I didn't want to be part of. I didn't know anything about protecting someone, and the idea of being with *that* man all the time pretty much scared the crap out of me.

His words ran through my mind. "There's that, or that you'll fall madly in love with me." I clamped my eye lids shut. That was the last thing that was going to happen. Why would he even say such a thing? Was it because I refused to talk with him before? I was a nobody who knew nothing about him, and didn't really want to.

Okay, as a woman, I did actually have hormones and a brain. So yeah, he was extremely attractive and sexy as hell, and the thought of being held in his arms was an incredibly heady thought, but I wasn't like most women. That concept shouldn't appeal to me. I wouldn't let it appeal to me. He was out of my league. Way out of my league. Besides, I didn't fall in love. I had once, and I'd lost everything because of it. Never again.

Maybe he had said that to bait me. He couldn't really want me to like him, could he? Or maybe his ego was so large that he couldn't understand the concept of someone not wanting to fawn all over him and fall at his feet.

By the time I got back to the station, I convinced myself that he was not serious and that he was just trying to annoy me. I could deal with annoying; I'll show him annoying.

I went into the station, but it was already later than I thought, and there were very few people left inside. I heard Jimmy in his office and walked down the hall.

"Hey, Jim," I said as I entered. I collapsed into a chair in front of his desk.

"What the hell is going on? Why did the chief give me all your cases?" He eyeballed me over a case file that he had spread wide open on his desk.

I shook my head. "You're not going to believe this." I got up and closed the door. "I've been assigned undercover. I'm gonna work as a security guard to figure out who is making death threats against someone."

"Who are you working for?" He leaned back slowly in his chair.

"This is the part you won't believe. It's Ryan Palmer." I waited for his reaction. His eyebrows shot up, and his mouth hung open.

"*The* Ryan Palmer?" he asked in disbelief, "As in the same one you rescued from the airport? And then the car wreck?"

"Yep, the one and only." I shook my head turning away from him as I remembered the sparkle in Ryan's eyes.

"So what do you have to do?"

I took a deep breath. "It looks like someone close to him is making threats. I don't know all the details about it yet, but they want me to move in and stay by his side. Try to figure out who is doing it and why."

"Are you still going to be working here?" he asked as he started to swivel back and forth in his chair.

"No, the chief wants it to look like I've taken a leave of absence. I have to move into the house tonight. Then I start tomorrow." I glanced up and saw something flash across his face.

"You're moving in with him?" His chair stop moving, and I bit my lip.

I knew he wouldn't like it. I wasn't crazy about it myself. "Yeah, and speaking of which, I need to get going." I stood. "I have to go through my files and get the rest of my stuff for you. I'll leave my passwords, too, in case you need something off my computer. I'm sorry about all of this; it's not like you don't have enough to do."

He stood and walked over to me. Jimmy was about six inches taller than I was. A comfortable height when we were in front of each other. He studied me intently for a few moments.

"How long are you going to be gone?" he asked quietly, pushing a lock of hair behind my ear.

"I'm not sure, hopefully not long, but they hired me for up to six months." He peered over my shoulder and blew out a breath before he stepped closer.

"Am I going to get to see you?" he slid his hand along my cheek, and I leaned into it smiling. Jimmy and I had something going. I wasn't sure when it had started, or what exactly it was, but we saw each other from time to time. No one knew, and we kept it as quiet as we could. Most people never questioned seeing us out since we worked so closely together. It just appeared as two co-workers going out for dinner or a beer.

"I don't know when I'll get time off or what I'm going to have to do, but I will let you know." I tipped my head back so I could peer into his green eyes better.

"I don't like the fact that you're going to be living there with him." What could I say or do? Nothing really, so I only shrugged.

"Don't worry about it. I'll figure out what's going on and be back soon. Look, Jimmy, I have to go." I started to turn away, but he pulled me into his arms. His kiss was deep and much more passionate than it normally was, especially here at work. Normally, he might sneak in a kiss here or there, but this was different. It was as if he didn't want me to forget it.

I was breathless when he let go of me. I removed my arms from around his neck where they had found themselves drawn, gave him a lopsided grin, and stepped away to open the door.

"I'll talk to you later, Jimmy."

"Jackie," he said, and I turned around. "Be careful with him." He seemed so serious that it made me nervous. I laughed quietly.

"Jimmy, I'm always careful." I turned and was about to walk out of the room when I stopped and surveyed him again. "Hey, Jim, do me a favor and don't believe everything you might see, okay?" He narrowed his eyes, and I knew he would question my words; so, I walked out before he could. I wasn't sure why, but I didn't want to tell him about the whole girlfriend thing.

In my office, I went through my files, took notes, and made sure all of my information was in order so that I could hand them off to Jimmy. I wasn't sure how long I'd been working when my cellphone rang.

I glanced at my phone, taking in the phone number on the screen. Instead of it being a caller ID number telling me who was calling, it was my phone number, well, a virtual number anyway. A virtual number was a telephone number that was not directly associated with any particular phone company. It's harder to trace, and I used it for work quite often. I had one for personal use, too. You could have multiple virtual numbers all ringing to one phone, or even ringing to multiple phones.

This particular virtual number told me it was work related. I was going to have to forward this number to Jimmy while I was on my leave of absence. "Hello," I said as I put it to my ear.

"Jacquelyn, is everything alright?" I heard the man's voice on the other end of the line and froze.

"How did you get this number, Ryan?" I sat back in my seat.

"My attorney gave it to me earlier. I guess your chief must have given it to him. I was worried about you. I thought you would be here by now."

I glanced up at the clock and saw that it was almost ten o'clock. I had been here for five hours.

"Sorry, I got caught up at work. I'm leaving here shortly, but I still need to go home and get my things. Maybe I should just get packed and come by in the morning."

"No, I want you here tonight," he replied quickly.

I thought for a moment. "Why? Is there something going on that I need to know about? Are you all right?" Maybe they got another threat and needed me to start now instead of tomorrow.

"No, I'm fine." He hesitated. "I just want to know you're here."

His earlier comment echoed through my mind again, but I dismissed it. "Look, it will be better if I come tomorrow. It's going to be a while, and I'm tired. I want to get a good night's sleep, get my things packed, and then I'll be out first thing in the morning." I might have to work for him, but I was not going to let him control me.

He was quiet for a few seconds, mulling over my words. "Fine, but be here as early as you can. I'll see you in the morning." He hung up before I could respond to him. *Needy much?* I shook my head, dropped my cell-phone on the desk, and closed the file I was looking at. He was like a moody child, one-minute laughing and grinning, the next sullen and pushy. I forced thoughts of him out of my mind and finished what I was working on.

A few minutes later, I dropped the last case file onto a pile with the others and made my way down the hall to Jimmy's office. The room was dark. He must have gone home without saying anything else to me. I set the files on his desk and walked back to my office to turn off my lights.

It felt strange walking out of the station; almost as if I were leaving for good. I examined the building as I pulled out of my parking space. I knew I would be back, but somehow, it felt like my life was about to be seriously altered.

After arriving home, I packed some of my things. Luckily, I had already done laundry, so most of my clothes were clean. I put them in piles and then climbed into bed to get some much-needed sleep. I would get up early and pack them into bags.

As I lay down on my pillow, I dwelled for a moment on the fact that I was going to work for Ryan Palmer. Everyone thought he was an amazing, talented, funny, and yes, a very sexy actor. I'd never commented to anyone about him, and not a soul knew that every night since I'd first met him, as I laid down to sleep, his face came to my mind, his eyes filled my thoughts, and I drifted off to sleep.

Tonight was no different. Although, instead of seeing him lying in a hospital bed or standing in an airport terminal, he was sitting on a couch smirking at me with sparks lighting up his blue eyes.

My alarm went off at four forty-five in the morning, just as it did every workday. I showered, threw my clothes into two suitcases, and then made sure I locked up the house before I left. I would call my neighbor and have her grab my mail and keep an eye on my place.

I drove out to Ryan's estate. It was about thirty minutes from my house and was nestled among rolling green pastures. The vibrant sunrise was shining on the front windows of the house as I drove up the winding driveway. The colors were reflecting brightly off the glass. I could barely see through it because of the reflection, but I was able to make out someone standing on the third floor. The person faced my direction, looking down on me. I knew instantly it was Ryan and my heart skipped a beat.

As I climbed out of my truck, I watched him. With the sun shining in, it formed a hazy halo around him. He looked like the god I had commented on during my press release. I swallowed. *What in the hell am I doing here?*

He walked away, and I wasn't sure where he had gone. I directed my attention to the front door as I heard it open and Troy stepped out.

"Jacquelyn, good morning!" he called from the entrance. He walked down the three stone steps that led to the walkway and out to the driveway as I made it around to the back of my vehicle.

"Good morning, Troy." Smiling at him was easy. He was a very attractive man and when his lips spread in a wide grin, his whole face lit up. I opened up my hatch just as he reached my side.

"I'm glad you're here. I wasn't sure how much longer I could keep him calm." He laughed as he spoke and reached in to grab one of my suitcases.

"Why isn't he calm?" I questioned as he put the suitcase down and reached in for the other one.

He laughed again. "He's been pacing since you left. He was afraid you weren't coming back. I doubt he even slept last night."

I grabbed my laptop bag out of the back and closed the hatch. I didn't know what to say.

"Come on, let's get your things up to your room before we have breakfast. The team will be here around eight, and we'll start going over everything then."

I followed him into the house and up the stairs. I didn't see Ryan, but I knew he wasn't far away. My heart was still beating more rapidly than I wanted it to. I took a deep breath as we stepped up onto the third-floor landing. Troy started to walk across the bridge that led through the atrium, and I stopped—probably right where Ryan stood earlier—and looked out through the window at the beautiful sunrise.

It took my breath away as I scanned over the land. "Wow."

Troy glanced over his shoulder and stopped, following my line of sight. "Pretty awesome view, isn't it?"

"Yeah, one of the best I have ever seen in this area." I took another moment to absorb it and figured I would probably get a chance to see many more of them, so I turned back at Troy and smiled. "Where's my room?"

"Right down here. Ryan's room is at the end of the hall, and I am across from you." He walked to an open door, and I was hoping he didn't hear me stumble when he mentioned Ryan's room. I looked up and saw a door at the end of the hall. I was going to be right next to him. I swallowed again and hoped Troy couldn't hear that either.

I followed him into my room. It was bright and much larger than I expected it to be. The windows faced east, allowing the colorful sunrise to shine in. Troy set my suitcases down and turned to me. I stood just inside the door and took in the room.

It was decorated simply, but elegantly, with dark woods and shades of greens and purples. If I had been the one to decorate this room, it would have probably been almost exactly like this, but nowhere near as expensively.

"Hope you like it. Ryan had it redone recently. Your bathroom is through that door, and the other door is your closet." He pointed to the two doors off to the side, and I nodded. Ryan had just redone this room. *Had he done that for me?*

"It's beautiful," I said almost breathlessly, "Thank you."

"Hey, don't thank me. Thank your boss." He grinned and then moved toward me. I stepped aside so that he could get to the door. "You get yourself unpacked and then come downstairs. I'll be out back on the patio. It's a beautiful morning, so Ryan wants to eat breakfast out there."

I acknowledged him, and he left me alone to get settled. I guess what Ryan wanted, Ryan got. I shook my head and moved to one of my suitcases. It didn't take me long to get my stuff put away and to lay out my toiletries in the gigantic spa-like bathroom. It was larger than my whole bedroom at home. As I was zipping up my suitcase to put it away, I felt someone behind me. I spun around and found Ryan standing against the doorjamb, his hands shoved into his battered blue jean pockets.

How did his eyes always have a way of making my heartbeat faster? He was wearing a light blue T-shirt today that brought out the little flecks in his eyes.

"I hope your room is all right," he said casually.

"It's beautiful, thank you," I responded. I didn't know what else to say with him studying me the way he was. There was a hunger in his eyes that I didn't understand, or maybe I didn't want to.

He pushed off the doorjamb and came toward me, stopping a foot in front of me. "Nowhere near as beautiful as you are."

My heart pounded against my breastbone, my palms felt damp. I wiped them on my pants gently. I didn't know what to say and I wasn't sure I could speak if I tried. I could see that he did have circles under his eyes, making what Troy said about him not sleeping a little more believable.

He took another step closer as he reached up to touch the side of my face, his knuckles brushing over my cheekbones. I felt a pulse of energy run through my body as his hand slid over the sensitive skin. I couldn't move as he came closer to me.

He stopped just inches from my face. His eyes were intent on mine, his breath fanned over my lips, a slightly minty scent as it caressed me. My heart thumped so hard that I was certain he could hear it. I couldn't help but lick my lips and swallow. He came closer to me, our lips a breath apart.

I didn't know what I was doing. I honestly didn't want anything to do with this man, this movie star god who had everyone doing exactly as he asked. But I also didn't want to step away. A part of me wanted to know what it would be like to feel his lips on mine, to feel his arms around me. The intelligent, coherent part of me was ready to shove him away. It knew that everything this man was about was not something I should get involved in.

Finally, the side of my brain that controlled my intelligence came to life and shoved the hormonal side back to where it belonged. I moved away from him just as he began to descend on me.

"Can't blame a guy for trying, can you?" He sounded smug, and the urge to punch him in the face made me clench my hands. "I came to tell you that breakfast is ready." He turned and walked out of the room without saying anything further.

When he was gone, I sat on the edge of the bed and dropped my face into my hands. Oh, good Lord, this man was going to be the death of me!

RYAN

*I*t was around seven when the front gate called up to say Jacquelyn had arrived. I stood in the atrium and watched her dark blue Jeep move quickly as it came up the hill and stopped out front. She sat in the driver's seat peering up at me, her hands gripping the tan steering wheel. I was tempted to run down and pull her into my arms. She was finally here! But I didn't. Instead, I spun on my heel and went back to my bedroom.

I hadn't slept much last night as my mind whirled around with the thought that she might not come back. What if she didn't? What if she refused to do this? She had to, didn't she? I mean, I did pay her township an outstanding amount of money to have her services. I finally decided that if she was asked to do something, she would, so she'd be back.

It wasn't just that I wanted her here with me; I really did need her help. Things were getting crazy on the sets, and rumors were starting to leak about the things that were happening. I didn't need any more negative publicity. This year had already been a nightmare with the press.

Troy and Jackie were talking in the hallway, and I reached to open my door with a grin plastered on my face, but I refrained at the last second. I needed to give her a little time to settle in. When Troy sent me a text saying breakfast was ready, I figured it was as good a time as any to go say hello.

She spun around the moment I stepped through her doorway. Her instincts were incredible, but I already knew that. The look on her face and the light color of her eyes caught and held my attention. We appraised each other for a while before I finally asked her what she thought of her room. I had remembered the earthly look of her the first time I saw her and had purposely had this room decorated to reflect that.

She said the room was beautiful, but she had no idea what beauty was. I looked it straight in the face. Fresh, vibrant, and earthy. That was what beauty was, and she was it to a T. There wasn't an actress or model alive who compared to the woman in front of me.

A few short steps and I stood before her. "Nowhere as beautiful as you are." Without even a thought, I stepped closer, drawn to her by the need to feel the soft skin of her cheek. I had to be closer. I no longer wanted to imagine the feel of her lips; I needed to feel them, along with her tongue sliding over mine, and her arms holding me tightly. I had dreamed of this woman for months, and I finally had her within reach.

I shouldn't have stopped. I should have just moved in to take what I fantasized about. She would have responded; I could feel it, see it in her eyes. The way she explored my face and opened her mouth as the space disappeared between us. Her tongue flicked out to wet her lips, and that alone told me what I needed to know. Maybe I was hoping she would come to me. But she didn't. Just before I seized the moment, she stepped out of my reach.

I shrugged. "Can't blame a guy for trying, can you?" My voice came out all wrong. I knew I sounded like an ass, but I didn't want her to know that her rejection had stung. "I came to tell you that breakfast is ready." I spun and left the room.

In the hallway, I leaned back against the wall, willing the vibrations in my legs to stop. Maybe if I had her, just once, this irrational need would go away. I shook my head and pushed off the wall when my subconscious whispered, *once will never be enough.* With a sigh, I made my way down to the patio.

Everyone from the team who stayed at the house had already gathered around the table. "Morning, everyone. Jacquelyn will be down in a few moments; she was just about finished unpacking." I took a seat and reached for the huge stack of fluffy pancakes that sat in the center of the glass table.

"I hope you didn't freak her out," Roseanne said.

"I didn't freak her out, Rose, relax." I rolled my eyes and grabbed a few pieces of bacon. We all turned toward the back of the house when we heard footsteps hit the flagstone patio.

She took my breath away as she came to an abrupt stop. The plate of bacon suspended in the air as I was about to put it back down. A moment of unease passed over her features, but she scanned the table and seemed to shift her shoulders and gain control.

Troy stood up. "Jacquelyn, come sit over here." He pointed to a chair next to him and moved to hold it out for her.

"Thanks, Troy." She smiled up at him. "You can call me Jackie. Jacquelyn can be mouthful."

She sat down and shared another smile with him. I forced myself to take a bite of my pancakes and not react to the jealousy that rushed through my veins like acid.

Troy started the introductions. "Jackie, you met Roseanne yesterday. This is Drew and Robbie. They're part of our security team. Drew is the other bodyguard; if for some reason we can't be with Ryan, then he'll take our place. He is usually with us whenever we travel and will continue to do so while we figure things out. Robbie is in charge of our transportation logistics, and he makes sure things are always secure whenever or wherever we travel." Jackie acknowledged each person with a quick nod. I sat quietly watching the exchange while I pulverized my pancakes.

"Roseanne is our assistant. She does a lot for us, and she is always around to make sure we have what we need. She's especially here to help you." Jackie quirked an eyebrow up at Troy as he continued, "If you find you need something, anything, then she will get it for you or find out how to get it if she doesn't have direct access."

"Morning, Roseanne." The smile Jackie shared with Rose was the brightest I'd seen grace her lips, and I almost bit my tongue while I chewed on a piece of bacon.

"I can't wait to work with you, Jackie. I love those CSI shows, so this is going to be so cool watching a real detective figure this all out." Roseanne gushed out the words with excitement, causing Jackie to laugh. The sound was musical, and Troy and I exchanged a quick glance.

"It's really not as exciting as it looks on television, but you work in the movie business, so you should already know that." They shared another laugh.

"Yeah, I know. But that's TV, this is real life!" Even I laughed at how exciting she made it all sound.

"So, is this the whole team?" Jackie asked.

I was chewing so Troy answered. "No, this is only the part of the team who knows exactly why you are here. We have eight other people, but they mostly work the sets and scene areas." He reached over and picked up the coffee carafe that was out of her reach and handed it to her.

"Thanks." She poured herself coffee, and I watched as she scanned the table for the creamer, pouring a generous amount into her cup. "So, what do the other people think I'm here for?"

Everyone looked at me, except for Jackie who was stirring her coffee. When no one said anything, she glanced around the table and saw them all watching me. She picked up her coffee and took a sip, observing me over the rim of her cup with a raised brow.

I swallowed the lump of pancakes in my mouth as everyone waited for my reply and took a sip of coffee to help wash it down. "Well, they are going to be told that you're here because we've been seeing each other since the airport incident, and I wanted to keep you close; so I gave you this job."

She raised her other eyebrow to match the first one and set down her coffee. "Have you told them that yet? I don't think that's very practical." A ping-pong match would not have had as many heads turning back and forth as our conversation did.

"No one knows you're here, and we didn't tell anyone else that you were coming. Only the four of us, my agent, and my attorney know what we're doing," I said carefully.

She scrutinized me for a long few moments. "I suggest that you tell people that we started seeing each other after the car accident. I would not have gotten involved with you after the airport incident because it was an open case, and you were a victim. It wouldn't have been right. The time of your accident would be more appropriate since Mr. Patrick had just been sentenced."

I mulled over what she said and chewed on the side of my cheek as I sat back in my seat and stared at my almost empty plate. Obviously, she did things by the book, and I couldn't fault her for that. I nodded absently. "Okay, we'll tell people that we started seeing each other in January then. How's that?"

She stared at me hard. "So we are actually going to pretend that we're dating? As in a couple, a *real* couple?"

"Yes." I braced myself for her backlash, but she clenched her jaw and stayed silent. So silent, it began to make me nervous. I was trying to come up with something else to say when she finally spoke.

"Why? Why do I need to do that? Why can't I just pretend you gave me this job as a thank you for saving your life?" She picked up her coffee again but didn't bring it to her lips. I noticed the cup was shaking slightly about the same time she did, I watched her set it back down.

I realized, with a certain amount of satisfaction, that I wasn't the only one who was nervous. "Well, because the person who is threatening me seems to have a problem with the women in my life." The sound of her laughter filled the quiet morning air and startled a bird off a nearby branch.

"That doesn't surprise me." She shook her head and looked down at her plate. She hadn't eaten anything yet. "Have you ever thought about not having a woman in your life? The problems might stop, you know."

"Aren't you going to eat?" I asked her, ignoring her question. That one had gotten a little too close for comfort. I always found that I was much happier when I had a woman around me, until she got on my nerves, at least.

"No, I don't eat breakfast. Coffee is fine." She turned to Troy. "So, you think me pretending to be with Ryan is going to flush this person out?"

"Yeah, that's exactly what we're hoping. We figure that if they try anything, you might be able to figure it out quicker since you'll be so close to Ryan." She examined me for a moment over the table. "Ryan needs to stay focused on the movie, so while he's focused on that, you will be around and can watch out for him. But…" He stopped and shot me a look.

"But, what?" Jackie asked and flicked her eyes between the two of us.

Troy hesitated for a few seconds, and everyone stopped eating. "You're going to have to pretend to actually like Ryan." Her shoulders rose and fell as she inhaled deeply and let her breath back out slowly.

"I don't think I'm that good of an actress," she said quietly, and everyone at the table but me chuckled. I focused on my plate for a moment before I lifted my face up. She was grinning at me, so I knew she was just joking. I laughed softly, relieved, and shook my head at her.

"Fine. How much am I supposed to act like I like you? Am I supposed to be totally smitten by you, or just like you, like you?" She had a mischievous look on her face as she asked.

Totally smitten I wanted to say. "Maybe someplace in the middle. You're not the only one who's going to be acting here, you know. I'm going to have to pretend to like you, too."

Everyone burst into laughter, except for Jackie who scanned the table. "What did I just miss?" she asked.

Troy put his arm around her shoulders and pulled her close. "Nothing, girl. You missed nothing." Troy continued to pull her close until he made eye contact with me. I must have had a look on my face because he immediately pulled his arm off her and went back to eating.

"The people here will know that this is all an act, along with Ryan's agent and a few other select people. We want to keep it as quiet as we can since we think it's someone on the set," Roseanne stated. "Everyone here we absolutely trust. We've all been with Ryan for years."

"Is it possible that it's one of your other security team members?" She looked around the table, taking in Robbie and Drew at length.

Troy answered. "There is a good possibility of that. That's one of the reasons why we didn't tell them about you coming. We'd like it to just look like Ryan brought you on as his girlfriend to keep you close and to give you something to do while he's working." She nodded at his reply.

"So, when does all this start?" Jackie picked up her coffee cup and took another drink. She looked more relaxed now.

"Right after breakfast," Troy said, "Some of the other team members will be here and then we have two interviews set up for later today. You will be there for both of them, and while you aren't going to be in the interviews, we want them to see you and know that you're around. The sooner we can get the rumors flying, the better."

She closed her eyes and breathed deeply a few times. With a quick shake of her head, she opened her eyes. "So much for my calm, quiet life," she muttered, but we all heard it and exchanged glances.

"What about the notes that you've received? When do I get to see them?" She turned to me, but it was Roseanne who replied.

"I'll show you all the stuff we have tomorrow when we go to the set, because they are all in Ryan's trailer. Troy and I will fill you in on all the events that have led up to this."

"Today, just start getting to know people. Keep your eyes open and see what you think of everyone," Troy stated.

Troy's cell rang, and he checked the screen and stood up. "Excuse me, I need to take this." He walked back into the house.

Roseanne, Drew, and Robbie got up after Troy left and excused themselves. I watched them walk away and pushed my chair back from the table, dropping my napkin on my plate.

When I looked up, she was watching me. "You have no idea how much this is going to impact my life," she said quietly.

I didn't know what to say, so I shrugged lightly.

Her eyes sparkled hotly for a moment, and I realized that shrugging probably wasn't the best thing to do. It was pretty insensitive on my part.

"You are going to have to be honest with me, Ryan. You're going to have to talk to me and tell me things that are going on. Are you going to be able to do that?"

"Yes." I stood, and she followed my lead. After pushing in her chair, she turned to look out over the property behind us.

"It is beautiful here." Her voice was soft. I walked up behind her, afraid I would miss a single word she said. She stiffened at my approach just as I heard voices inside the house heading our way.

"Show time, Jackie. You ready for this?" I whispered behind her as I stepped closer to her back and put my hands on her elbows.

Her entire body tensed. "Relax. I'm not going to hurt you," I said softly as I wrapped my arms around her from behind, gently laying my hands over her stomach; the skin was taut under her shirt. *Was that from tension, or did she have abs of steel?* For a moment, I relished the feel of her in my arms. She fit perfectly, but I knew she would. To me this was not acting, but I needed her to think I was doing my part. I didn't want to scare her away.

The voices grew closer, and she moved her hands up to her stomach where my forearms crossed over. She put them over mine. I moved one of my hands to her shoulder and pushed her hair off her neck so that I could lean in and kiss it just as two members of our team walked out through the door.

Her skin smelled so sweet and felt so soft under my lips. I couldn't help but kiss it a second time, and when I pulled my lips back, I slowly flicked my tongue out and over her neck. I felt her shiver, and a small sound came from her mouth.

"You liked that," I whispered in her ear, nudging it with the tip of my nose.

She turned her head to the side and looked me in the eyes. "I'm a better actress than I thought," she whispered under her breath, though her eyes were playful.

"Hey, Ryan," Bill yelled from the door. I didn't let go of Jacquelyn but pulled her along with me as I turned.

"Hey, Bill. I think they're going to start the meeting in the study." I held Jackie tightly, probably tighter than I needed to, but I was enjoying the feel of her in my arms too much to let up.

Bill was eyeballing us and absorbing everything. He was the perfect person to watch this because I knew he liked to talk. He'd start the rumors immediately.

"Okay, thanks," he said and stood there a moment longer. I spun Jackie slowly into my arms. She looked surprised when I did it, and I know she was even more surprised when I pulled her tightly against my chest and kissed her hard.

She didn't respond at first, but then, I felt her body melting into mine ever so slightly. The sound of Bill laughing faded as he went back into the house. I should have ended the kiss then, but my mouth had a mind of its own. I held her tighter, savoring the way her tongue ran over mine, the way our lips melded together, and the way her body fit perfectly against mine. When I finally stepped back, my knees were weak. She smirked up into my eyes.

"Yeah, I'm a much better actress than I thought." She winked and pulled out of my arms.

If that was acting, I was in deep trouble. I watched her hips sway as she walked away, and I could feel my heart pounding in my chest.

JACQUELYN

$\mathcal{I}$ walked away from Ryan with my heart thudding loudly in my ears. Did I really just kiss him like that? Holy crap, I really did. I still felt the imprint of his lips on mine. The way his tongue tasted sweet from the pancake syrup as it entered my mouth.

How I got into the house and found the bathroom was beyond me. I shut my eyes as I leaned my head against the back of the door.

When I opened them up, I stood in front of a large oval mirror. The face staring back was flushed, eyes wide, and lips slightly swollen. And here I thought Jimmy's kiss last night had been passionate. It didn't even come close to the knee weakening one I just shared with Ryan. What an amazing difference, especially when I knew Jimmy actually cared about me and Ryan was only acting.

I finally got my heartbeat under control and splashed water on my face. The scent of his musky cologne filled my nose as I splashed the warm water on my skin. I ran my hands through my hair and tried to focus on what I needed to do, and *not* on what I had just done.

When I was firmly back in control, I opened the door and heard voices down the hall and to the left. I followed them until I found the room that Ryan had called a study. It was a large open room with shelves of books lining one wall. I wondered if the books were just props. Ryan didn't seem like the type to read much more than his scripts.

Like the family room I had been in last night, this one had various seating areas. Roseanne, Drew, and Robbie were already there, along with the guy named Bill who had shown up on the patio. He was checking me out, and I tried not to blush under his energetic scrutiny.

Troy entered behind me and pointed to a seat just off to the side. If he hadn't pointed it out, I would've headed there anyway because it gave me a good view of everyone. Four other people joined the meeting, and Roseanne quickly introduced them to me.

Bill worked security around the trailers where Ryan got dressed and rested. He had others who worked with him. Markus was in charge of technology and took care of the headsets, computers, and cellphones everyone used. Brady was a crowd control guard and made sure he knew where crowds were and gave Ryan a heads up on when to avoid a certain area. The last one introduced was Brian; I wasn't quite sure what Brian did. Roseanne never explained it to me.

Any one of these four could be involved in the threats against Ryan. They would start at the top of my list. It was Markus and Brian who seemed the most concerned with my presence.

Bill kept smirking at me, and Brady didn't pay any attention to me after shaking my hand. I listened carefully while they talked with Robbie about the start of production tomorrow and what concerns they had, who else would be on the sets, what equipment they needed, and where the shooting was taking place. I didn't ask any questions, although I had quite a few. I wanted to make it look like I was the dumb blond girlfriend who was just along for the ride.

It was easier to learn things if people didn't suspect you were investigating them. The meeting was wrapping up when Ryan walked into the room.

He winked at me, and everyone saw it. I couldn't help but blush as the memory of our kiss bounced back into my mind the minute his face came into view. He walked over and stood next to my chair.

"Are you guys done with her? My interviews are starting soon, and I'd like Jacquelyn with me now. It's about time that everyone knows about us." He chuckled huskily and rubbed the top of my shoulders. Everyone joined in with the laughter except Markus and Brian, who shared their own private glance.

Troy said I was good to go, and they had a few more things to talk about and he would fill me in later. I stood beside Ryan as he slid his warm arm around my waist and led me out of the room. I told myself that I put my arm around him only to make it look good. Yep, that was the only reason.

"So, what did you think?" Ryan questioned me as we meandered down the hallway and out of earshot. He still had his arm around me, and I tried to pull away from him. He held on tighter, though I wasn't sure why since there was no one around to act for.

"It was interesting," I said as I peered at him. He stopped moving and halted me by curving his fingers around my waist. His eyes were sparkling and shadowed, and his lashes were full and dark. I leaned back and realized it was because he was wearing makeup. It was strange to see a man who already had such a perfect face made up to look even more handsome.

"Interesting? That's all you have?" He frowned as he focused on me.

I blinked. "Yes, it's interesting to hear how it's all done. How they coordinate everything for you."

We were at the end of the hallway just inside the atrium, and the room was bright. The pupils of his eyes were small, making the blue even brighter and bolder since there was so much more of it to see. I knew he was going to kiss me before he started to move toward me, and I was torn between meeting him halfway or stepping back—my logic battling my hormones.

As he got closer, I saw his eyes flick to the side real quick, I heard footsteps on the marble floor. Okay, so we were back to acting. I wrapped my other arm around his neck and raised my face so that his lips brushed mine.

It would have been the perfect kiss, gentle and slow, if it wasn't for the fact that my heart wanted to explode out of my chest. His left hand caressed my cheek while his right arm stayed around my waist holding me to him; our hips fit snuggly together, and my chest pushed against his hard chest. His right hand slid up to the nape of my neck, holding my lips tightly to his. He wouldn't have to worry; my hormones had no thoughts of ending this anytime soon on their own.

"Excuse me, Mr. Palmer, but you are going to ruin your makeup if you keep that up." A female voice startled me back to reality, and logic began to crash in. His lips rose up in a smile, and he pulled away with a chuckle.

"It's worth having it redone for a kiss like this, Marie." Together we turned to face her, and I noticed she had a small strained smile on her older face.

"Marie, this is Jacquelyn. Jackie this is my makeup artist. She's the one who makes me gorgeous." He led me over to Marie, and we shook hands.

"Not hard to make you gorgeous, Mr. Palmer. I have a good palate to use." She laughed kindly as she shook my hand.

Marie openly examined my features. "You'd be a perfect palate too." Ryan still had his arm around me. "The newspaper photos didn't do you justice."

I blushed, and she laughed. "Oh, and she blushes, too! That's perfect."

"She is a perfect palate, isn't she?" Ryan gazed down at me with a little too much heat in his eyes. I rolled mine at Marie, trying to ignore the feelings that he awakened in my hormones. She laughed a husky sound.

Ryan turned and looked out the front door. Two vehicles pulled up in front of the house, and Troy walked in behind us.

"Ryan, where are we doing this interview?" Troy asked as he entered.

"Are you guys done in the study? We can do it in there." Troy nodded and walked outside to speak with the people who were climbing out of the media vans.

"Jacquelyn, let's go sit on the patio until they're ready for us." He began to lead me away, but Marie grabbed my arm.

"Do I need to do some makeup on her? Is she in the interview?" she asked Ryan.

He considered me for a moment. "No, she's perfect just the way she is." My breath caught in my throat at the sound of his voice and the sexy look in his eye. Damn, he wasn't a good actor; he was freaking fantastic! No wonder he was one of the most popular film stars these days.

"It's a pleasure to meet the woman who is not afraid of evil. Hopefully, you can keep this guy from finding anymore," Marie chortled as Ryan led me away.

The whole fear no evil comment had been a constant source of comment since the incident at the airport. I didn't understand why people couldn't let that go. I ground my teeth when my back was to her.

Ryan led me to the patio, and I pulled away from him as soon as we walked out the door. I sighed.

"What's wrong?" he asked as we made our way over to the table where we had eaten breakfast.

"Nothing." I shook my head and sat down, resting my arms on the glass table. "Why did you tell reporters that I didn't fear evil?"

He studied me for a minute and sat down crossing his left leg over his right at his knee. He contemplated the scenery for a few moments before turning back to me. "That day in the airport, it was all that I knew about you. You walked right in between that man and me. I could only see your back and the words that were written there. I couldn't believe that someone would just walk in front of a man with a gun when it wasn't part of a script." He shook his head. "How did you even know he was going to do that?" He uncrossed his legs and sat up closer to the table, laying both of his forearms down on the glass.

I shrugged. "I watch people. He was obviously up to something. I saw him when he came in; he was acting nervous and watching your group. The way he was moving and examining you told me something was up. I could tell there was something in his jacket, so when he started to move toward you, I did what I did." I shrugged again and looked away, out toward the back of the property pasture.

"I never did thank you for that," he said quietly.

I laughed. "Oh, yes you did! All the flowers, cards, and phone calls you sent, and then at the hospital." I shook my head remembering all of the stuff I had received from everyone.

"Why didn't you call me?"

I sighed and hung my head. "I told you before. There was no reason to call you. I knew you were grateful. I just wanted all the attention to go away."

"I saw the press conference that you did. Would you really have done the same thing for him if the tables were reversed?"

I pushed away from the table and sat back against the seat. "Of course I would have. He's a person, and I protect people. If you saw the interview, then you know that."

He studied me for a minute before we both got lost in the beauty of the pasture beyond the house. A few minutes later, Troy walked out onto the patio.

"They want to take a few pictures of the property. Do you mind, Ryan?" Troy asked as he joined us.

"No, that's fine," Ryan said as he stood.

"Why don't you and Jackie take a little walk out that way? Hold hands; make it look good. Hopefully, they will get some shots of you two and help get the information out there," Troy suggested as I stood up, too.

Wow, is this what normally happened? Staged romance to make the public think things were going on...*was it always only for publicity?*

Ryan reached over and took my hand silently. We didn't say anything as we walked side by side down the four slate steps and out toward the pasture where the horses grazed.

It was a beautiful spring morning with fresh, clean air. A light breeze blew but the sun felt warm on my skin. Not quite as warm as my hand that was in Ryan's, but warm enough.

As we wandered toward the fence, I thought about what was going on around him. "Tell me, Ryan, what kind of threats have you gotten?"

He surveyed the fields. "Mostly notes." He shrugged. "The water bottle was the first thing that actually happened, although the notes have shown up in some pretty strange places."

"Like where?"

"Restaurants I've dined at. I got one at the airport once, and then one at my parents' house while I was visiting them."

I considered what he said for a few minutes. "Were these places that you went to often?"

"No, not really. I rarely go to my parents, they usually come visit me." He stopped near the wooden fence on the edge of the pasture, pulling my hand so I was closer to him.

"Is that something that you announced you were doing? Something you told the press about?" I watched him closely.

"No. I try to keep my parents out of the spotlight."

I thought for another moment. "When you make your plans and your reservations, how do you normally make them?"

"I either call, or Troy does." He wrapped his arm around my waist and reeled me in.

"On a cellphone." My heart thumped wildly as my body rested against his.

"Yeah, what else?" he said and laughed.

"Do you have your cellphone on you now?" I asked while I tried to put some distance between us. He made it hard to think when our bodies were touching. Now that we were actually discussing the real reason I was here, I wanted to concentrate.

"No. I don't carry it around when I'm at home. Why?" He held me tighter, keeping me from putting the distance between us that I wanted.

"Good, I want you to stop using your cell. If you need to use one, use mine. I'd keep your phone off unless you absolutely need to have it on." While our fingers were still laced together, he brought my arm up to the small of my back forcing me to arch my chest toward him. My hips made contact with his, and a wave of heat washed from my head to my pelvis. Damn hormones!

"Why? You want to know whom I'm talking to? I promise I won't call any other women while you're here." His face was mere inches from mine. My other hand absently went to his hip while his other hand lightly caressed my face, his thumb gently rubbing over my bottom lip.

"I don't care who you talk to. You can call all the women you want. I just want to make sure your phone isn't compromised," I whispered as he brought his face closer. His eyes flashed something for a brief moment, and I wondered if he would pull back.

"There is no other woman I want to talk to right now, only you." He breathed out the words just before he put his lips to mine. His hand squeezed mine tightly behind me and then let go so that he could splay his hand across my lower back. Once he released that hand, it automatically came around and landed on his shoulder.

It was so easy to kiss him, and after only two kisses, my body craved his. He shuddered as my fingernails trailed lightly over his skin.

I heard the whistle, and I assumed Ryan heard it also, but we didn't break off the kiss right away. A few moments later, another whistle came louder, and Ryan chuckled huskily as he pulled away.

I was breathless as I peered up at him and followed his line of sight to the back porch. There were five people standing on the patio, and one of them had a camera pointed at us. Troy waved his hand in the air to motion us back.

I rested my forehead on his chest, my eyes closed while I tried to regain what composure I could while still in his arms. I heard his heart beating, and his labored breath. I was glad to know that I wasn't the only one who felt like they had just run a marathon.

Ryan took my hand and we began to walk back. "That probably gave them some good shots. They will be splashed all over the place by the end of today." He sounded proud of himself, and I had to remind myself that he was only doing what he did best: acting.

This isn't real, Jack, remember that. I let him lead us back to the house. *It isn't real; it's just an act.*

RYAN

I watched her walk away from me as my heart raced. I had never met a woman who could make my heart beat as though adrenaline coursed through my veins non-stop. I followed her into the house and watched as she walked around the corner into the hallway. Roseanne smirked as I came closer.

"Do you need to excuse yourself to the bathroom, too?" she asked and chuckled. I grinned back at her and walked down the opposite hallway. I went into my personal study to read some of my lines for tomorrow's filming. I still had a couple of hours until the interviews started.

When I walked into the study, my cellphone was ringing. I usually left it on the desk when I didn't need it. I hated carrying it, and knew that people who really need to get in touch with me would call Troy. I looked down at the caller ID and saw that it was Kayla. I listened to another ring and debated whether or not to answer it. In the end, I let it go to voicemail and ignored it as I picked up my script for the scenes I would be working on tomorrow.

I heard a phone in the house ring. A few minutes later, there was a knock at my door; it opened before I told them to enter. I looked up to find Marie, my makeup artist and stylist.

"Mr. Palmer, Ms. Rainey is on the phone for you. She said it's important."

"Fine, I'll take it in here." I glanced at my watch. "You almost ready for me?"

"Yep. When you're done with your phone call, you know where to find me." She turned to leave and closed the door behind her.

I took a deep breath before I answered. "Hey, Kayla, what's going on?" I was short with her because I didn't feel like entertaining her today.

"How come you didn't answer your cellphone?" She sounded pouty. "I haven't talked to you in days. I thought we were going to rehearse a couple of the scenes?"

"I've been busy, Kayla." *And avoiding you.* "We'll have time to rehearse them later. Did you need something because I'm kind of busy right now?"

"I know you have those two interviews today. Did you want me to come over? I could help you out with them, be your moral support." Her voice was all cheery as she spoke.

The only reason she wanted to be here was so that she could try and slip into the interview herself. Or, to make them think we were still seeing each other. I wasn't interested in either of those options.

When I declined, she pressed on. "Are you sure?" She sounded pouty. How did a woman sound pouty on the phone?

"I'll see you on the set, Kayla." I said goodbye and hung up before she could say anything else. I wasn't trying to be an ass but, as usual, it came out that way.

I left the study and made my way down the hallway to a room I had turned into a simple salon and makeup station. The set wasn't too far from here, and I preferred to do most of my dressing at home. Besides, interviews were something that happened every day, so it was good to have an area like this at home. I sat down in the chair and talked with Marie while she worked.

Marie had been working for me for about a year, but she still continued to call me Mr. Palmer. She said it was a sign of respect.

After Marie styled my hair and put on enough makeup so that I wouldn't look washed out in the interviews, I climbed out of the chair and made my way to the large study to find Jacquelyn. I wondered how she was fairing with the group.

I entered the room and found her sitting off to the side. I wasn't happy that she was pushed off like that, and I would talk to Troy about that later.

Jackie left the room with me, and I took advantage of the small hallway to keep her close. "So, what did you think?" I asked her as we walked.

I really was interested in knowing her thoughts and her opinions of my team.

I looked down at her as we stood in the atrium. There was something so warm and earthy about her and, with the sunlight shining through the glass, it made me feel so comfortable to be beside her. Maybe that's why I wanted to kiss her, even though no one was around. I started to move closer, and I had the feeling that she was going to step back. She surprised me when she brought her lips to mine. It was the perfect kiss for a romance movie, inviting with just the right amount of magic to cause sparks to fly.

It felt so easy to deepen the kiss and hold her against me. The feel of her soft skin under my hands was like satin as one of them slid up to hold her neck from behind. Her soft flowing hair tickled the back of my hand.

"Excuse me, Mr. Palmer, but you are going to ruin your makeup if you keep that up," I heard Marie say as she entered. I knew she'd been coming down the hallway, but until she spoke, I had put her aside, concentrating on what was in front of me.

"It's worth having it redone for a kiss like this, Marie." And I meant every word of it.

After I told Troy we would do the interview in the study, I led Jackie outside to the patio. I liked to get fresh air before I did interviews. I wanted the feel of the sun on my skin before I switched it over to the brightness of the artificial lighting they used.

I noticed that she tensed up when we got outside. "What's wrong?"

"Why did you tell reporters that I didn't fear evil?"

I shook my head because even now, six months later, that whole scenario blew my mind. Finally, I was getting my chance to ask her about why she had done what she had. "How did you even know he was going to do that?"

She took it all so lightly, and I wondered how she did that. I couldn't understand how she looked at it as just a job when it was my life she was talking about.

The sound of her laughter warmed me as she put her chin up and the sun shone down on her face.

"Why didn't you call me?"

She sighed but didn't look at me when she answered. "I told you before. There was no reason to call. I knew you were grateful. I just wanted all the fanfare to go away."

It was obvious she had no idea how much that event had affected me. It changed me in ways I didn't know I needed to change. I realized then that I was just an idol to people, and I was not important to anyone in particular. I wanted to be important to someone, not just some handsome actor everyone fawned over.

Troy joined us, and we discussed pictures for the interview and of the house. I figured it was a good time to get Jackie into a romantic setting without it being so obvious, so we walked out toward the white fences.

Although my thoughts were on romance, Jackie brought it back to business with questions about the threats I'd received. We talked for a few minutes about it all, but I really had other thoughts in mind. It was hard not to have these thoughts when she was right next to me.

I pulled her close and locked her arm around her back as we came together. As our bodies contacted, she told me she didn't want me using my cellphone. Was she jealous?

"I don't care who you talk to. You can call all the women you want. I just want to make sure your phone isn't compromised." So, she wasn't jealous. Once again, she was doing her job. Well, time to change that.

"There is no other woman I want to talk to right now, only you." When my lips touched hers, I felt the electricity spike through us both. She wound her arm around my shoulders and slid her hand to my neck. The feel of her hand on my skin caused me to shiver, and I ignored the whistle in the distance. When Troy whistled again, I knew I needed to stop before I started giving the photographers more than they needed. I had been ready to lay her down on the ground and make love to her right there.

I looked away from her as soon as the kiss ended, trying to suppress the rising heat in my body. As we'd hoped, a photographer was standing on the patio taking shots of us together. Interestingly, I found I didn't like the intrusion when it came to my time alone with Jackie. For the first time, it felt as if my privacy had been truly invaded. I knew this was all supposed to be an act, and the scene we just put on was for this specific purpose, but I suddenly wanted to protect Jackie from what we just shared.

Still, I knew that we'd just done what we set out to do. "That probably gave them some good shots. They will be splashed all over the place by the end of today." This is all for a purpose, and we did what we had to for that, nothing else. *Yeah, right!*

The photographer continued to shoot pictures of us as we walked back to the house. When we got closer, I put my hand up and told them that was enough. At least the man was decent enough to stop when asked. Some photographers weren't so kind. It was probably only because he already had some seriously intimate photos to use.

I introduced Jacquelyn to several of the people who were there for the interview. "Mr. Palmer, is Jacquelyn going to join us for the interview? You know we would love to get her thoughts on your latest filming," the producer said. I was about to answer when Jackie spared me.

"Thank you so much, but to be honest, I'm not much for interviews. I'd prefer to just watch. Maybe another time we can do that." I caught her eye and winked just as Marie grabbed me to freshen up my makeup.

Troy made a beeline for Jackie the moment I was busy. It was probably a good thing not to leave her alone with all those people.

"So you seem to be pretty serious about this girl," Marie stated as I sat back down in the chair, "I have seen you with a lot of women, but I have never seen you quite so intimate in public before."

I chuckled. "I guess I can't help what I feel." *And exactly what was that?* Marie studied me in the mirror and picked up a brush; with a small, tight smile, she went to work touching up my makeup.

Jacquelyn wasn't in the room when I returned, but as I got settled in for the interview, I saw her come in and stand to the side. She leaned against the wall the same way she did the first time I saw her in the airport, with her arms crossed over her chest. She wasn't looking at me; she studied the room. Her eyes were steady as they scanned, and I realized that she had automatically gone into work mode.

For a few minutes, I observed her as she took in the room, but I brought my focus back to the interview when I finally needed to. The first interview went well, and before I knew it the second one was about to start. I didn't have much of a break in between, and no chance at all to talk to Jackie.

She stood against the wall for both interviews, always watching the people. If she watched me during the interview, I didn't know it. When the last one was over, I went to see Marie who quickly took off the makeup. Then I went in search of Jacquelyn.

I found her on the third-floor balcony looking out through the atrium's glass at the sun. It was getting lower in the sky, and the colors were exploding around it as it neared the horizon. She seemed lost in thought as I approached her. Her expression was intense and far away. I was hesitant to step closer, so I stopped a few feet away.

With my hands resting on the wooden railing, I watched as the sun began to set. She didn't move. She just kept staring straight ahead; I wondered if she even realized I was there.

"I know you don't eat breakfast, but do you eat dinner?" I asked casually as I glanced sideway over my shoulder at her. Her eyes unclouded as if she was coming out of a deep sleep.

"Oh, Ryan, I'm sorry. I was lost in the view." She peeked quickly over at me before turning back to look out the window. Then she stopped and turned to focus on me. This time, as her eyes traveled over my facial features, I found myself not moving, afraid to break the intense examination she was giving me.

"Hey, you guys want Chinese? I'm gonna call in an order," Troy yelled from the bottom floor. Jackie and I locked eyes for a moment longer before she glanced over the balcony.

"Sure, that sounds good," she yelled down.

When Jackie headed toward the stairs, I reached out to grab her arm. "Jackie, wait."

"Not now, Ryan." She shook her head and pulled out of my grasp easily.

I watched her descend and wondered what was wrong and why it bothered me that I didn't know.

JACQUELYN

$\mathcal{T}$he way the interviews were conducted was interesting, especially the starting and stopping of the cameras to make sure they got the best views. The reporters asked endless questions, some over and over again, to make sure it was the way they wanted it, or Ryan wanted it.

There were a lot of people in the study, and while I kept one eye on Ryan, I watched the others in the room, too. Always scanning, always searching for something that might seem out of place. I observed Markus when he entered the room at one point. He didn't see me, and it gave me a chance to really examine him. He was watching Ryan closely. Almost too closely.

For a few minutes, he listened to the interview, and then got on his cellphone and messed around with a few things before he looked straight up and into my face. I gave a tight smile, but he just glared at me for a few seconds, then turned and slithered out the door. I didn't like him, and I wasn't sure if it was because I just didn't like him, or because there was something not quite right about him.

While the interviews proceeded, I half-heartedly listened as Ryan answered endless questions about his latest movie, the one he was starting to film tomorrow, and the questions they geared to get more information about me. It took everything I had to keep from running from the room as people glanced over at me time and time again. One of the interviewers tried to get me to come in front of the camera, but I adamantly refused as politely as I could.

I was exhausted by the end of the interviews and wondered how Ryan still looked perfectly relaxed after hours of dealing with all this crazy activity. I had to remind myself that this was his life; being in front of a camera and acting for people was his job.

After the interviews, Ryan was whisked away. I would have followed, but I saw Troy walking out with him. I quickly disappeared from the production staff that was packing up and made my way upstairs. I needed a few minutes alone to think.

My intent was to go up to my room to ponder everything from today, but when I got to the top landing, the colors of the sky stopped me, and I stood gazing out the window over the pasture behind the house. The sun was setting and if I thought the sunrise was breathtaking, I had no words for the sunset. I was immediately lost in the moment as thoughts invaded my mind.

I knew that within a few hours, the photographs that were taken of us would spread quickly all over the internet and on every TV station. What would my friends think about all of this? Man, I hadn't even called Rebecca to tell her about it. She was going to freak out. I also knew, she wouldn't be the only one. I would not be surprised to hear from Jimmy tonight as soon as the news got out.

My thoughts kept going back to the kiss that we shared out near the pasture. The kiss that had devoured part of my soul and melted my toes as it warmed my insides close to a boiling point. What did we look like as we stood in the throes of passion?

Those pictures would be flashed all over the world, and I would forever be known as one of Ryan Palmer's women. That thought irked me, and I needed to figure out how to protect myself in all of this. How could I keep my heart from becoming involved with a man I could never have?

That was easy. My past kept people at a distance. I couldn't let anyone close to me. I had no choice. Would this cause a problem? Maybe. I had to figure this out quickly before *they* got involved.

I learned a long time ago to keep people at a distance and to keep my heart detached. I would never trust myself to love someone again; I couldn't afford to. That was why Jimmy and I had stayed so quiet about our relationship. He understood.

With Ryan in my life, it could be more dangerous for us both physically and mentally. I couldn't afford to bring harm upon him.

My past haunted me to the point that I wondered if I would ever be free to love someone again. Would there be a time when I could trust that no harm would come to the person I loved?

Ryan startled me out of my depressing thoughts, and I realized how low the sun was. How long had I stood there lost in my haunted memories?

"Oh, Ryan, I'm sorry. I was lost in the view," I murmured as I glanced at him. I meant to turn right back, but the last of the sunlight coming through the window made him glow. His face was so beautiful in this light. Yeah, I know men shouldn't be beautiful, but at that moment, he was. *I could fall in love with that face. Ah, hell!* I was already in love with that face. It was the man inside who scared me to death; but falling in love was not an option, and this was just a job.

After answering Troy, I turned to head downstairs, but Ryan reached out and grasped my arm. I quickly removed my forearm from his hand and kept walking.

"Not now, Ryan." I couldn't say more at that moment, and I didn't think I would be able to handle another long, elegant kiss without breaking down completely. The look on his face said he wanted exactly that, and more. I couldn't give him more. Not now, not ever.

I found Troy in the kitchen glancing over a menu. "So, what did you think of today?" he asked as he pushed the menu toward me.

I climbed up on a stool and picked up the menu to look over my choices. Hong Kong Chinese, good pick; I ordered from them myself. "You guys do a lot of those?" I asked as I pushed the menu back his way. I knew what I wanted, the same thing I always got.

"Quite a few at the start of a production, and then after he finishes filming, we do a ton of them." He smiled. "What do you want?"

"Shrimp cashew and an egg roll, please." He wrote it down and smirked. "What?"

"That's the same thing Ryan always gets." He lifted his head up. "You two actually have more in common than you think."

I snorted. "Yeah, okay!"

He walked around the kitchen island to stand next to me. "I think you'd be surprised by him if you gave him a chance."

I considered what Troy said for a moment. *A chance for what?* I pressed my lips together, unsure of how to answer.

"Just keep an open mind, Jackie, and give him a chance." He put his hand on my shoulder as he spoke and squeezed gently. He was a very touchy man, and normally, I didn't like that, but I really clicked with Troy and his touchiness didn't bother me for some reason. I still didn't know what to say, so I acknowledged with a single nod.

"I'm going to go call this in and then send Drew out to pick it up. We'll eat in the family room so that we can watch TV and see if you guys show up on the seven o'clock entertainment news."

I sighed without realizing it. I was staring at the counter when Troy turned and came back to me. "Are you okay?"

"Yeah, I'm fine," I lied. What could I say? It didn't matter to them that my township sold me out to be a call girl to Ryan. It didn't matter to anyone other than me that while I did this, my heart and my soul were going to be hurt, and my reputation would be put out there with all those other groupie women.

Troy squeezed my shoulder again and walked away. I put my forehead down on the cold marble of the counter after he left the room. I could not imagine what my friends were all going to say when they heard about this. And what about Jimmy? I knew I was really lost in thought when, for the second time that night, someone was able to walk up on me without me knowing.

I jumped when a hand touched my shoulder, and I reached for the small of my back where I normally kept my off-duty weapon, but I wasn't wearing it today.

Ryan stood in front of me with his hands up in a defensive position after he took a quick step back. "Sorry, I didn't mean to startle you."

I relaxed back onto the stool. "Sorry, Ryan. I didn't hear you come in."

"Obviously." He pulled up another stool and sat beside me. He was close enough that his knee brushed the side of my leg. He didn't move it away. I couldn't handle the feeling of his leg touching mine, so I shifted my legs away from his. If I thought he wouldn't notice, I was wrong. His face registered something, but I wasn't sure what it was.

We sat quietly for a moment, and I watched him from the corner of my eye. He was studying me as I pretended to stare at the stainless-steel fridge. He reached out toward me, and I tried not to flinch when his hand came to my neck. He was only reaching for my pendant.

"What saint is this?" he asked as he fingered my small silver medallion.

"Saint Michael," I replied as I peeked at him.

"Are you Catholic?" He cocked his head.

"No, but just because I'm not Catholic doesn't mean that I don't believe in the power of it."

He looked confused. "What power?"

"The power of protection. Saint Michael is the protector of law enforcement." I met his gaze, and he nodded slowly in understanding.

He let go of my pendant. I felt it slap back against my skin softly. It was warm from the heat of his fingers, and it reminded me of when his hands were on me earlier. I squirmed on my seat as he reached for my arm, but I realized he was just reaching for the wristband I was wearing, not my hand.

"What does this say?" He pulled my arm closer so that he could see it better.

"Heroes Live Forever." The touch of his hand on my arm was hot, and my heart thumped like a drum in my chest.

"I take it this has to do with law enforcement, too? Why is it black and blue?" He fingered it slowly. The tips of his fingers slid over my skin as it left the silicone of the band and touched my wrist. Could he feel my pulse beating more rapidly?

"Yes, I wear it as a reminder of all the officers who have been killed in the line of duty. The black wrist band is for mourning, the thin blue line represents the officers banding together."

He considered my words. "Banding together? Like protecting one another?"

I laughed quietly and shook my head. That is what most people thought. "The thin blue line does represent police officers banding together, but not like people think. If you were to take all the good people and put them on one side, and then took all the criminals and put them on the other, and then you lined up all of the police officers shoulder to shoulder in the middle, you would see the thin blue line between them."

"The line between good and evil?" he asked softly.

I swallowed heavily and pulled my hand back. "Yeah, something like that." I turned away so that I was facing the fridge again.

From the corner of my eye, I saw him as he reached out to touch my hair. I couldn't stand to let him touch me one more time, or I wasn't going to be able to control myself. I slipped quickly off the other side of the stool to put distance between us.

"Ryan, there is no one here to act for. Do us both a favor and remember that I'm only here to do a job." I saw hurt cross his face, and I almost apologized for it. Instead, I told myself I didn't care, and I started to walk past him to leave. He put his arm out to stop me, and it caught me right around the waist.

I tensed, staring straight ahead. What was he going to say? When he didn't speak right away, I turned to him slowly.

"Do you think this is only an act, Jacquelyn?" he whispered.

My fingers itched to touch his face, to sooth the desire by running my hands over his shoulders and kiss his lips, but I clenched my teeth for a second and pulled his arm off my waist.

"That's exactly what it is, Ryan. That's all it is. You paid handsomely for my professional abilities, and that's it." I moved away before I could see the reaction on his face.

When I entered the hallway, my knees almost gave way. I put my hand out on the wall to steady myself. It was just an act. Don't believe that he wants anything more than to use you for his own publicity and safety.

I made it into the family room on unsteady legs just as Drew walked in with the food. I wasn't particularly hungry anymore, but I knew I needed to eat. I hadn't eaten all day with watching the interviews and keeping an eye on everyone.

Ryan joined us shortly after I did, and I was careful not to look his way. I made sure that I sat in a chair that was slightly off to the side where he wouldn't be able to sit next to me. Troy handed out the containers and gave me a plate so that I could pour out my food.

"Chopsticks or fork?" Roseanne asked as she walked over to me, holding both out for my selection.

I like chopsticks, but my hands were still shaking so I opted for the fork and dug into my food, realizing I was a lot hungrier than I thought.

There was casual conversation in the room as Troy turned on the television, and we all brought our attention to the screen to watch the entertainment news.

I almost choked on a mouthful of my egg roll when a picture of Ryan and I standing out by the pasture flashed up on the screen.

"Looks like Ryan and his heroine have finally come clean about the secret relationship they've been having for the last few months. Our photographers caught them having a private moment at his new estate near where Detective Jacquelyn Liveon used to work. Sources at the department say she is currently on leave, and they are not sure if she will be returning."

I could do nothing but stare at the screen as they flashed pictures of us sitting on the porch, kissing out by the fence, and walking hand and hand toward the house. We looked relaxed and, I hated to say this, but we actually looked good together. I managed to swallow the food in my mouth as I listened to the announcer.

"Before a scheduled interview with Ryan Palmer today, our photographer was able to get some shots of the couple who appear to be very close and quite happy together. Ryan stated in his interview that they have been secretly seeing each other since January after his car accident. He finally decided to come out in the open since the relationship is becoming more serious."

I flicked my eyes to Ryan. *Serious?* Did he really tell them serious? I guess I had been too intent watching the people around him during the interview to actually listen to his answers. I focused on the television as one more close up of us filled the screen in a very intimate kiss, our arms wrapped tightly around each other. *Well, hell!* That photograph sure made it look serious. My skin was on fire as the blush crept up my neck.

"Ryan Palmer told us today that Detective Liveon has taken a leave of absence from her job to be close to him during production and to allow them time to further develop their relationship. He also stated that she will be working on his security team since she seems very capable of keeping him safe. Be sure to tune in tomorrow night when we air Ryan Palmer's full interview about the filming of his upcoming movie which starts production tomorrow."

We were all glued to the screen, even as the broadcaster moved on to another story. At the same moment, everyone started laughing, high fiving, and went right back to eating. Ryan caught my eye and then looked away.

"I think that turned out good. Ryan, those pictures look real, man!" Drew said as he shoveled food into his mouth.

"Oh, they looked real because they were," Roseanne laughed. Ryan and I both turned to her before we glanced at one another again.

"Roseanne, we were just acting," Ryan said sternly as he looked back at her.

I was about to back up his statement when my cellphone vibrated in my pocket. I knew by the length of the vibration that it was a text message and not a phone call. I reached down and pulled it out just as another message came through. *Crap! Here it comes.*

I set my plate down on my lap and unlocked the screen. Becca had sent me a message, along with Brad, and, oh, here's one from Steve, too. Before I could even read Becca's message, I got another one. This time it was from Susan.

I sat back in my seat and put my head against the cushion behind me. Four more messages popped up on my phone as I sat there staring at it. I opened the message from Becca, and it read, "WHAT THE HELL IS GOING ON?" And, yep, she really did write it in all caps.

I typed back, "Relax, explain later." Then I started flipping through the other messages that either asked me what was going on or made comments about the steamy kisses they had seen.

Becca answered me back before I got done reading the rest of my messages. "NOW!!!"

I really didn't want to answer her right now, but I knew she would bug the hell out of me if I didn't. "Give me a minute," I typed back. I set my plate down on the table next to me and stood.

It wasn't until I stood that I noticed everyone watching me. "Is everything all right, Jackie?" Troy asked.

I shook my head. "You guys just exploded my whole world, and you think I should be all right with it? No, I'm not all right." I lifted my phone as I felt it vibrate in my hand long and hard telling me a call was coming through. I knew without looking who it was.

"If you will excuse me, I need to try to explain, no wait—I need to lie to my boyfriend, my co-workers, and my best friend about why I have supposedly been hiding this from them for months." I turned and walked out of the room without looking at any of them again.

I took a deep breath and answered the phone as I stepped out onto the back patio. "Jimmy," I said quietly.

"Mind telling me what the hell is going on?" Anger laced his words.

"Remember what I told you before I left?" I said softly as I began to pace the patio.

"What? About not believing all I see?" I heard a thump coming from his side of the phone, and I wondered if he had just thrown something. "Can I tell you it was pretty damn hard not to believe it while I was watching it? What's going on, Jack?"

"Jimmy, you know I can't talk about what I'm doing undercover. Just know it's not true. You of all people need to know it's not true." I was trying not to actually beg him to believe me. It wasn't until he called that I realized just how much this was going to impact the relationship we had. What guy would want to see his sometime girlfriend in the arms of another man, much less plastered all over the news?

"You can say that, Jack, but that looked pretty damn real. Is that why he wants you there? So he can flaunt you all around to make people think you're his girlfriend?" I heard anger like I'd never heard before radiating in his voice, and yet I suddenly felt as though I needed to make excuses for Ryan.

"Jimmy, it's not what you think. He's not flaunting me around." I spoke quietly as I stood staring out at the dark sky.

"But he is making it look like you're his girlfriend, right? How long has this really been going on?" he asked me pointedly.

My eyes burst wide open. "What do you mean, how long has this been going on? I just came here today."

"Yeah, it sure looked like it was a first kiss to me." I didn't even know how to answer him. I knew he was going to be upset. I could understand that. And if I had been able to talk to him about it, I would have explained it, but I couldn't. I never expected him to be this upset though.

"Well, good luck, Jack," he said quietly.

"Wait, Jimmy!" But it was too late, he already hung up the phone. I looked at my phone and almost threw it out into the field. "Son of a bitch!"

Before I could do or say anything else, my phone rang again. "Hey, Becca," I said as I answered it.

"What the hell is going on?" She got right to the point.

"I can't go into details, Becca," I said slowly.

"What the hell do you mean you can't go into details? I want every freaking single detail!" she yelled into the phone. I would have laughed if I hadn't felt like I had just betrayed everyone I knew.

"First, I hear today when I show up for work that you have gone on a leave of absence. Then, I see you on the freaking TV kissing the most gorgeous man alive."

"Look, Rebecca, I'm tired. It's been a very long day. All I can tell you is that I'm working undercover. You need to keep that quiet. Everyone is supposed to think I just took some time off to relax, but I'm working."

"Yeah, you're working all right!" She laughed, and I had to smile.

"That's not what I meant. Look, I'll call you in a few days and try to explain some of this." I turned around to find Ryan standing against the house in the shadows. His arms were crossed, and the emotions on his face were closed tightly as he watched me.

"Wait! Before you hang up, you have to tell me something. Was it amazing?"

I knew what she was asking. As I stared at Ryan standing in the shadows, I remembered every moment of that kiss in the pasture. I could feel the heat from his body even now as we stood ten feet apart. "Yes. I'll talk to you later, Becca." I heard her laughter in the background as I hung up the phone. I turned my phone off; I couldn't deal with anyone else tonight.

I met Ryan's stern look. "What?" I asked when he didn't say anything.

"Why didn't you tell me you had a boyfriend?" He pushed off the wall and came to stand in front of me. I didn't want to be this close to him, so I took two steps back.

"First of all, you didn't ask, and secondly, would it really have even mattered to you?" I probably said that a whole lot angrier than I meant to, but I was upset about Jimmy. I never wanted to hurt him.

"No. It wouldn't have mattered," he replied quietly, as he pulled me to him. I pushed against his chest, suddenly afraid to be in his arms.

"When I want something, I take it. I want you, Jackie, whether you think I am acting or not. I want you." The heat in his eyes was blazing and as his lips crushed on mine, I wanted to pull away. Every cell of my intelligent brain was telling me to do that, but instead of pushing him away, I gripped his shirt where my hands were on his chest and fisted it tightly.

I would regret the decision to do this, but right this second, with the memory of that kiss from earlier burning in the back of my mind, and the smoldering look in his eyes, I couldn't fight the flames of fire that licked between us.

His hands dug into my back as mine slid up his chest and wound around his neck. Our lips meshed angrily together as our tongues dueled, and our breath mingled hotly. His hands roaming over my body as if they had a mind of their own, and only so much time to commit my curves to memory

"Ryan? Oh, damn. Sorry!" Roseanne stumbled over herself as she stepped outside and saw us locked in an extremely hot embrace. We broke away quickly, both of us shocked to have gotten so out of control.

"What, Rose?" Ryan said huskily as he turned to her.

"Ummm, Beth is on the phone for you." She glanced between the two of us. Ryan looked over his shoulder toward me, and his eyes said a hundred different words, all of which made my body want to melt.

"I'll call her back—" he started to say, but I stopped him with a hand on his arm.

"No, Ryan. You need to take that, and I need to go to bed. It's been a long day for me, and I need to get some rest so I can do my job tomorrow." I walked away from him before he could say anything else.

The thought of actually resting was absurd, but I knew I needed to get away from him before I was unable to stop. This man and his kisses were like an addiction, and I was becoming a willing addict craving that one last hit, and knowing one more would never be enough.

RYAN

I was torn and battle weary; torn from wanting Jacquelyn and weary from the constant battle of emotions that consumed me when she was around.

Earlier when she had stood staring out at the sun from the third floor. There was pain in her eyes. When I had tried to stop her to talk, she pushed me away. She didn't understand that I wanted to know what the pain was about; I wanted to take it away for her.

Those feelings were strange and new to me. I had never gone out of my way to be there for someone else. For my friends, yes. But for a woman? Never. Since high school, I had been a typical playboy, seeking females to keep me company and suit my needs. It only got easier the more popular I became. There had never been a woman in my life who made me want to be a better person, until now. That realization struck me hard.

I found her in the kitchen lost in thought once again. Her head was resting idly on the marble of the counter. Her silky hair fanned out like a curtain to hide her face. She didn't hear me enter, and when I softly touched her shoulder, she spun around and put her hand behind her back.

The look in her eyes was alert and alarmed all at the same time. I put my hands up and stepped back quickly. She regained her composure and relaxed back on her stool. I pulled another one closer and sat down, angling myself so that I could not only see her, but my leg would casually touch hers. She moved her legs away to avoid me, and I felt a pang of regret.

When she had sat there staring off into space. I took advantage of the moment to take in her profile, the gentle slope of her nose, the fullness of her lips, the soft curve of her chin. My eyes trailed down to the necklace she wore.

I had listened to her talk about her necklace and her bracelet. These small things let me see a side of her I didn't know about and made me want more.

I knew she cared about people and valued humanity. But I never realized how that spread throughout the law enforcement community. I personally always looked at cops as the guys who wrote the tickets and took out the trash. It was time to change my views.

As I had studied her and thought about what she said, I reached out to move her hair back behind her ear so that I could see her face better. She'd stood quickly, and I sat up straight, surprised by her quick movement.

"Ryan, there's no one here to act for. Do us both a favor and remember that I'm here doing a job." Her voice was solid and steady. Didn't she realize that she was more to me than just an employee? How could she not know that I was feeling things for her that were real? That this wasn't all just an act?

When I'd entered the family room later, I found her seated slightly off to the side and in a single chair so that no one could join her. In the kitchen, I had decided I would give her some space and accepted my food from Troy, finding a seat closer to the television.

Everyone was talking about the start of tomorrow's production, and there was a sense of excitement in the room, although it didn't seem to include Jacquelyn or me.

Troy turned on the TV and flipped it to the entertainment station that had been out at the house today. I heard Jackie cough sharply when the first picture showed up on screen, but I didn't look at her. I was too engrossed in the images they displayed. She was beautiful in the photographs, and she looked perfect standing beside me.

The picture of us kissing out by the fence was so incredible it took me right back to that moment. The image on the screen could have been a promo poster for a movie it was so intimate and natural. The memory of her in my arms rocked me to the core as I saw the pictures they flashed across the screen.

When they finished the story, I was afraid to look at her. What would she have in her eyes? On their own accord, my eyes flicked to her quickly, she was staring at me, her mouth slightly open, her face flushed.

"I think that turned out good. Ryan, those pictures look real, man!" Drew took a huge bite of his food.

"Oh, they looked real because they were," Roseanne laughed. Jackie and I both considered her for a moment before we looked back at each other.

"Roseanne, we were just acting," I said quietly.

Jackie started to pull something out of her pocket while everyone watched her. It was her cellphone, and the screen was lighting up. She set her plate down and started moving through screens on her phone. I wondered who was sending her messages. I heard the vibration of the phone from the other side of the room, and it was almost constant.

She started to type. Her face held conflicting emotions while her shoulders and back were straight and tense. Everyone was observing her as she stood, still typing on her phone.

"Everything all right, Jackie?" Troy asked, aware of her mounting tension as we all were.

She shook her head, her voice soft and husky when she spoke. "You guys just exploded my entire world and you think I should be all right with it? No, I'm not all right." She glanced at her cellphone as her screen lit up brighter, and the vibration radiated through the air again.

"If you'll excuse me, I need to try to explain, no wait…" She closed her eyes for a split second to gather herself, and then said, "I need to lie to my boyfriend, my co-workers, and my best friend about why I have supposedly been hiding this from them for months." She spun and walked out of the room.

I glared at Troy. "Did you know she had a boyfriend?"

"No." He looked as shocked as I did. "I had no idea. We asked around, but no one seemed to know anything about her having a boyfriend." He seemed almost as upset as I was.

What if she really did have a boyfriend, and she hadn't told him about this? What would he be thinking? Did I really care? Not really, but was I such an ass that I wanted to hurt someone else to get what I wanted? With Jackie, yes, I think I was enough of an ass to hurt anyone who got in my way.

I put my plate down on the table and looked toward the door. Should I go out there and talk to her, or should I wait until she comes back in? I wasn't good at waiting, I got up and went to the sliding door, stepping out while her back was to me.

I stepped into the shadows as she spoke again. "Jimmy, it's not what you think. He's not flaunting me around."

Her body was tense. "What do you mean, how long has this been going on? I just came here today."

He must have been wondering if this really had been going on since January. The kiss they'd shown in the pictures looked a hell of a lot more intimate then just a casual getting-to-know-you kiss. If I was on the other end of this, I wouldn't have believed it was an act either.

I heard him speaking, although I could not make out his words.

"Son of a bitch!" She spit out the words and stared at her phone. Did he just hang up on her?

I kept watching. I was seeing a different side of her right now, and I wanted to know every part of her. I knew she was upset, and she'd probably be even angrier once she realized I was here.

She didn't have long to wait before her phone rang again, and I listened to the brief conversation she had with what sounded like a girlfriend. I watched her shoulders slump as she spoke. Midway through the conversation, she turned and saw me leaning back against the house. I didn't move.

She was in partial shadow, but my eyes adjusted enough to the darkness that, as I watched her, I knew she was staring back at me. She hung up the phone. I watched the screen go black before she slid her phone into her pocket.

"What?" she asked quietly.

"Why didn't you tell me you had a boyfriend?" I pushed off the wall and moved toward her while a variety of emotions tossed around in my mind. When I stopped, she took two small steps back.

"First of all, you didn't ask, and secondly, would it really have even mattered to you?" *Ouch!* But she was right. Hadn't I just figured that out for myself?

"No. It wouldn't have mattered." My voice was husky, and I pulled her to me before she could move away. I needed to show her that I wanted her, that she was more than just an employee. "When I want something, I take it. I want you, Jackie, whether you think I'm acting or not. I want you."

I expected her to fight me, and for a second, I thought she might. Instead, her body responded to mine, and I suppressed a shiver of anticipation as she pulled me closer. The kiss should have engulfed us both in flames; that's how hot and intense it was.

I was lost in the feel of her body against mine, of her tongue dancing in my mouth, her hands straining against me to hold me tighter. I never even heard Roseanne step out through the door as my hands ached to touch every inch of her.

"Ryan? Oh, damn. Sorry!" Roseanne exclaimed as she found us locked together. We jumped apart like two guilty children.

"What, Rose?" I said breathing heavy, my voice much lower than normal.

"Sorry, Ryan," Roseanne said after Jackie disappeared inside.

I shook my head. "It's all right, Rose. It's probably better that you did walk in on us." I pushed my hand through my hair and tried to calm down my raging hormones.

"I didn't expect to walk in on that. I figured you were talking to her. What did she say about her boyfriend?" Roseanne spoke casually from beside me, giving me the time I needed to calm down.

I laughed. "Nothing." I put my hands on my hips and looked out over the pasture. "I didn't give her a chance to talk." I shook my head and looked down at my feet.

"You are one pushy man, you do know that, Ryan? You realize that she is probably the strongest woman you've ever come up against, so if you want to win her heart, you better figure out how to stop being so damn pushy." Roseanne tried to joke with me, but what she said was true, and we both knew it.

"Yeah, you're right, Rose." I turned to her and put my hand on her shoulder, squeezing gently before I walked into the house and toward my study so that I could take Beth's call.

In the office, I picked up the phone as I sank down into my leather chair. "What's the word?" I said in the way of a hello.

"I have gotten about twenty-five phone calls and emails since that story hit the air. It seems as if everyone wants to know if that really is her, and if it's really true." She laughed generously over the phone.

I wasn't sure what to feel or say just then.

"You can expect quite a bit of paparazzi to be at the movie set over the next few days to see if it really is true." She laughed again. "I gotta tell you, Ryan, those were some steamy pictures! Better than some of your movie ones!"

"Yeah. Thanks, Beth. I'm glad the word is getting out there; that's what we wanted." I nodded, trying to convince myself that it was still what I wanted. "I'll talk to you tomorrow. I need to try and get some sleep. It's going to be an early morning and a long week ahead of us."

"Sure, Ryan. I'll be in touch with you tomorrow. Will you have your cellphone? Or should I call Troy?"

"Call Troy. Jackie doesn't want me to carry my phone right now." I leaned back in my chair.

"Isn't that a bit controlling?" she asked, and her words irritated me.

"No, Beth. She's doing what I'm paying her to do. She thinks my cell-phone might be bugged or something, so she doesn't want me to use it."

"Oh, all right then." She drug out the last word in a snotty way.

After I dropped the phone on my desk, I decided that Jackie had the right idea; it was time to turn in for the night. Walking up the stairs, I wondered if Jackie was still awake. I stopped at her door and listened quietly, but I didn't hear anything. I thought briefly about knocking, but in the end, I walked to my room and shut my door for the night.

JACQUELYN

I heard him outside my door, and I held my breath. The hormonal side of me wanted him to knock while the logical one was scared that he would. His footsteps moved away from the door, and I released the air from my lungs. It was better that he left, it was better. Yep, it was better. *Who am I trying to convince?*

I changed into pale lavender cotton lounge pants and put on a camisole top to match. The comforter was deep green and burgundy, I ran my hand over it before turning it back. I snuggled into the sheets and rubbed my cheek against the pillow; the coolness was refreshing while the heated exchange kept playing in my mind. It was a king-sized bed, much larger than my queen at home, and lying on my side, I realized how alone this huge mattress made me feel. I pushed myself toward the middle to make it seem not so large.

In my mind's eye, the images of today flashed on the back of my eyelids: When I arrived and saw Ryan standing at the top of the hallway, the banter at the breakfast table, the amount of work the interviews took, and the heart-stopping kisses we shared by the pasture and on the patio.

Those kisses out by the fence had been for show. They were to give everyone an eyeful. The images splashed across the TV screen reminded me just what kind of a show it was, and how—even to me—it looked like more than just an act. We shared a very intimate moment that normally would have been meant only for us, and now it was being flashed all over the world. How did people in the public eye put up with such nonsense? And why did the population feel it was so damn important to know?

I pushed the thoughts out of my head and forced myself to think of a dark circle. A circle that kept getting larger and darker as it filled my mind. I forced the random images of Ryan that tried to push through out of the circle. Slowly, I gained control, and my body relaxed into sleep.

If only I was able to keep that dark circle in my mind as I slept. If I could have, it would've kept the other images away, but they slowly crept into my mind as my body relaxed into a deep slumber. Memories of my life drifted quickly; explosive images mixed with sad moments. Dreams of love and loss played over and over causing me to toss and turn throughout the night.

My alarm went off at four thirty in the morning and I untwisted myself from the sheets. More than once, I had woken up. The fleeting memories had fallen away each time, but the feelings they produced did not. It had been a long night, but I still felt I had gotten enough sleep to deal with what I'd need to do today. I didn't really have a choice, did I?

Troy told me we were starting early, and I wanted to make sure I was ready to go and could meet with him to find out any last-minute details about what was to come today before we left for the set.

I showered and dressed in tan cargo pants and a purple polo shirt. Troy told me to dress comfortably in whatever I wanted; there was no dress code on the sets. I lived in cargo pants when I was wasn't dressed in slacks for work. I pulled on a pair of hiking boots and strapped my off-duty holster to my ankle. I put my sub-compact Glock into the holster and made sure it was secure. My straight blade was strapped to my other ankle and I pulled it out of its sheath to double check that it was clean and ready.

When I left the bedroom, I found the rest of the house still dark. I could hear someone moving about down below. I hoped it was Troy because, without coffee, I wasn't quite ready to face Ryan. I made my way down to the kitchen and started the coffee. While it was brewing, I sat down at the counter and finally went to check my messages. I had thirty text messages and four voicemails.

I sighed and began to read through the text messages. Most of them were comments from friends and co-workers about what they saw on television. Some people commented about additional photos they saw online. I even had a couple of people send me the pictures. I bypassed the photos without even looking at them and put my phone down.

When the coffee was done and as I was pouring, someone walked into the kitchen behind me.

"There is nothing like the smell of coffee in the morning...except bacon. Well, bacon and coffee. Hmmm." I glanced at Troy over my shoulder and watched him rub his face with both hands. I reached up and grabbed another mug for him.

With our coffee in my hands, I turned around and set his down on the counter in front of him.

"How are you so awake this early in the morning?" he asked as he fought back a yawn, "You're even dressed already."

"I'm used to getting up early." I shrugged. "I have trained myself that when the alarm goes off, I wake up. It's part of the job."

"As long as I have been in this business, I still can't get used to it." He took a sip of his coffee, and I watched the steam drift up around his dark, handsome face.

"What are your thoughts on who's trying to get to Ryan?" I studied him carefully. I couldn't rule anyone out, and if Troy was one of those who knew all of Ryan's whereabouts, then he was on the list. At least for now, anyway.

He took another sip from his mug. "Honestly, Jackie, I don't know. It doesn't make sense. The notes have all been left in odd places where Ryan randomly shows up. There doesn't seem to be a rhyme or reason to it."

"I know that you help make his arrangements. Is there anyone else whom you might have told about where he goes?" I took a sip from my mug while keeping my eyes on him.

He shook his head and shrugged with one shoulder. "No. I keep most of Ryan's plans to myself. Roseanne knows, but I know it's not her."

"What makes you think it's not her?" I asked, tipping my head to the side. "Is she interested in him? Maybe jealous of the women he brings into his life?"

He laughed. "Roseanne? No way! Rose treats him like a kid, and to be honest, she's not exactly into the male type."

My eyebrows shot up. "Oh, okay. Yeah, maybe we can take her off the list then." I shared a laugh with him.

"She is definitely off the list."

"Is there anyone else Ryan has been seeing lately who might have ended on a bad note?" Not that I really wanted to know about the long list of women that had been part of his revolving door, but if this person was making comments about him being with women, then it was probably someone scorned.

"Wow, where do I even begin?" He scratched the side of his face.

"You can begin by pouring me coffee." We both snapped our necks to the side. Ryan was leaning against the doorjamb, watching us.

"Don't you think you should ask me those questions?" Ryan's normal husky voice was more raspy than normal, and I noticed an irritated look on his face.

I sat up straighter on the stool. Someone got up on the wrong side of the bed. "Well, I planned on asking you those questions, too, but you and Troy will both have different opinions of the women in your life."

He walked into the kitchen and sat down on the stool next to Troy's. "Why would our opinions be different?"

"Because he sees them as women in your life. You see them as, well," I cleared my throat, "let's just say you see them in a different light." I really didn't want to talk to him directly about his sexual relationships.

"You mean to say that I see them as women I have slept with?" His voice carried a trace of sarcasm.

I raised an eyebrow, "If the shoe fits."

"Well, for your information, I don't sleep with every woman I go out with." He climbed off the stool and started to pour some coffee. I glanced at Troy and found him inspecting me.

"Ryan is right, he didn't sleep with every one of them, just most of them." Troy chuckled, and Ryan turned to scowl at him. "Sorry, man, but the truth is the truth, and if it helps to stop this, then Jackie needs to know."

Professional, be professional, Jackie. "Troy is correct. Your sexual history is of no concern to me, but the women you were involved with are." It was Ryan's turn to raise a skeptical eyebrow.

"Really? Not your concern, huh?" His eyes bore into mine. Did this man's eyes ever stop sparkling?

Before I could respond to Ryan, voices carried in from the hallway, and Drew and Roseanne entered. "Jacquelyn, are you ready to go? Troy will stay here with Ryan. We want you to come with us to the set and have a look around. It will give you a chance to get familiar with the area." She stood at the door waiting, dressed in jeans and a colorful blouse.

"Yep, I'm ready." I slid off the stool and took one last large gulp of my coffee before depositing the mug into the sink. "We will finish this discussion later. You both might want to make a list of women who have come through Ryan's life that haven't exactly been happy to be put back out." I smiled to ease the sting of what I said and turned to walk out the door.

"Hey, Jackie, those letters that Ryan received are at the set. I'll make sure you get them today," Troy called out as I started to turn the corner.

"Sounds good, Troy. And make sure I get your lists as soon as possible." I called over my shoulder, trying to avoid Ryan's aggressive look as I left.

"Whoa, now I could make a nice list for you," Roseanne commented as she followed me outside.

"Good, you do that. A woman's insight would be useful in this, too." We exchanged a quick look before I followed Roseanne out front. We decided to take my truck over to the set and the ride only took about fifteen minutes. I didn't even realize they were filming a movie in this area. Tells you how much I stay out of the everyday patrol dealings.

RYAN

*A*nother night of tossing and turning left me on edge. I sat on the side of my bed and rested my head in my hands, rubbing my eyes with the heels of my palms. It was going to be a long day, and Marie was not going to be happy that I had bags under my eyes.

After a quick shower, I made my way downstairs. I knew Jackie was already there because her bedroom door was slightly ajar, and I peeked in to find the bed made and the smell of her light perfume filling the air.

I heard voices in the kitchen and recognized that they belonged to Troy and Jackie. When she asked for a list of the women I had been involved with, I felt self-conscious. How many women would end up on that list? The answer was too many, way too many.

After she left for the set, Troy turned to me. "If you want her to figure this out, you're going to have to tell her about all of them."

"There aren't that many," I lied.

He threw his head back and laughed. "Like hell there aren't! You're like a sailor, a lady in every port."

I ground my teeth, because in a way it was true, but I still felt I needed to deny it. "I was with Kayla for a while."

"Speaking of Kayla, I got two phone calls from her last night. She is pissed, man. Pissed."

Crap, I forgot about telling her what was going on. Of course, I wouldn't have told her the truth, but I should have told her about Jackie before she saw it in the press. "Sorry, I forgot to tell her."

"Yeah, thanks for that. I had to deal with her screaming in my ear on one phone call and then calling me back up sobbing on my proverbial big strong shoulder for the second one." He stood and patted me on the back. "You can thank me later."

I groaned. I knew I could avoid her for a little while, but we were set to shoot a scene early next week. She was a co-star in the film, and while she had a much smaller part than mine, hers was an important one.

"Do you think she might be behind all these threats?" Troy asked as he leaned against the counter and crossed his arms.

"The thought has crossed my mind, but why would she do that?" I rested my chin on my palm and leaned on it over the counter, wondering if Kayla could be the one behind all this.

He shrugged his wide shoulders. "It could be her. She did get really jealous when you were trying to find out who Jackie was after the airport incident." He cocked his head to the side. "Wasn't it right after that when you told her she wasn't moving in here?"

"Yeah, it was. Having a guy hold a gun on me made me realize a few things about life, and I didn't want to waste any more time with her. I'm going to be thirty-four soon, I'm almost ready to settle down. You know, start a family."

The laughter burst from Troy and snapped me back to reality and out of the little fantasy I was indulging in, the one of Jackie standing on the back patio with a baby in her arms. Was I ready for that and was she the one I wanted to share it with?

"What's so funny?" I asked as I sat up straight.

"You!" He stepped forward and put his hands on the other side of the kitchen island from where I was sitting. "Man, I never thought I would see the day when you didn't want your bachelor status and were talking about kids and a wife. You sure you didn't get some brain damage in that car accident a few months ago?"

I rolled my eyes at him. "I'm not saying I'm ready to do that right now, but it started me thinking, and I knew Kayla wasn't the woman I wanted to do that with."

He lowered his voice, saying, "But Jackie is?"

Was she? Who the hell knew? "I don't know. I'm crazy about her, more than crazy about her, but I have no idea how she feels." I thought for a moment. "Yeah, maybe."

I sat staring at my hands, lost in thought. Could Jackie and I really have a relationship? Would she even be interested in something like that with me? The bad part about it was I knew she didn't like the glitz and glamour of my lifestyle; she hated the attention. Was there any middle ground where we could build a foundation for a future?

Once again, Troy broke me out of my thoughts. "You about ready to head out? There's an early meeting with the producer and director this morning. Plus, I want to make sure Jackie is all set up."

I downed the rest of my coffee, wincing as the hot liquid burned the back of my throat, and got off the stool.

"Do you think this is going to work? I mean, Jackie figuring out who is making these threats? It could be Kayla. I guess I should talk to Jackie about that." I left my cup sitting on the counter and followed him out of the room.

"I think if anyone can, it's her. However, you have to be honest with Jackie, man. And, yeah, I'd tell her about Kayla."

"I will. I just wish the truth wasn't so damn long and messy."

Troy turned to look at me when we got to the front door. "You really like this girl, don't you?" I stared at him not sure how to reply. He pulled the door open, and we walked out to the waiting limo.

"I've never seen you worried about what a woman thinks." He climbed in and I slid in beside him. "Hell, I've never seen you get so damn posses-sive either."

The door closed. "I'm not possessive!"

Troy turned to stare at me. "Get real man. If I even touch her, you have daggers in your eyes."

"No, I don't." I looked out the window. Was I really possessive?

"Yeah, and Rose told me about the little display outside last night. She said you guys were getting hot and heavy out on the patio." He let that sink in before he continued. "You have never been one to stake a claim, but I sure think you were driving one last night."

Was he right? Was I staking a claim on her? That wasn't what I meant to do. Oh hell, that was exactly what I meant to do last night when I crushed her to me after her phone call with her "so called" boyfriend.

I didn't want another man in the picture. I wanted her to be mine and only mine. Why, I don't know; but ever since I first saw her, I have been looking at my life in a different way. For the first time, someone else mattered to me.

I didn't know how she felt, not really. I knew she was attracted to me; I could see that in her eyes and feel it in her kiss. Nevertheless, I had no idea what she really thought. And why the hell did it bother me so much?

Troy took a few phone calls while we rode to the set, and I dwelled on my feelings and wondered what hers were. The limo dropped us off at my trailer, and I scanned the parking lot as we got out, automatically searching for her in the throngs of people moving around. When I didn't see her, anxiety rippled through me.

Troy slapped me on the back as we moved to the trailer door. "I'll find her, relax." Damn, he knew me too well.

Troy walked in my trailer, put his headset on and started calling out for Roseanne right away. I could tell by the one-sided conversation that she was set up and headed back here. The tension I felt lessened while I was in the bathroom.

Marie was going to have fun with me today. I shook my head as I examined the reflection in the mirror over the black marble sink. I had dark circles under my eyes that were going to need some serious magic to get rid of them.

I felt, more then heard, the trailer door close, and finished washing my hands. I stepped out and turned to see Jackie examining the trailer. When she looked at me, her eyes didn't make it to my face, but caressed every inch of visible skin on my chest. Her face flushed as I leaned against the wall. The way she checked me out made me feel lightheaded.

I finally cleared my throat and explored her face as it grew pink with embarrassment. I moved slowly toward her, feeling like a panther stalking its prey.

She didn't move as I grew closer and never broke the intense gaze that we were locked in. I touched her cheek and gently stroked her lips with a kiss. How easy it would be to pull her into my arms and push her down on the eight-foot couch to our side. The image of us making love right here, with the bright lights and mirror over us, tempted me to lock the door.

But here and now was not the right time. Yeah, I wanted her, and right this second. I saw in her eyes that she wanted me, too. When it finally happened, it wouldn't be a wham-bam-thank-you-ma'am; it was going to be a long night of passion. I was going to enjoy every single inch of her beautiful body and make her cry out my name over and over again.

Right now, we both had work to do. Speaking of which, I told Jackie, "Troy has the letters you wanted to see in the back room. They are in the drawer next to the bed on the left side. You can look at them later when you get a chance."

"Okay, thank you." Her voice was soft, husky and I lowered my head for another sweet kiss.

The door yanking open broke the intense connection we were sharing. Without thinking, I pulled Jackie to my side and stepped back. She didn't fight it and even melted against me just the slightest bit. Did she feel anything for me other than lust, I absently wondered as I faced the giddy green eyes of my agent.

"Well, well, well..." I watched Beth look Jackie over carefully. "You're cuter than I remembered."

JACQUELYN

They issued me a parking pass when we arrived that gave me the right to basically park wherever I wanted. It was kind of like being in a police car; we didn't really care what signs said, we parked where we had to, when we needed to. Roseanne gave me a quick tour of the trailers, and I met some of the other people who worked security for both Ryan and a few other actors.

A lot of people stared at us as we walked around, and I heard people whispering more than once. I knew they weren't talking about Roseanne and I being there. I was the topic of conversation, and I cringed internally each time I noticed. I wish I could put blinders on everyone like they do on horses to make them see straight ahead so they don't notice anything else. I could use that right now. The rumors had obviously spread quickly here on the set. Man, the things we did for undercover work. I wanted to sigh and hang my head, but instead, as Roseanne showed me around, I smiled as if I was happy, almost giddily, while my nerves zinged through me.

Many of the people we passed appeared to be talking to themselves, and I wondered if everyone in the business was just crazy. Shortly after, I realized they all had headsets on. I took in the excited hustle and bustle that surrounded us and found myself sucked into it. Roseanne said that the first week and the last few days were the most exciting.

We meandered over to a trailer that I was told, was Ryan's, when Bill and Brady walked around the corner.

"Morning, ladies," Bill called out brightly, a huge grin splitting his face. It was hard not to return the smile, ever since I first met him, he had been in a good mood.

"Morning, Bill. It's Brady, isn't it?" I said to the guy standing next to him. I knew who he was, but I was still trying to gauge him up.

He nodded but said nothing. This guy was the complete opposite of Bill. I mentally noted the fact that he didn't even attempt to look me in the face.

"Roseanne, Markus wants you to bring Jacquelyn over to the tech trailer to get set up with her gear as soon as you can."

"Thanks, Bill, we'll head over there now," Roseanne replied and took my elbow to pull me along. Bill grinned again as we left and walked into the trailer. Brady watched me for a moment before he followed Bill. He is either very shy, or I make him extremely nervous.

Roseanne chatted about what was going on around the area as we walked. She pointed out other trailers and people of importance. I was glad I was detail oriented and had a good memory because there was a lot going on that I needed to remember.

Just as we were about to enter another trailer, we heard someone yell for Roseanne. She smiled and waved at the woman and told me to head in and find Markus while she went to chat with her.

I wasn't sure if I should knock or not before I entered. Figuring that people probably came and went from here all the time, I decided to just let myself in. I opened the door quietly and stepped up the two steps into the trailer.

There were counters and cabinets around most of the room. Music played from a radio on the counter, and it masked the sound of my entrance. On the far side sat a table with several chairs around it. Markus sat with his back to me. His dark hair was cut just above his collar with a thick wave to it. He was reading a message on his cellphone. I moved up behind him quietly.

I watched him as he typed, "She should be here soon" and hit the Send button. The hairs on the back of my neck stood up. It wasn't what he wrote, I knew he was expecting me, it was the text program he was using on his phone that caused my skin to prickle. As the seconds ticked by to five, my suspicion was confirmed. I watched the screen change from words to little tiger paws.

He was using an application called TigerTalk—an encrypted text software that can't be traced. It's the kind of software generally used by drug dealers and cheating spouses to hide the text messages they send between parties. The words sent by text would appear on the other person's phone when connected and would immediately disappear after a predetermined time. It could be a few seconds or an hour, depending on how the person programmed their settings. There was no way to trace these text messages.

Why would Markus need to use such software? I heard a soft ping come from his phone, and a message popped up from someone named LaLa. "Is everything set for her?"

I watched as he typed out, "Yes, all set." and hit the Send button again. The original message had already turned into little paw prints on the screen. I took a step back from him, realizing that if he found out I was directly behind him, then he would know I saw what he typed. My steps were unheard as the music and computers running drowned out any sound my feet made on the floor.

I reached behind me and slowly turned the doorknob, pushing the door open slightly then pulling it closed with a nice hefty click. Markus spun around in his seat. He was obviously surprised to see me already standing inside the room.

I smiled. "Morning, Markus. I believe I was supposed to come here for my gear?"

He considered me closely for a moment and put his phone down on the table just as a small ping came through his speaker. He looked at his phone and then flipped it over so that the screen faced down.

"Yeah, I have several things for you." He walked over to the counter and opened a box. Inside was a radio, headset, cellphone, and charger.

"Set the radio to channel five. That's the channel our security team uses. I assume you know how to use a radio, so I won't explain, but if you have any questions, just ask." He put the radio down and picked up a phone. "This has been programmed with everyone's numbers so all you have to do is scroll through the contacts." He handed all of it to me, and I clipped the radio to my belt while slipping the phone into a pocket of my cargo pants. I had no intention of using the phone, but I would keep it, just in case. The headset I would situate later when I could thread it through the back of my shirt.

"You bring the radio back at the end of the day so they can charge here." He pointed to a shelf behind me where a bank of about fifty charges sat. Some had radios in them, some were empty or charging extra batteries.

"Thanks, Markus. Anything else?" I asked politely as I put the headset and phone charger into one of my other cargo pockets.

"Nope, that's it. If you find you need something else, or something doesn't work correctly, let me know."

As I inspected him and took in his dark brown eyes, I realized that they alarmed me. His eyes had no depth. They were flat and cold, almost lifeless. I almost shivered, but I controlled the urge and moved away from him.

"Okay, thanks," I said quietly and stepped back from him. This person was not someone I would put my back to. I continued to step backward until I absolutely had to turn to get out the door. The entire time I moved I kept my eye on him as he did on me.

When I closed the door behind me, shutting out the lifeless look in his eyes, I finally shivered. That man bothered me, there was no doubt about it. Knowing that he was using encrypted software on his phone and talking about me only brought more suspicions to mind. Normal people didn't use that software for everyday conversations. He was up to something, and right now, he was at the top of my list of suspects, right in front of Brian. But why did he bother me so much?

Roseanne was still talking to the woman from earlier and they stood closely together laughing and sharing personal glances. Troy's words echoed in my head from earlier that morning, and it appeared I was looking at the proof of that. As I approached, Roseanne took notice of me and called out, "Did Markus hook you up?"

"Yeah, he did." I tried to smile, but it was forced. Markus's dark, malicious eyes flashed through my mind.

"This is Mandy," Roseanne said introducing me to her friend.

I shook her hand as a bright, beautiful smile radiated off her. "It's a pleasure to meet you, Mandy."

She was a gorgeous woman from head to toe, and I wondered why she wasn't in front of the cameras instead of working behind the scenes. "The pleasure is all mine." Her sweet, tinkling laughter made Roseanne smile and bite her lip.

"Jackie, where is your headset? Didn't Markus give you one?" Roseanne turned her attention back to me.

I reached into my pocket and pulled it out. "No, he gave me one, but I wasn't going to sit there and drop it down my shirt in front of him."

"Does he give you the creeps, too? He's got the strangest eyes!" Roseanne said as she reached out for the headset. Obviously, I wasn't the only person who picked up on him. *Good to know.*

Roseanne pulled the collar of my polo shirt away and dropped the cord down the back, tickling my skin as it snaked down my spine. She didn't give me a chance to pull the shirt tails out myself, quickly tugging at the back of my shirt and reaching up to grab the cord. I chuckled as I'd normally never let someone touch me quite so personally, but it didn't even seem to faze her.

She moved things around on my belt. I figured it was easier to let her do it, and I held my arms out of the way so that she could get it set up. She probably didn't realize that I had used these things before, or how many years I had worn ample gear around my waist that had "just the right spot" to sit. I'd adjust it all once she was done.

I heard a small buzz emanating from the earpiece that hung over my shoulder. I lifted it up to my ear and slipped it in, reaching for the radio to adjust the volume. I thought this place was busy before, but all of a sudden, the area around me got a whole lot busier. All those people who had been talking to themselves came into focus, and I realized they'd been having intense conversations with other people.

With the ear bud firmly in place, I felt like I was back on patrol. Static came and went along with crackling, both of those punctuated by different voices asking for something or someone. I flipped through the channels, listening for a few seconds to make sure I was able to pick them all up.

I felt at home with this in my ear, like I was back to doing my job. I grinned.

"Just make sure you only talk on channel five. That's our channel," Roseanne said as she started to tuck my shirt back in.

I laughed and stepped away from her. "I can do that, Roseanne. Yes, Markus already told me about the channel."

"We should get back to the trailer, Ryan will be here soon." Roseanne said as she reached out to put her hand on Mandy's arm. "See you later, Mandy."

"Where is Jackie?" a male voice came over the headset just seconds after she had spoken. Roseanne and I shared a raised eyebrow look and laughed.

"Troy, we're on our way back to the trailer now. I assume Ryan is there?" Roseanne answered by pushing a small button on the wire from the headset.

"Yes, he is, and he wants her here," Troy replied quickly.

I sighed. And the show begins. "I take it Ryan doesn't have a head-set?" I asked Roseanne as we made our way back through the lot where the stars' trailers were all lined up.

Roseanne laughed. "No, we don't allow him to play with our toys."

"Thank God," I said dramatically, and we both burst out laughing again.

"Jackie, you on here yet?" Troy's voice filled my ear.

"Yes, Troy. I copy you. Do you need something, or are you just concerned I might not know how to use the technology?" Roseanne snorted beside me.

Troy laughed as he keyed up on the headset. "No, just making sure you're hot."

"Yeah, I'm hot, but we already knew that." Roseanne snapped her head to me with a look of surprise.

"Yes, we know you are." His laughter reached us both and Roseanne grinned beside me. "See you in a few minutes."

"I can't believe you just said that." Her laughter was contagious; I couldn't believe I said that either.

"Have you ever been on a movie set before?" Roseanne asked as we walked along.

"Nope, can't say that I have. I know we've had a few movies filmed out here and our patrol officers would assist with traffic and stuff, but I have never been around one."

"Well, I hope you find it interesting. I do. I think it's amazing how many times we have to do scenes over and over again and then when the director finally puts it all together, so much of the scene ends up sitting on the cutting room floor, or they use the first take of the thirty that were shot."

"I'm sure it will be interesting." I thought for a second before I spoke again. "Roseanne, what do you really think of Markus?"

She blew air through her lips as though she was blowing bubbles in water. "He's weird."

Weird, yeah, that would describe him pretty well. "How long has he been working with you guys?"

"Hmmm…" Apparently, she was thinking. "We hired him on the last film, so about eight, maybe nine months ago."

"Do you know someone named LaLa?" I watched her as she screwed up her face trying to recall the name and coming up empty.

"LaLa, no I don't think so. Why?" She turned to me and looked away.

"No particular reason, just wondering."

When we got to Ryan's trailer, she turned to face me before reaching for the knob. "Look at you, getting all into investigation mode."

I glanced around us to make sure we were alone. "That is what I'm being paid to do."

"And other things," she added.

"I'd rather not think about those other things right now, thanks," I muttered and put my hands into my pockets.

"Ryan's not a bad guy. He really does like you, you know."

I swallowed and was about to say something when the door opened and knocked Roseanne off the first step and into me.

"Oh, sorry, Rose," Troy called out as he stepped out quickly and grabbed her arm. She had slammed right into me, and thankfully, I got my hands out of my pockets in time to catch her or we would've both landed on the ground.

"Damn, Troy! What's the freaking hurry?" She pulled out of Troy's hold.

"Sorry, I was just opening the door to look for you ladies. Jackie, go in and calm him down, please."

After I rolled my eyes, I stepped around Troy and Roseanne and climbed the three steps into the trailer.

The inside took me by surprise. After being in the tech trailer, this one was amazing. The floor was hard wood, and the track lighting made it shine as if it were wet.

There was a small bar area to the right and the cabinets looked like mahogany and were as clean and shiny as the floor. The granite counter sparkled along with the crystal decanter and glasses that sat along the back edge.

I continued to inspect the inside and turned to the left. Along the right wall was a long beige couch with big fluffy pillows. A mahogany coffee table sat in front of it and across from it, attached to the wall, was a 60-inch television. Holy cow! This place must cost more than my entire house!

Mirrors on the ceiling reflected the images back down and made the room look even bigger. At the end of the trailer were two doors and a small galley-style kitchen, but even that area was fancier than what I lived with.

One of the doors opened, and Ryan stepped out wiping his hands on a towel. He was wearing a button-down blue shirt, and it was completely undone. My breath caught in my throat as I got the first glimpse of his bare chest live and in person.

I'd seen it in the movies, and it was incredible there, but I had no words for what I was looking at. His skin was smooth with gentle slopes of muscles, toned to perfection and begging to be touched. My palms dampened at my sides, and I slipped my hands back into my pockets to control the shaking that had started for some unknown reason. *Yeah, right.*

Ryan leaned against the wall, a towel hanging limply from his right hand. The shirt pulled away from his left side as he leaned and gave me the view of his perfect abs running along his body. He cleared his throat, and I jerked my stare from his body to his smiling eyes. My cheeks started to warm as a blush stole across them.

He pushed off the wall and moved lazily toward me. His feet were bare and made no noise on the glossy floor. I forced myself to swallow the excess saliva that gathered in my mouth.

"If you keep looking at me like that, I'm going to be late to the set." His voice was deep and smooth as he stopped directly in front of me. My chin rose as he grew closer, my head tipped back so that I could keep looking him right in those beautiful eyes.

His musky fresh scent stirred my senses alive, and I wanted to lean in and inhale him deeply. He grasped my chin gently between his thumb and a knuckle and slowly lowered his lips to brush them against mine. I took the moment to draw his scent deeply into my chest, holding it there while he feathered another kiss over my partially open mouth. The tip of his tongue had barely reached out for a taste, but deep in my gut it burned.

He straightened slowly, watching me. I was lost in him and a sudden realization struck me: I was in a whole lot of trouble.

He lifted one side of his mouth in a lazy grin, my heart galloped out of my chest. Yep, right away from me and any chance in hell that I had at getting out of this without a scar on it when I finally captured it and put it back inside my body; the chance of that was now long gone.

The trailer door opened, and Troy, Roseanne, and another woman walked in. Ryan slipped an arm around my waist and pulled me to his side.

"Well, well, well…" the woman said as she inspected me from head to toe. "You're cuter than I remembered."

She walked over to Ryan and kissed him on the cheek. "Hello, Ryan."

"Jackie, this is Beth, my agent. What are you doing here?" She dropped her large, garishly styled purse-slash-briefcase down on the floor with a loud thunk.

"Is that any way to talk to the person who gets you these gigs? I came to see her in person, and I have another script I want you to look at." She plopped on the couch behind her, lifted her feet up, and dropped them onto the coffee table. Bits of dirt and dust dropped off the bottom and onto the wood.

I looked at the dirt briefly and felt like it was a sign of things to come. *Great, just great.*

RYAN

"Hello, Ryan," Beth said after placing a sloppy kiss on my cheek.

"Jackie, this is Beth, my agent. What are you doing here?" She wasn't supposed to be at the set. In fact, she never came to location unless it was an emergency.

"Is that anyway to talk to the person who gets you these gigs? I came to see her in person, and I have another script I want you to look at."

"Would you mind getting your dirty feet off the furniture?" She rolled her eyes dramatically but put them back on the ground. "Since when do you ever deliver a script in person? That's what FedEx is for."

"Do you have any coffee? I took the red-eye to get here this early. Aren't you happy to see me?"

I glanced at Roseanne and was about to ask her to go get Beth some coffee when she spoke. "One coffee coming up, anyone else?"

"No, thanks," I replied and directed my attention back to Beth as Roseanne bolted out the door. "You know I love to see you, Beth. I just don't get why you're here."

She stood and pulled her black blazer back into place. "I told you, I wanted to see her for myself."

Absently, I pulled Jackie tighter to my side, and she slipped her arm around my waist. The tips of her fingers brushed the skin just over the top of my waistband and sent a jolt of sensation right to my groin.

"So, Miss 'I fear no evil,' it's nice to finally meet you." I felt Jackie stiffen at my side, but she responded politely enough.

"A pleasure to see you again, Beth." She held her hand out to Beth without leaving my side, and Beth flicked a glance my way before shaking it.

"Oh, that's right, we did meet briefly in the hospital after you rescued him from the car accident. I forgot about that." She grinned like a tiger about to attack Jackie. Then she moved her eyes back and forth between us and observed how we were standing.

"You two keep up the act when you're alone, too. Good idea. Probably makes it easier to do it in public if you rehearse in private."

"Maybe it's not an act," I replied slowly and felt Jackie tense beside me.

Beth threw her head back and laughed. "You and her together? For real? Yeah, all right, Ryan. Go ahead and have your little affair or whatever it is, and then we can move forward."

I wasn't sure which one of us had a stiffer spine after that comment left Beth's lips. I gently squeezed Jackie's hip where my hand rested.

"That was rude, even for you Beth," I spit out.

She was about to answer when Troy stepped into the conversation. "Ryan, they're calling for us in the director's trailer, we need to go."

"All right." I pulled away from Jackie and walked over to where I'd left my loafers. I slipped them on while I buttoned my shirt.

When I started for the door, I reached for Jackie's left hand while Beth grabbed her right arm. "Leave her here with me for a few minutes. I want to get to know her."

Something flashed in Jackie's eyes, but it appeared more like determination than concern.

"It's all right, Ryan, you go ahead. I'll stay here with Beth while you're in your meeting."

"You sure?"

"You have Troy by your side right now." She gave me a smile and lifted her chin. I leaned down and kissed her. "So, yes, I'm sure," she said after I released her lips.

Troy pulled me toward the door. "They are waiting for us, let's go."

I glanced over my shoulder as I stepped down and saw Beth and Jackie practically glaring at each other. They looked like they were about to go into battle, I wondered who would win. Maybe I should have insisted that she come with me.

"She'll be fine. They need to work things out for themselves."

"Yeah, but I'm not sure she's used to sharks." Troy laughed beside me, and we stepped up the stairs into another trailer for the meeting.

"She may not have dealt with sharks, but the woman carries a gun, I wouldn't worry," Troy whispered as we joined the rest of the group there.

When we finished the meeting, Troy nudged me and said quietly, "Heads up, Kayla's here."

"Are you serious? She doesn't have a scene until next week. I don't have time for her crap right now."

"I don't think you need to worry, sounds like Beth handled it."

I turned to gape at him when we stepped outside. "Beth?"

"Yeah, from what Rose just told me, Beth told her to take a hike and leave you alone." He grinned.

"I thought they were friends? Beth always said that Kayla and I should settle down."

"Well," he shrugged, "maybe Jackie caged the shark." We passed a few of the production crew as we walked and exchanged casual hellos.

"Somehow, I don't see Beth picking Jackie over Kayla," I said dryly.

"It's a good thing that you have the choice then, huh?" He slapped me on the back, and we stepped into my trailer. Beth and Marie were sitting on the couch chatting when we walked in. I looked around for Jackie, but she wasn't there.

"She left when your dragon lady tried to get her hooks into her," Beth said casually.

"What do you mean she tried to get her hooks into her?" I snapped.

"Kayla came in here all self-righteous telling her to get away from her man, and your new lady handled it like a pro."

I leaned back against the bar and crossed my arms. "What's that supposed to mean, Beth?"

Beth came to stand in front of me. "It means she put Kayla in her place. If you're a smart man, and I believe you are, you won't screw this up. That woman is good for you, probably too good for you."

I tried not to wince at her last words, for she was most likely correct in her assumption, but I was more interested in how she put Kayla in her place. "What did she say to Kayla?"

She cocked her head to the side. "You are going to have to ask her the particulars, but I will say she left Kayla standing there with her mouth hanging open. That's not something I've ever seen, and it won me over. I like the girl." She grinned, and I shook my head. This was a first.

The details would have to wait, because Marie rushed me into the chair to get my makeup done so that I could head over to wardrobe. We were starting the first scene in less than an hour, and she had a lot of work to do.

Troy spent the time talking on his cell while Marie and I chatted casually in front of the mirror in the back room. I wasn't sure where Beth had disappeared to, or Jackie for that matter.

Just about the time we were done, Markus walked into the room. "Hey, Ryan, you have your cellphone on you?"

"No, sorry, forgot it at home, why?"

"Oh, I just wanted to update some data on it, no biggie. I'll get it next time." He turned to walk out, and I studied him. I had never been comfortable with him, but he was highly recommended for the job. When it came to the technology for our team, he was right on; but suddenly the conversation I had with Jackie about my cell made me wonder about him and what exactly was on my phone.

Marie finished up with me while doing a good job of hiding my dark circles. That is, after she gave me a five-minute lecture about the importance of getting my rest. Tsking over me having Jackie at the house keeping me awake at all hours.

Troy and Drew showed up to get me to wardrobe, and I chuckled as I got dressed in the police officer's uniform that I was wearing for the scene. As I put the vest on and then the shirt over it, a strange sense of pride washed over me. This is what Jackie is used to wearing, and it made me feel just a tad bit closer to her.

As we piled into a white van with tinted windows along with eight other people, I asked Troy, "Where is Jackie?"

"She'll be over soon. She and Rose are going over some stuff and the list that she made."

I ground my teeth. I wish I could have spoken to Jackie before Rose gave her a list.

Troy barked out a laugh. "Chill man, I saw the list. It isn't as bad as you think."

"Yeah, whatever," I muttered. I forced thoughts of my past and of Jackie out of my head and began to focus on the scene we were about to do.

It was a major scene in the parking lot behind a building. Sheila Burke, who was the female lead, and I were starting off with an intense moment right off the bat. This scene would set the tone for the rest of the movie, a paranormal love affair that was forbidden.

We arrived on scene, and only four of the actors were part of the filming today. Sheila, Devon Storms, Erik Walters, and I would spend the day getting the scene set to perfection. I huddled around the other actors to start working through the choreography. For the majority of the scene, it was just Sheila and me. When it was time for Devon and Erik, Shelia and I would be in the background. Like I normally did, I got lost in the job and didn't think of Jackie until Sheila and I were supposed to share our first kiss.

I had kissed a lot of women on sets, never having a problem acting out the passion I was supposed to be feeling. Today, as I moved in to share our first kiss, I hesitated just long enough for the director to yell, "Cut!" and start the scene over.

Just as we got to the kiss in the fourth take, I pulled back and called cut myself. A rumble went through the crowd of workers and onlookers.

I scanned the crowd. "Where is Jacquelyn?" I called out. Heads turned and whispers were shared, and then I saw her stepping out of the director's tent, confusion evident on her face as she met my eyes.

"Excuse me for a moment, Sheila. Please don't take this personally, but I need to get in the mood." I stalked toward Jackie.

The people between us parted. "What's wrong, Ryan? Are you all right?" Jackie asked, concern written clearly over her features.

I went directly to her, sliding my hands to the side of her face, lifting it so that I could lower my lips to hers. I heard her gasp as her hands came to rest on my biceps.

I put all the passion I felt into a gentle loving kiss.

When I pulled back, her eyes were dazed, and murmurs spread like wildfire. "Sorry, but I needed to get into the mood, excuse me for what I'm about to do."

"What you are about to do," the director called out from behind Jackie, "is get back on the set and give Sheila the same exact kiss you just gave her."

I grinned at him before I planted another soft kiss on her lips before going back to my position.

There was a smirk on Sheila's face when I returned. "I'm not sure we can duplicate that, but let's try."

I winked at her and took my place. The next take was worth keeping, and with all the softness and passion that I had shown Jackie, I acted it out with Sheila.

Although it came across on film as passionate and sweet, I felt nothing when I kissed Sheila. My emotion stemmed from the one I had shared with Jackie just moments before.

I was lucky that I was working with Sheila. She was a five-star actress and wasn't offended in the least. If that had been Kayla, heads would have rolled.

The director gave us a break after we finished the scene, and I searched for Jackie in the crowd and found her standing near the food table. I grabbed a bottle of water and a protein bar as I joined her.

"This is going to sound really stupid, but what is the name of this film?" she asked as I walked up.

I pulled back the wrapper on my bar, taking a bite and chewing it before I answered her, "Garda."

She laughed. "I thought that scene looked familiar. This is based on that paranormal book *Garda, Welcome to the Realm.*"

"You know it?" I asked before taking another bite.

She stopped walking and turned to me. "Of course, I do. Have you ever met Stacy, the author?"

"Not yet, she's supposed to stop by the set one of these days. How do you know about it?"

"Ryan, she works two townships over from here. I've worked on investigations with her."

"Seriously?" I asked around a lump of chewy protein bar.

"Yes. I love that book! I got to read it when she first released it. This is so cool that I get to see you filming it." She pulled her phone out of her pocket. "Sorry, I gotta send her a message and tell her."

I finished my snack and reached for her wrist. "Do that later. Right now, I want your undivided attention for a few moments."

She let me pull her closer, and I slipped her arm around my waist and held her close.

"Wait, I have a question." She pulled back before I could descend on her.

"What?" I stopped halfway to her lips.

She gazed at my mouth for a moment and swallowed. "Why are you filming this in the day when that scene is at night?"

I chuckled low in the back of my throat. "It's called filters. Now stop talking about work and kiss me."

She turned her head away from me and scanned the people around us. I saw her eyes pass over something and then return to it. She locked her jaw before turning back to me and stepping up on her tiptoes to close the gap between us.

If the director had thought the last kiss was good, he would have been blown away by this one. The noise and the people around us disappeared as we got lost in the kiss and each other.

Someone passing by us jostled us, reminding me where we were. I slowed the kiss and pulled away. Her eyes were dazed, her lips swollen. She bit her bottom one and considered me for a moment.

"Sorry, forgot where we were," I whispered as I rested my forehead on hers. She made a sound in her throat that seemed to agree with my comment.

With a deep, steady breath to get myself back in control, I put space between us, but kept my arm around her waist and led her off to the side where there were fewer people.

I saw her shake her head and roll her shoulders back, most likely trying to gain control over her own senses, as I was.

"So what did you think of the filming?" I asked as we stopped by the edge of the parking lot.

"Very interesting to see how it all works. I never had any idea how many times you have to go through a scene to get it right. It gave me a better appreciation for the cost of a movie ticket." She peered around the area, taking everyone in again.

"There is a lot that goes on behind the scenes. That scene was pretty easy. We should be able to wrap this one up within the next hour or so if Devon and Erik can get through their lines."

Her eyes opened in surprise. "That was easy?"

"Wait till you see a fight scene. The choreography that goes into that takes a long time or a car chase scene, that gets intense, but I don't do those. I have a stunt double for that."

"What—afraid you might get hurt?" she teased.

I laughed and took a swig from my water bottle. "No, Beth just doesn't want to lose her biggest money maker quite yet." I chewed the inside of my cheek for a moment and swallowed. "Speaking of Beth, I hear there was some excitement at the trailer this morning. I'm sorry about Kayla."

"Pfft..." She waved it off. "No big deal; I handled it."

"Yeah, that's what Beth said. What did you tell Kayla anyway?"

She peeked at me and then looked away to scan the area again. "Doesn't matter. I don't think she'll bother me again."

"No way. If you want me to spill all the ladies I've been involved with, then you can tell me what you said to Kayla." She blushed but didn't respond and basically refused to look me in the face.

"Jackie," I laughed, "come on, I want to know what you said." I pulled her so that she was facing me.

She tilted her chin to look me in the face, her teeth biting down on her bottom lip. "How about we talk about that later?" She stood on her tiptoes and put her lips to mine.

It was the second time she had made the first move, and a little thrill of excitement raced through me. It wasn't a big kiss, but it lasted for a few seconds. When she pulled back, she wrapped her arms around my neck and put her mouth close to my ear.

"We have people watching us. I thought I would help out our story."

I ran my hand up her back and tugged her hair so that she pulled her face away from my ear. "You can help out like that anytime you want." I kissed her again, this time holding her close so that it was more passionate.

I heard them calling for us to get back in place, and I reluctantly let her go. Both of us were slightly breathless, and I noticed her pupils were dilated. I kissed her on the tip of her nose and helped her stand back up straight.

"I have to get back to work."

"All right, I'll see you later," she said shyly as she turned and walked to stand someplace out of the way.

JACQUELYN

$\mathcal{B}$eth and I considered each other for a few moments after Ryan and Troy left. It felt as if we were gauging one another to find the best way to attack. Personally, I was looking at this as if I would question a suspect.

"So," she said slowly and sank down on the sofa, "Why don't you have a seat, and let's talk."

I didn't feel like sitting; I did my best thinking while I was on my feet. But standing over someone was never a good idea, unless you were trying to intimidate them. I didn't want to come across that way to her. For some reason, I didn't want to be on this woman's bad side.

I walked around the coffee table and sat on the couch, resting my hand on one of the fluffy tan pillows that lay haphazardly between us.

"Tell me, Jackie, why did you get involved with the incident at the airport?" She turned and watched me carefully.

"I would have figured you saw the press conference. I saw someone who needed help, and I did what I had to do." I shrugged.

"There was no other reason?" She tapped her bottom lip with a well-manicured fingernail coated with a deep burgundy color.

"No," I simply responded.

"You weren't trying to get his attention? Get a little fame out of it?" She scrutinized me while she spoke.

I laughed quietly to myself. "No. If you didn't notice, I disappeared as soon as I could and didn't want anything to do with the spotlight, or Ryan. That's not my thing."

"You know, Ryan looks at you as some type of guardian angel or something, especially after you rescued him from the car accident." Beth clasped her hands casually in front of her while she turned to sit sideways on the couch, facing me with one leg slightly drawn up under her.

"I didn't rescue him; I was on my way home and just happened to be the first one to tumble over him. Again, I did what I was trained to do, and nothing more."

"I don't know about that." She got quiet for a moment. "He still thinks of you as the woman who fears no evil."

I shook my head and looked away. "That drives me crazy. I have fear just like everyone else."

"You know, I noticed that when you write your last name down backward, it spells no evil. Have you ever noticed that?

I laughed. I hadn't thought about that since I was in elementary school, and we had to write our full name down and find out how many words you could make with the letters of your name. I had always felt sorry for the people with short names like John Smith. "Yeah, I knew that."

"Rather fitting, Detective Liveon, don't you think?"

I shrugged. "I'm not sure what that has to do with anything."

"You don't? Hmmm, I think it has everything to do with things. Like the fact that you are here now. Why is that?" She squinted as she waited for my answer.

"You know exactly why I'm here." The words came out more tartly than I intended.

"Do I?" She cocked her head and her kinky brown hair fell away from her face.

"I'm here because I was hired to do a job, and nothing else."

We stared at each other, and I wondered if she heard the small piece of the lie I had just spoken. It tasted bad on my tongue. While I was here doing a job, the woman in me felt that I was also working on something else. I just didn't know what that something else really meant.

"I think you want more from Ryan then you are letting on, that's what I think."

"It's a free world, and you are welcome to your own thoughts. Just don't make more out of them than they are." I stood up, ready to leave this conversation behind.

The door opened and Beth and I both turned to see a very angry woman stomp up the steps, her four-inch heels slamming on the hardwood floor. Damn. Kayla. I braced myself for the onslaught I saw coming when I met her eyes.

She moved to stand right in front of me. With her heels, she was the same height as me, and we faced off. Her eyes dripped with venom as she bore them into mine.

"What the hell do you think you're doing with my man?" I heard the door open again but didn't turn to see who it was. You never took your focus off an enemy and, right now, that is exactly what this woman was.

"Excuse me, Kayla, but what are you talking about?" I asked politely.

"You know exactly what I'm talking about!" she shouted into my face. I fought the urge to step away because I realized I would gain more if I stood my ground against her. She could very well be the one sending the threats.

"I'm sorry, but I don't see a ring on your finger." I glanced down at her hand to make a point. "Did I miss the announcement of your wedding vows in the latest tabloid? Because the last time I checked, Ryan was a free man."

"He is not free! He's mine! We've been together for a year! If you weren't such a mundane woman looking for a cheap thrill, you wouldn't be anywhere near him. He's just using you for some stupid publicity stunt! You do know that, don't you?" she spat. Her shoulders were visibly shaking, and the anger welled up in my chest.

I forced the violence I wanted to unleash on her down before speaking. "Did those pictures really look like a publicity stunt?" I raised an eyebrow at her. "Because you see, I was there. And it sure didn't feel like one. It felt like a man who wanted a woman, and she shared the desire."

"You bitch! He could never want someone like you!" She stepped back to launch a well-aimed slap across my cheek, but I saw it coming and moved faster.

I grabbed her wrist, her eyes popped open wide. "Someone like me? You mean someone who doesn't want a damn thing from him, except to make him happy? You mean a woman who doesn't want to steal his spotlight, but would rather watch from the sidelines. A woman who is real, not filled with Botox and silicone?" I pushed her wrist away, and she lost her balance and took a few steps back.

"You ever try to touch me again, and I'll have you arrested for assault. Stay away from me, and stay the hell away from Ryan; he doesn't want you anymore and he's not your man. He's mine."

I turned to Beth who still sat on the couch, but now her mouth hung open and an excited look was in her eyes. I nodded to her. "Beth, we'll finish our discussion later."

I turned from her and found Roseanne grinning near the steps. "Roseanne, don't we have some work to do?"

Roseanne giggled, and I fought the grin that tried to escape my lips. We walked out of the trailer, slammed the door behind us, and moved away quickly.

"Holy shit! I can't believe you just said that to Kayla! That was freaking awesome! Oh my God!" She laughed and jumped up and down beside me. We moved down a few trailers, and I slipped between two of them. Rose kept moving until she realized I left her side and backtracked to find me bending over with my hands on my shaking knees.

"Jackie, are you all right?" She put her hand on my back, and that's when I lost it. Laughter started deep down inside my belly and forced its way up. Roseanne joined in with me and, before we both knew it, we were hysterical, and tears ran down our cheeks.

"I can't believe I just said that to her!" I sputtered in between gulping breaths.

"I have never seen her speechless before, that was absolutely incredible. Wait till Ryan hears what happened; he is going to be amazed."

The thought of Ryan sobered me. "No, don't you dare tell Ryan what I said in there." My hair whipped back and forth around my face as I shook my head vehemently.

"Are you kidding? If I don't tell him, Beth sure will! Besides, why don't you want him to know?"

Why didn't I want him to know? Duh! Because I basically just said that this wasn't a job, that this was real, and I had feelings for him and I was willing to fight for him. Damnit!

"Please, don't tell him," I begged her and grabbed her arm to make sure she understood.

She peered at me carefully. "You really do like him, don't you?"

"No. No, it's just…" I stammered.

"It's just that you really do like him," she finished and beamed at me. "If you didn't, you wouldn't be turning as red as a fire truck right now."

I dropped her arm. Oh, crap. I stood there and stared at the dirt on the ground, my hands on my hips.

"Hey, I won't tell him about what you said." She hesitated for a moment, "Or how you feel. But I think you might be in for a surprise, because you're not the only one who has those same feelings." She raised her eyebrows twice. "If you know what I mean."

The slamming of a door echoed back to us and we both stuck our heads out past the edge of the trailer and watched as Kayla stomped away. Beth was grinning from ear to ear while she watched Kayla's retreating back. When Kayla disappeared, Beth turned and walked in another direction.

"I've never seen Beth look so happy," Roseanne whispered next to me. I had no idea why she was happy, and to be honest, that thought alone scared the hell out of me.

"I have to go back to the trailer. I forgot to grab the notes Ryan said he had for me."

She pulled a slip of paper out of her pocket. "Here, I made that list you wanted about the women he was involved with."

I looked at the piece of paper as if it was a snake about to bite me. "It's not as bad as you might think." She pushed it closer, and I reluctantly took it and slipped it into the pocket on my thigh. Not as bad as I might think? Or was it worse?

We got back to the trailer, and I walked to the bedroom door and pulled it open. Holy cow! The bedroom was huge. How do you fit a king-sized bed in a room like this and still have space to walk around? I glanced at the dark wood cabinets and a matching dresser, along with a sitting area and a small table. Another mirror covered the ceiling, and a shiver raced down my spine at the thought of lying on that bed staring up into it with Ryan beside me. Whoa, girl, none of that.

I straightened my back and walked to the nightstand. On top of it was a framed picture of an older couple. The man looked like an older version of Ryan. It must be his parents. I picked it up and sat down on the bed; melancholy rolled over me as I thought about how much I missed my own parents.

I put the picture back down and pulled open the small drawer. Three envelopes sat on top of other papers, and I pulled them out by the edges. I doubted that there would be any prints on them from the person who sent them, but still, I would check.

I set them on the top of the nightstand and looked around for something to fold them into. I stared at the dresser for a minute and then walked over to it. In the second drawer, I found what I wanted—a pile of T-shirts. I pulled one out, walked back over to the bed, and unfolded it. I placed the envelopes into the center and wrapped them up. I would have one of my crime guys look at them for me.

I turned to close the drawer of the nightstand but paused when I saw a newspaper clipping poking out, the word evil barely visible on the edge. My fingers shook slightly as I lifted the papers covering it and found several newspaper clippings of the incident at the airport. He had saved them. On one of them, he had underlined my name, twice, in red.

I went to set them back down and saw a photograph under the clippings. It was a shot of me at the press conference.

Should I be worried about this? Was there an underlying obsession happening here? Had Ryan made up the threats as part of a plan to get me here?

Roseanne walked in and interrupted my thoughts. "Yeah, he has quite a stash of those. He was kind of obsessed with finding you after that happened."

I turned to her while I eased the drawer closed. "You know stalking is a crime."

"Not if you want to be stalked," she said quietly. I didn't bother to reply, because even though I hadn't wanted to be in contact with him before, I wasn't fighting it now.

"Did you find what you needed?" she asked when she realized I wasn't going to reply to her last comment.

I lifted the shirt. "Yep. I'll get someone to take this back to my lab and check it out."

"Okay, I think one of your guys is down near the edge of our tent town. Let's go find them, and then I'll take you over to the set."

We found one of my patrol officers doing some traffic control near the edge of what they called "tent town." They weren't really tents, but it did look like a camp with all of the trailers parked here. I asked the officer to take it back and have one of the crime lab guys process it and let me know what they got. He slipped it into a plastic evidence bag, shirt and all, and sealed it before tossing it into the front seat.

Roseanne and I climbed back into my truck and drove over to the filming location. I found a spot where I could watch the area and still see him. Troy was wandering around and talking on his phone. He waved when he saw me, and I returned it before turning back to the action in front of the cameras.

I was impressed with what I saw. Not just Ryan and his acting, but the actress and the way the people behind the scenes moved and made things happen. The director sat inside a black draped tent. There were four different screens in front of him, each one showed a different view of the scene.

I watched with more interest than was warranted as Ryan moved toward Sheila, his co-star. I hadn't realized that Ryan was portraying a police officer in this film. Sheila and Ryan were in a very intense and romantic part of the scene when Ryan paused. The director in front of me grunted. He told the actors to start over.

When Ryan himself yelled cut, the director threw his hands up in the air. "What's his problem?"

"Where is Jacquelyn?" Ryan called out loudly from the set. I must have made a noise, because the director turned to look at me.

"Well, go see what the hell he wants so that we can get this finished," he all but barked at me. I spun and moved out of the tent.

Ryan caught my eye the moment I appeared, and I was drawn by the vision he made as he moved toward me. The uniform he wore was a standard police dress uniform. The gear he wore around his waist emphasized his strength and commanded power. I had always been a sucker for a man in uniform, but never had a man affected me so deeply.

I squeaked out a few words and asked what the problem was. Was there a threat on the set I hadn't seen? Did something happen that I hadn't picked up on?

He gripped my face gently and planted a passionate kiss on me. My head spun, and my heart raced as our mouths meshed and our tongues dueled. Not once did I think about the thirty or so people who stood around us staring.

I was so moved by the kiss that I could only nod my head when he mumbled to me, "Sorry, but I needed to get into the mood, excuse me for what I'm about to do."

When the director's words reached my ears, I cringed. Ryan gave me one more small, gentle peck before he turned and strutted back to his place on set. My eyes trailed down the back of his body from his strong shoulders, to his thin waist with the heavy equipment wrapped around it, and then his firm buttocks. Oh, I was so far gone.

I saw Sheila grin and make a comment to Ryan and just like that the filming started again. This time, I watched the kiss from where he'd left me. My legs still shook, and I feared if I tried to move, I would fall flat on my face.

As Sheila and Ryan gave in to the onscreen passion of the first kiss, I wondered if we really looked like that. My mind recalled a photo we had seen on TV only the night before, and I realized that we looked even better than they did.

With that single take, the director was happy with the outcome. I was still close enough to his tent that I heard him say something about me being around for all future romance scenes to keep Ryan in the mood. I felt the heat creep into my face as I scanned the area and saw others glancing at me with knowing looks.

I moved away from the tent and toward the food table. I needed a drink, but water would have to do for now.

When Ryan joined me, we talked about the film. I was happily surprised that I knew exactly what they were filming. Stacy was a detective in another township not too far away, and we had worked on several cases together. We'd even gone out for dinner a few times to unwind and discuss our jobs. Ryan pulled my hand away from my phone before I could send her a message and drew me close to him. My knees began to shake at his close proximity. I wasn't sure how much more of his passionate kissing I could handle before I caved completely and lost myself in him.

I scanned the area. Most people were doing their own thing; while some glanced at us, there was one person who caught my attention. Smoldering hate burst from her eyes toward me. I'd show her that things were over between them. I pulled away from her evil glare and brought my lips to Ryan's. Once our lips touched, nothing else mattered.

How easily I could get lost in the feelings he evoked in me. I had to find a way to get my bearings back. Talking about his work, or thinking about the real reason I was there, was the best way. He must have thought the same thing because we turned the conversation back to the filming.

When he went back to work, I noticed Kayla was nowhere around, and I was glad she disappeared. I wasn't ready for a repeat performance with her just yet, especially in front of Ryan.

Beth happened to wander my way and stood next to me. I did a double take and braced for the cutting words that I expected to come out of her mouth.

She stood with her arms casually crossed over her chest, her line of sight on the scene. "I'm impressed. I have never seen anyone put Kayla in her place before."

I peeked at her from the corner of my eye, but didn't respond.

"I think you're good for Ryan, and whether you want to admit it or not, you're not just here for the job. It is quite obvious that you are here for the man, too."

I turned to look at her straight on. She glanced at me with her eyebrow up. "Am I correct in my assumption?"

I exhaled. "I don't know." We both turned back to the scene in front of us and stood quietly for a few moments. I watched Ryan as he joked with Sheila and winked at me when he saw me observing him.

"Well, I think you'll figure it out soon enough. In the meantime, what is it they say in your line of work?" I peered at her, unsure where she was going with this. "I've got your back." She winked and turned away. I watched her retreat and chuckled quietly to myself. I guess that was good, right?

RYAN

The scene with Erik and Devon went smoothly, so we moved on to another scene where Corey, the role Sheila plays, returns from the grave much to my character's surprise.

Again, before the intense kiss in the scene began, I sought out Jackie and tugged her into the director's tent. The director smirked, but turned around to give us a moment as I planted a hungry kiss on her. My entire body hummed with the current we created as I walked back to Sheila, who tried not to grin.

When we were done, I searched the area for Jackie. She was nowhere to be found. Troy and Drew escorted me back to the trailer so that I could change out of the costume I was in. How did real cops wear that stuff all day, every day? When I had peeled the vest off my body, I stretched like a cat, thankful to have it off and not confining my movements any longer.

I asked where Jackie was and was told she had gone back to the house to do some work. I skipped my shower there and climbed into the limo to get home. Even though I was focused on the scenes we were filming, Jackie's face found its way into my mind on several occasions. I wanted to feel her in my arms again, and not just to get me in the mood for a scene.

I locked my jaw, concerned by the way I needed her to help set the mood. I had always been able to get in the right frame of mind in the past; so why was it so different now?

I walked into the house when we got home and wandered around. Jackie wasn't in the kitchen or living room area. I looked out the back and found her sitting on the patio, papers in her lap, her legs stretched out on another chair she had pulled closer. She was on the phone, and the wind tossed her hair gently around. A smile lit up her face and warmed the inside of my gut as she laughed.

"She's a beautiful woman," Troy said quietly as he stood beside me.

That she was. She leaned her head back and laughed harder. Who was she talking to that made her so happy? Did she make up with her boyfriend? Or was it a friend?

A feeling very close to jealously replaced the warm feeling in my gut, and I turned and strode away.

"Where you going?" Troy questioned as I moved to leave the room.

"I'm going to go take a shower. Can you make sure dinner is ready soon?" My voice was clipped, and I didn't wait for an answer before I strode purposefully out of the room.

I climbed the stairs to the third floor and stopped on the balcony. I could see Jackie still sitting out on the patio talking on the phone, but now she was going through the papers in her lap and making notes. What was she working on? I spied on her for a short time and then went to clean up.

Before I came back down, I sat on the bed and pulled out a notepad. Roseanne had already given Jackie her list, and I was sure that Troy probably had, too. I needed to write mine up. I sighed. How many years was I supposed to go back? Kayla and I had been together for a while, so other than a few social events, there hadn't been many other women this last year. But before that, damn, there were a lot of woman. Did I list the ones I had just dated, or the ones I had been sexually involved with? The list was almost the same though.

I stared writing down the names, thinking of the women I had been involved with over the last three years. I didn't have to go back further than that, did I? I ended up with a list of nine women. Obviously, I had been playing the part of a true Hollywood playboy. That thought embarrassed the hell out of me, and I ripped the paper off the pad, folded it, and slipped it in the back pocket of my jeans.

I found everyone sitting on the patio. The sun was setting low on the horizon, and the colors were muted in the sky because of the thick clouds that were rolling in. We would get some rain tonight.

Suzette, my chef, placed our dinner on the table as Roseanne, Drew, Troy, and Jackie gathered around to grab a seat.

Baked chicken over pasta with a light sauce and salad were on the menu tonight, and the scent of the food made my stomach grumble as I moved closer to the table. I took the empty seat next to Jackie, she glanced up for a brief moment. Something dark rolled through her eyes that I couldn't read, but then she turned her attention back to putting food on her plate.

I examined her casually from the corner of my eye as she ate with enthusiasm and joined in on the friendly conversation at the table about the day's events. I was ecstatic about the way she made herself so comfortable here and got along with everyone. She kept her attention on them, but I knew she was very aware of me.

Our legs brushed under the table once, her fork stopped momentarily halfway to her mouth. Did she feel the same warmth that traveled up my thigh from where our legs had connected? I saw her lick her lips and swallow before she put the food into her mouth. *Ah, to be that fork.*

Jackie's eyes were everywhere but on me, and I wondered why. Dinner was a nice affair, everyone was relaxed and sharing funny stories about things that happened on the set that day. Roseanne spent most of the time talking because she has the ability to be just about everywhere, unlike Troy who stays by my side almost relentlessly and Jackie who remained very focused on the investigation throughout the day.

I noticed that the conversation stayed off of Beth and Kayla, and I wondered how I could go about asking what really happened.

"So, Jackie, what did you think of my agent?" She stopped eating and glanced pointedly at Roseanne. She finished chewing her food slowly and lifted her napkin to dab her lips. I figured it was more of a maneuver to search for the right words than proper etiquette.

"Beth?" she asked quietly, as if she didn't know who I was talking about.

I leaned back in my seat, watching her struggle slightly with how to handle this. She knew exactly where I was trying to take this conversation.

"Beth is very nice," she said and pushed some pasta around her plate with the fork. She peeked up at Roseanne and Troy. I wasn't the only one surprised by her choice of words.

"Nice, huh?" I paused for a moment. "You are about the only person I know who has ever called her nice." I leaned on the table and pushed my plate back so that I could rest my elbows on the glass. "So what did you ladies have to talk about?"

She shrugged and put some food into her mouth, placing more attention to the last few pieces of noodle on her plate than on anyone around us. "I don't know; she just wanted to get to know me, I guess."

"Really, now?" I said it slowly and cocked my head to the side to get a better look at her face. Her cheeks were pink, and I fought back a grin.

She wiped her mouth with her napkin, tossed it onto the plate, and sat back making direct eye contact with me for the first time since we started dinner. "No, actually she wanted to know if you were any good in bed."

Roseanne burst out laughing, but when she saw the threat of violence in my eyes, she quickly put her hand over her mouth to smother any further noise. She did not succeed.

Jackie was staring hard at me when I met her eyes. She raised an eyebrow waiting for my response. "You're not going to tell me the truth, are you?"

She shook her head while she exhaled and shrugged. "There is nothing to tell, Ryan. She asked me a few questions, and we were just finishing up when—" she caught herself and peeked at Roseanne while biting her lip.

"When what? When Kayla showed up?" I encouraged her to keep going. I was dying to hear what happened. Someone on the set told me Kayla had been so pissed she wasn't watching where she was going and walked around a corner and right into a guy carrying a bunch of electrical equipment, knocking him over. She screamed at him, making a huge scene, and then stomped away.

"You are making this a bigger deal than it has to be. Why is that?" I saw her lock her jaw and grind her teeth, but I pressed on. "Rumors are flying all over the set. If it's no big deal, then tell me what you said so that I know what the truth is."

She tipped her head back to look up at the darkening sky and closed her eyes. My eyes traveled down her neck, and I envisioned kissing every centimeter of her skin there. I inhaled quickly.

"Forget it." I pushed the chair back from the table and tossed my napkin down. "If you don't want to tell me, fine." I shrugged roughly and growled. "Fine." I stared into her eyes, the blue of her irises turning almost a steel gray as anger filled them. I knew the feeling; I wasn't too happy myself, that she wouldn't tell me. I turned to leave and remembered the list I made.

I spun back to her again, absently noting that everyone, except Jackie, was staring at me as if I had two heads. I pulled the paper from my pocket and dropped it in her lap. "The list you wanted."

To her credit, she never looked away from my intense scrutiny and the note lay on her lap against one of her hands, but she didn't reach for it. I walked away before anyone had a chance to speak.

In my study, I pulled out my script from the desk drawer and flipped it open to the scenes for tomorrow. I had to force myself to focus on what I was reading, because my mind kept wandering back to the muscles and tight skin of her neck and what her eyes would reveal when she read my list.

I poured myself a scotch and kicked my feet up on my desk as I scanned through my lines, reminding myself about how the flower shop scene was supposed to go.

I read through the scene four times when I felt eyes on me. I looked up and found Jackie standing in the doorway, her arms crossed over her chest, her shoulder leaning against the doorjamb. I flushed, remembering the way I threw the list on her lap and stomped away like a child.

"I know you're working, and I'm sorry to bother you, but I need to speak with you for a few minutes, if you can spare the time." She didn't leave her spot, and I noticed she hugged herself a bit tighter as she spoke. Did I make her nervous? Or was she afraid of another one of my childish outbursts?

"I could use a break. Come on in, Jackie." I put my feet back on the floor and flopped the heavy script on the desktop. I got up and poured myself another scotch. "Would you like a drink?"

"No, thank you. I don't drink." She made her way to the desk and took a seat in front of it.

"Why don't we talk over here?" I pointed to the couch and chair in front of the fireplace. "Why is it that you don't drink?" I asked, as I put the lid back on the bottle and moved toward the fireplace.

She shrugged. "Just never really got into it." She sank into the dark leather couch and sighed heavily. "Okay, that's not the truth. I don't drink because my father was an excessive drinker. Not a bad drunk, he just drank a lot sometimes and did stupid things."

"So because your father drank, you don't?" I settled on the opposite end of the couch.

She turned so that she was sitting sideways, her legs curled under her. Her feet were bare, and I was tempted to reach out and pull them in my lap.

"In my job, turning to a bottle is easy. The stress of the job can easily feed an addiction. I'm careful not to pick up a drink when I'm stressed. Don't get me wrong. I do enjoy a beer here and there, and I will drink when I'm out in a social situation. I just don't drink at home, and I never drink alone."

We studied each other, and I rolled her words over. She doesn't drink at home. Was this home to her? She had only been here for two days. Could she feel that comfortable here?

"That's understandable." I was happily surprised that she shared that level of personal information with me. "So, have you tried to get your father help?"

Her eyes darkened drastically, and her hair fell like a curtain around her face as she bent to examine her hands. She picked at a nail while she frowned. "My parents are dead." She cleared her throat and looked up; pain was vivid in her eyes, but there were no tears. "And before you ask, I don't want to talk about it, and I know you're sorry."

A shiver passed over her, she pulled her legs tighter underneath of her. "Okay, I won't ask, and yes, I'm sorry to hear that."

She nodded and scanned the room. I watched her battle some internal demon for a moment and decided it would probably be best to change the conversation.

"So, you wanted to talk to me?" I asked casually, taking a sip of my drink. I swallowed the warm liquid.

She inhaled and exhaled deeply before she turned to face me again.

"Yes. I looked at your list. It wasn't much different than the ones I got from Troy and Roseanne."

Well, that was good to know. "All right, so what do you need to know?"

She looked me right in the eyes. Her composure was back now, and the inner strength she normally carried filled her expression. She was suddenly all business again.

"How many of those women did you sleep with?" She didn't even blink as she spoke.

I cleared my throat uncomfortably. "Almost all of them. I didn't sleep with Blair; she was just a casual thing. Turns out she was into women, not men. We just went to some social engagements together because she needed a male escort."

"Thank you for your honesty. Which ones did you break up with yourself?"

I took another sip while I contemplated the answer. "Susan, Tiffany, and of course, Blair, all decided that it wasn't going to work out for one reason or another, so that leaves six that I personally ended things with."

"Kayla being one of them?" She tilted her head to the side as she asked.

"Yes, Kayla wasn't too happy about it; obviously, she's deluded and still thinks we're together." I thought for a moment while I swirled the brown liquid in my crystal glass. "Do you think Kayla could be the one behind all of this?"

One shoulder came up in a small shrug. "She could be, but I'm interested in knowing more about the other five. Have any of them contacted you recently?"

"Monique did, and so did Diane. When they heard Kayla and I had split, they both got in touch with me."

"Why did you stop seeing them?" She turned on the couch so that her back was against the side and pulled her knees up until they were almost touching her chest. Her arms wrapped lightly around her legs; her fingers laced gently together. She looked so beautiful sitting there that I couldn't remember what she just asked me. I played back my memory to recall her question.

"Initially, Diane said she wanted to get back together with her previous boyfriend. We hadn't been dating for very long, so we ended things. But I guess it didn't work out with her ex after all, so when she heard that Kayla and I split, she asked if we could try it again. I told her I'd call her sometime, but I hear she's already back with him again.

"Monique and I were like oil and water. We dated a few months, but we spent more time fighting over stupid things than getting along. When she called me, I told her I was too busy with this new film coming up and didn't have time for a relationship."

She rested her chin on her knee, and my heart skipped a beat. She looked so comfortable sitting there, but I could see the wheels turning in her mind.

"And the other three women?" she asked quietly.

"Clare, Jillian, and Melissa." I shrugged. "This probably sounds petty, but they were just pretty faces to have on my arm for premieres and such. When we split, they all went on their way. I stay in touch with Melissa and we're friendly, but I'm not sure what happened to Clare or Jillian; but neither of them seemed upset by my decision or have tried to contact me in ages." I tipped my glass back and finished my drink. "So what are your thoughts?" I stood to go get a refill but ended up setting my glass on the table and sat back down, this time closer to her. She looked at the back of the couch where my shoulders rested. I was close enough that I could reach out and touch her now.

She pulled her legs tighter to her chest, her fingers turning white as she gripped her knees. I pried her hands apart, then grabbed the leg of her pants and pulled it so that it lay over my lap. The second leg followed, and I rested my hand gently on her shin. She folded her hands on her lap and avoided my gaze.

"I think I'll start by looking more into Monique, Clare, and Kayla." She met my stare with a shuttered gaze.

"What did you think of the notes?" I slowly moved my hand back and forth over her shin. Her eyes flicked to the movement, and I felt her legs tense.

"To be honest, I didn't read them. I found them and sent them to the lab right away. I didn't want any more fingerprints on them. I'll see them when they get back."

I stroked her leg a little higher, going from her ankle to just under her kneecap.

"Ryan, what are you doing?" she asked softly.

"Nothing, I'm just relaxing and trying to get you to relax, too."

She pulled her legs off my lap and spun on the couch to stand up. I grabbed her hand while she was off balance, and she fell onto my lap. Her breath rushed out as she landed in my arms and looked into my face, four inches away.

"What's wrong with wanting you to relax?" My voice was low, she glanced at my lips nervously.

"I don't relax when I'm working." She tried to push against my chest, but my arms wound around her tightly and I held her in place.

"Work is over. It's time to relax for a little while." I pulled her closer. "I want to kiss you again, Jackie."

Her gaze dropped to my lips and parted. I took advantage of that and reeled her in. The instant our lips met, the resistance in her shoulders relaxed, and she eased into the kiss. She still tasted of the creamy light sauce from dinner, and I felt a hunger not associated with my stomach come to life.

I speared my hand through her hair and tugged it back lightly, breaking the kiss to slide my mouth and tongue down the soft column of her throat, a sigh left her lips and added excitement to my veins.

"I want you, Jackie, like I have never wanted anyone in my life before," I murmured in her ear as I placed soft kisses under her lobe. I felt her stiffen before she pulled back and jumped to her feet.

My body felt lost with her sudden departure, and I reached to take her hand again, but she stepped away.

"Ryan, I'm sorry. That shouldn't have happened." She put her hands on her hips, her chest rising and falling, rivaling mine in speed.

I stood up. "Why not, Jackie? I know you want me. Do you think I can't tell?"

She scrutinized me for a moment, her eyes filled with a pain I didn't understand. "Wanting is not something that I allow myself to do. Ryan, I'm here to do a job, and while we are in public, I'll pretend to be your girlfriend. In private, that's not going to happen." She paused for a moment. "I'm not going to be girl number ten."

She spun around and practically ran out of the room. I brushed a hand through my hair and then down over my face. My past was coming back to haunt me. She didn't realize that not one of those women compared to her.

"What happened with Jackie? I just saw her run up the stairs." Roseanne's voice surprised me, and I twisted to see her.

"Who knows!" I picked up my glass and went back the bar, pouring more scotch into the crystal.

"What did you do, Ryan?" she asked as she flopped down on the sofa.

"I didn't do anything, Rose. Why does it have to be my fault?" I sank into the leather chair that matched the sofa. Her eyebrows were hiding in her bangs they were so far up on her forehead. "What?"

"Did you kiss her again? It seems like every time you do that, she runs from you."

"Why is that? I don't get it." I shook my head back and forth. "When she's around, hell, even when she's not around, all I can think about is having her in my arms, looking into her eyes."

"Oh, boy. Looks like Ryan has finally met his match and fallen in love."

"What?" I sputtered as I chocked on my drink. "I'm not in love!"

"Ha! Keep telling yourself that. You've been after this woman since you saw her standing right in front of you at the airport. Ever since then, you've basically stalked her and gave her this job just so that you could have her close. Now you can't keep your hands off of her, and you get all gooey and stuff when you talk about her."

"I do not get gooey, Rose."

"Like I said, keep telling yourself that." She grinned at me, and I sighed. Was I getting all gooey over her? Could I have fallen in love?

"I'm not in love with her, Rose. I barely know the woman." I leaned my head back on the chair, the cold leather felt good against my heated flesh.

"She found some of the things you clipped from the newspaper about her today. Said you were a stalker."

"What?" I lifted my head so fast, the room spun slightly.

"When she went to get the notes in the bedroom, she found a few of the clippings you saved about her. I think that freaked her out a bit."

I tried to remember what I had in the drawer. I hadn't been in there in a while.

"It's a good thing she didn't look in your drawer here. That would really freak her out." She sat up on the couch as if she was about to stand. "And by the way, she will never tell you what she said to Kayla, but it had something to do with how the kiss outside hadn't been fake. That two people who share that kind of desire can't fake it."

Roseanne smirked at me, and my heart thudded in my chest. Did she mean what she said?

"She also told Kayla that the reason you were with her was because she was real, and not full of Botox and silicone."

"She said that?" I was stunned.

"Yep, she sure did. Don't you dare tell her I told you." She started to walk out of the room. "Ryan, she likes you. I mean, she really likes you. Give her some time; she will come around. You guys are good together, so don't mess this up." She winked and left to leave me mulling over what Jackie said to Kayla.

Yeah, I did like that she was all natural and not some made-up Hollywood woman. But the thought that kept spinning in my mind was the other thing she said about desire. If what she said was true, she did feel it when she kissed me, and I would use that against her the best way I could.

I grinned to myself as I went back to my script.

JACQUELYN

$\mathcal{T}$he afternoon flew by, and I remained as far back from the action as I could. I continued to watch over Ryan, and the flurry of activity that constantly surrounded him. More than once, I got lost in his movements and the smile that radiated over his features as he worked and spoke with those around him. I mentally shook myself out of the dreamy world I found myself lost in and reminded myself that this was a job and as soon as I figured out the mystery, my life would go back to normal and Ryan would no longer be a part of it.

But what was normal? I guess it was the life I'd been living for the last six years, the everyday constant chaos of solving crimes and being alone. After all these years, you would think I was used to that, but standing here watching Ryan made me wonder if I could go back to that when this was all said and done. *Do I even want to?*

Roseanne called me over the headset and asked me to come back to tent town. I wound my way through the crowd of people on the set and found Troy, letting him know I was leaving, and that Drew was on his way over to take my place. Before I left him, he handed me a folded piece of paper. I knew what it was and slipped it into my pocket with the list that Roseanne had given me earlier.

With a deep sigh, I moved to my Jeep and headed back to tent town to meet up with Roseanne. The afternoon was winding down, and Roseanne wanted me to take her back to the house. She had things to settle for the next day's shoot, which required us to be in town where there were more logistical nightmares to consider with the stars of the show.

We told Troy where we were headed and turned our radios in at the tech trailer. Markus was nowhere around, and I took a moment to study the inside of the trailer carefully. Multiple computers sat on the shelves, and I bumped the mice one by one to find that each screen was password protected as I suspected they would be. I heard Roseanne's voice outside and quickly slipped out before she came in.

When we got back to the house, she grabbed her notebook and phone and sat down to start making calls, making sure that the area would be ready for them. All of us needed to stick close to Ryan tomorrow as we headed into town.

With Roseanne busy on the phone, I grabbed my own notebook from my backpack and wandered out to the patio. After getting comfortable at the table, I watched a few horses in the fields, their tails flicking back and forth at erratic intervals. How peaceful it was here.

I had been putting this off long enough. I pulled the two pieces of paper out of my pocket and unfolded the first one, Roseanne's list. She had ten women listed and stars next to two of them. One of those was Kayla, and the other was a woman named Monique. I wondered what the stars meant. Were those longer lasting relationships or ones where things had gotten rocky?

I opened up the note from Troy and found he had seven women on his list. Kayla and Monique were both underlined, and there was a question mark next to the name Diane. I debated on the list for a few minutes and reached for my phone, scrolling through my contacts. I pushed the button for Rebecca.

She answered on the second ring. "Please God, let me live in your shoes for one day." I laughed aloud when she finished.

"Sure, come right over, you can have it."

"Oh, don't make promises you can't keep!" She paused, and I heard her turn down the radio in her patrol car. "Did you really get sold out for a million bucks to work for Ryan?"

I stopped laughing. "Where'd you hear that?"

"The guys at the station were joking about it this morning. They printed a bunch of the pictures of you kissing Palmer and put them all over the wanted board."

"They did not!" I shouted playfully into the phone.

"Oh yeah, they did, although they took them down when Jimmy showed up. You should have seen his face when he saw them. He was so pissed that steam was coming out of his ears."

I could just imagine how angry he was to see those. I wish I'd been able to let him know ahead of time, although I did warn him not to believe everything he saw. But, as I'd told Kayla, even when I saw the pictures, I had to admit that it did look like a man and a woman who felt great desire for each other. And desire is exactly what I had felt when his lips took mine and his hands slid over my back. I suppressed a shiver at the memory.

As if reading my mind, Rebecca asked, "So it was awesome, huh?"

I threw my head back and laughed. "A girl doesn't kiss and tell."

"No way, you aren't getting out of this. Tell me, was it?" She practically shouted through the phone.

The grin that stole over my face was like the cat that ate the canary. "No, it was better."

"I hate you!" we cackled together for a moment. "So tell me, do you like him?"

"It's not like that, Rebecca," my voice grew somber. "We were just putting on a show, there is nothing else going on."

"Like hell there isn't!" She sounded indignant, and she knew me so well. "You've never kissed Jim that way."

That was true. The kisses I shared with Jimmy were calm by comparison and didn't have one tenth of the passion in them. I thought back on the possessive kiss he gave me before I left on my undercover assignment and realized I hadn't really felt anything during it. Not compared to the one I shared with Ryan. That lit my body up like a sparkler on the Fourth of July.

"Can we save this conversation for another day? I actually called you for some help." I didn't want to think about the feelings Ryan stirred in me anymore, not today.

"If you think I am going to let you go without every little detail, you're wrong. But since I am busy right now, and this conversation is better off over a beer and pizza, I'll let it slide for now. What is it you need?"

She was right. I would eventually tell her every detail, and it would probably be in our little hole-in-the-wall bar that we liked to hide in, but right now, I had business to discuss. "I need you to run a few names, see if anyone of them has any arrest records or if anything interesting comes up."

I heard her moving around, probably grabbing her clipboard from her gear bag on the passenger seat of her car.

"Okay, go ahead, I'm ready," she announced after a moment. I read off the women on the list, and she wrote each one down. "Why exactly am I doing this?"

I thought for a moment. If there was anyone I could trust, it was her. "I got hired to work with Ryan to find out who is threatening him. They think it's a woman from his past, so that's where I'm starting."

"All right, but why are you acting like his girlfriend?"

I exhaled deeply. "They seemed to think it was the best cover for why they suddenly have a cop around him. With what happened in the past, it seemed like a plausible excuse."

She was silent for a moment. "Okay, I can see that. I still think it's awesome, and you should take full advantage of being around that sexy beast."

"Really, Becca?" I replied with a chuckle.

"Come on, if you don't do him, you better call me so I can come over and get a shot! What I wouldn't do for a night with him. Whew!" I could just imagine her sitting in her car fanning herself because of her hot thoughts.

I ignored her comment and told her to call me when she got a chance to go through the names. We talked for a few more minutes about what was going on back at the department and then said our goodbyes.

Suzette was getting the table ready for dinner, so I stuffed my notebook and papers into my backpack and enjoyed the quiet evening as the sun set. I had no idea if Ryan was back or not until Troy joined me a few minutes later.

"So, Jackie, how was your first day on the set?" He squeezed my shoulder as he walked around me to take a seat on the other side of the table.

"Interesting to say the least." And I wasn't joking. The eerie feelings from Markus, the talk with Beth, the run in with Kayla, and watching Ryan on the set were all intriguing.

"I guess you recovered quickly from your run-in with Kayla." He took a sip of the beer he brought out with him.

I surveyed him for a moment. "It was no big deal," I finally responded. I watched his eyebrows rise, causing wrinkles to appear on his dark brown brow.

"It might not be a big deal to you, but everyone was talking about the warpath that Kayla was on after you walked out of the trailer." He looked down at his beer bottle and pulled on the edge of the label. "Can I ask you a question?"

I didn't think I could say no, so I just waited for him to go on.

He cleared his throat. "What do you really think of him?"

I pulled my gaze away from his and scanned the fields behind us. "It doesn't matter what I think, Troy. I'm here to do a job, and when I'm done," I turned my attention back to him, "I'm leaving, and Ryan goes on with his life."

"What if he doesn't want you to leave?" I pondered his words for a moment.

"Like all the rest of the women in his life, once he gets over this little hero-worship thing he has going, he'll get tired of me and move on." I shifted in my chair. "I'd rather be gone before that."

He leaned forward and set the brown bottle on the glass table with a clink. "You think he just likes you because of what you did for him? What did you call it, a hero-worship thing?"

"Troy, there is no other reason for Ryan to like me." I laughed, uncomfortable with the conversation. "I'm not in his league, this isn't my life, and I don't fit in. I'm not the kind of woman he needs."

He picked up his bottle, took a sip, and leaned back in his chair again. "That's where you're wrong. You are exactly the kind of woman he needs, and wants, in his life."

His words, needs and wants, rotated around in my skull and I didn't have a reply. Roseanne joined us a moment later, saving me from having to say anything further. The conversation put me on edge, and when Ryan appeared, freshly showered and looking all together mouthwatering, my heart skipped a beat and I couldn't look him in the eye.

Had Ryan told Troy he wanted me in his life? I couldn't imagine Ryan needing anyone, so I knew that part of Troy's comments were wrong.

Ryan's leg brushed against mine at the table, and I almost swallowed my tongue as the heat rushed up and down my thigh. I was unsettled through the rest of the meal. When Ryan pushed for me to tell him what I said to Kayla, my unbalanced emotions turned to anger. When he basically threw his list in my lap, I realized that he knew I was angry and my not talking to him had hurt him.

"Crap," I muttered after he left, I heard a snicker come from across the table. Troy excused himself to go do some work, and Roseanne and I pondered over the list a bit. The stars next to the names were people she felt might try to get back at Ryan. When I told her Troy had given me almost the same list and commented on those same people, she wasn't surprised.

I lifted the paper Ryan tossed on my lap and unfolded it. He had listed nine women on the paper, all written in a heavy print. The harshness of the writing reminded me of someone who was angry and trying to get a point across. Most of them were also named on the other two lists. I folded the papers and slipped them into my pocket, wondering why Ryan was angry when he made his.

I found Ryan in his office a while later. He was leaning back in his chair with his feet resting on the dark wood of the desk, his brow was slightly furrowed as he concentrated. His hair was mussed up, and he fingered a crystal glass with a dark caramel-colored liquid in it. My heart thumped against my breastbone as my eyes roved over his strong shoulders and lean legs.

He glanced up, and his face colored slightly. Was he embarrassed because I was watching him? He had to be used to that by now.

Although I told Ryan a little about why I didn't drink, but I didn't want to tell Ryan the truth. I didn't want him to know that years ago, I had fallen into a deep pit of despair and had found my courage to live in a bottle for a while. My life had fallen apart one night, and for months after that, I only managed to get by when I was under the influence of some strong liquid or another.

Jimmy is the one who finally got me to see what I was doing to myself, and gave me a shoulder to lean on while I gathered the strength to move forward.

I was surprised when Ryan answered my questions about the women as honestly as he did. Especially after I just lied to him, but then again, my life wasn't in jeopardy, so I didn't have to be truthful right now.

The more we talked, the easier it was to discuss, and I found myself oddly comfortable on the sofa next to him. His bright blue eyes stared directly at me most of the time. I was surprised when he stood up to return his glass but sat back down again and pulled my legs onto his lap. The back of my calves were on fire from where they rested on his warm thighs. His hand lay gently on my shin, and if I could have looked at my skin, I swear it would've been branded with his palm print.

I fought to hold back the feelings he created in me, the lustful images of him and I tangled on the couch and the hand that was doing lazy circles on my leg roving over my naked body.

"Ryan, what are you doing?" I feared speaking any louder than I did, not wanting him to hear the emotions crackling in my voice.

"Nothing, I'm just relaxing and trying to get you to relax, too." His voice was deep, husky, and soft. Little warning bells rang in my head: *Time to get the hell out of there.*

I started climbing off the sofa, but before I could get to my feet, I was on his lap, gazing into his heated eyes and feeling his hard body against mine. I tried to get away—okay, I tried half-heartedly to get away—but once he admitted that he wanted to kiss me, I was lost in the sight of his soft lips and the entrancing blue of his eyes.

He tasted of scotch and I soaked up the warm taste from his mouth. His hungry lips moved down my neck. I lost myself for a moment in the incredible feelings he stirred in me.

He whispered in my ear that he wanted me like no other woman. *Of course not; none of the other women on your list had saved your life twice.* The conversation with Troy raged back into my head, and I pushed away from him and stood up. My breathing was ragged, and my body was hot, begging for the release that it so badly wanted with him.

"Wanting is not something I allow myself to do," I told him, and my head screamed at my heart that it was lying. Wanting was all I could do! I could never give any more than that to a person. I made some lame excuse about not wanting to be girl number ten and fled the room.

Tears threatened the back of my eyes as I made my way upstairs to my room. With my mind in such turmoil, I didn't even stop to look out through the glass as I crossed the bridge.

After I closed the door to my room, I plopped onto the bed. My phone buzzed, I yanked it from my pocket and tossed it on the floor. I didn't want to talk to anyone. I wanted to wallow in self-pity.

I would never be able to fall in love with a man again. It wasn't that I couldn't, I could; and I feared that if I fell into Ryan's arms too many times in the peace and quiet of this house, that I would fall for this man.

He was a Hollywood playboy, a movie star god, and a multi-million-aire, while I was just a small-town police detective. I solved crimes; he created moments that pulled us away from reality. He was this incredibly gorgeous specimen of a man, and I was just an average looking woman.

But the most pressing point was that I was not free to love. I had done that once, loved with all my heart, and lost everything. I had been taught a lesson and knew that if I ever allowed another man into my heart, it would put his life in jeopardy. I wasn't just talking about a few notes, or a bottle of water with something in it to make you sick; I was talking about true death.

A death sentence had been put over me to punish me for doing my job. For the thousandth time since I had first fallen on the case in my second year on the job, I wished I had never been involved. Tears leaked from the corners of my eyes and rolled back into my hair. I would never be free to love again; all because I had put a stray piece of the puzzle together and one of the highest-ranking members of the mafia was now behind bars for life.

RYAN

I'm not sure how I got to sleep that night, but somehow, I did. When I woke in the early morning, I felt rested enough. Who couldn't use a little more sleep, huh? Like four or five consecutive hours?

I groaned as my feet touched the thick Berber carpeting on my floor and the heels of my hands ground against my eye sockets. Four was way too early, especially when you didn't fall asleep until after midnight. Marie was going to bend my ear while she did my makeup this morning.

With a grunt, I forced myself into the shower. The water helped to open my eyes, but it didn't take the sandpaper off the inside of my sockets.

I thought back to when I climbed into bed last night. Fantasies of Jackie lying beside me, my hands sliding over her soft skin and into her silky hair kept me tossing and turning. I thought about the last kiss we shared and how she pushed me away when I told her I wanted her like I had never wanted anyone else.

Her come back of being girl number ten had stung, plain and simple. Had I known a woman like Jackie would come into my life, I would have acted differently; I would have waited and not been such a playboy. *Yeah, right.* Who was I kidding?

I would have never thought it possible that an incredible woman like her would come into my life. She was someone who thought of others before herself, unlike me. She wanted to help them and make the world a better place. What did I do? I snorted in disgust as I washed my short blond hair. I entertained them, whoopee.

While the water washed away the shampoo, I wondered if I could ever be half the man she wanted. Okay, maybe I should rephrase that. I knew she wanted me, but could she ever need me? I felt like I needed her, and not just physically. Now that I had her beside me, taking part in my everyday moments, I craved more time with her. More time to see her smile, watch her work, see how her mind ticked, and find out more about her past.

I poured some liquid soap onto my hand while I wondered about her past. Other than talking about her father for a brief moment and knowing she was involved with someone, I didn't know anything at all about her life. I needed to fix that.

Maybe if I stopped thinking like a man trying to get her in bed, and acted like a friend, I could breach some of the walls around her and find out more.

I rinsed and grabbed my razor, deciding that would be my new goal: Get to know the real Jacquelyn Liveon.

Somewhere between washing and shaving, I found a new energy and rushed to finish dressing. I wanted to put my plan in motion.

When I got downstairs, Troy, Roseanne, and Jackie were in the kitchen sipping coffee and picking at some Danishes that Suzette had left out for them.

"Morning!" I cleared my throat to get rid of the huskiness and scanned over everyone with a grin on my face.

"Aren't you chipper this morning. Looks like someone got a good night's sleep," Roseanne quipped as she took a bite of a strawberry pastry.

I grinned. No one needed to know that I had barely slept, or that I had a new plan. I poured my coffee and made my way to the table, snagging a Danish from the tray as I sat down.

"How is everyone this morning?" I watched as they glanced at one another.

Troy put his coffee cup down. "Fine, and why the hell are you so awake?"

I shrugged and took a very small sip of my hot coffee. "Don't know. I just woke up in a good mood." I looked pointedly at Jackie, who raised one eyebrow just a tad and tilted her head to the side.

"Oh, damn!" Roseanne burst out and jumped off her chair. "I have to be in town in fifteen minutes. Jackie, are you coming with me?"

Jackie was about to rise and join Rose, but my words stopped her. "No, take Drew with you. I want Jackie with me today. Since we're going to be in town, I'd rather have her at my side."

Roseanne gave Jackie a pointed look, and Jackie shrugged. "I should stick close to him since we are going to be out in public. These are the kinds of places where something could happen."

Rose said her goodbyes and took off in search of Drew, who was always the last one downstairs.

"So, what's the scene you're doing today?" Jackie asked me as she wrapped her hands around her mug as if they were cold. She had pretty hands.

"We are doing the florist scene this morning and then we move to shoot one of the cemetery scenes this afternoon."

Her face paled. "Which scene?" she asked quietly.

I peeked at Troy. He was watching Jackie intently. "The one where Mitch talks to himself," I answered.

She inhaled deeply. "Okay, I was hoping you were not going to say the funeral scene. I'm sorry, but I'm not sure I can be present for that one."

"Why's that?" Troy questioned.

She looked at him. "Have you ever been to a police funeral?" We both shook our heads. "It's a pretty intense thing and can affect you deeply."

"How many have you been to?"

She looked at her mug, her fingers turning white as she gripped it. "Two. One was an officer who worked up north. I didn't really know him." She closed her eyes.

"Did you know the second one?" Troy asked as he leaned forward to see her face.

"Yes." She opened her eyes and lifted them straight up to meet mine. A pain as I had never seen blazed from her eyes. "The second one was for my fiancé."

Troy and I both jerked back in our chairs, shocked by her admission. Troy put his hand over her forearm. She kept staring at me, not even blinking. What could I say? There was nothing that would ease the pain so evident on her face.

"Well, when we get to that scene, we'll give you a few days off," Troy said moving forward in work mode. "Speaking of scenes, we need to get moving in a few minutes. I'll be right back."

Troy got up and left the room, but neither of us saw him leave. We were still focused on each other.

"I know this is just a job, and maybe there are some feelings that we have for each other, but it's because of that," she paused for a moment to catch her breath, "because of Logan's death that I can't get involved with you."

"Why does that have anything to do with us?" I almost reached out to her, but even from my seat, I could feel the hard wall around her that would rebuke my efforts.

"It has a lot to do with it. I'm sorry, but I can't explain it to you. I just need you to understand that we can never be more to each other than we are right now." She finally broke the eye contact and picked up her mug.

She finally admitted that she felt something for me, and in the same breath, she told me it would never work. I didn't believe that. We could find a way to work it out. In the meantime, I would respect what she was asking for and give her some space.

"Can I ask you a question?" I leaned back in my chair.

She shrugged, avoiding my intense stare.

"How did Logan die?"

At the mention of his name, she winced. "Ryan, I don't want to talk about this. I'm sorry."

I sat forward and reached across the table for her hand, she tensed, as I knew she would. "I understand what you're saying. I will try to respect your wishes, but just answer that one question, please."

She was quiet for almost a full minute, although her mouth moved as if to speak a few times. "He was killed, Ryan, along with my parents, on Christmas Eve six years ago."

My mouth fell open, and I knew there would never be a set of words I could string together that would make her feel better, or show how sorry I was. When she had spoken about her father passing away, I had no clue that she had lost her mother at the same time. And I had absolutely no clue that her loss was made even more painful by losing the man she loved and planned to spend her life with.

I suddenly understood her so much better: Her need to control, the way she was so careful and focused, and her ability to draw away from me when I got too close. It made a little more sense now.

"You guys ready?" Troy called from the doorway as he entered the kitchen.

She snapped out of her fog as if someone had flipped a switch, throwing a semi-smile on her lips as she pushed her chair back and stood. I had a much harder time dredging up the energy to stand. Would I be able to function if I had lost my parents and the woman I loved? I didn't think so.

She walked past Troy without a word as I finally found the strength to stand.

"You okay? You look like you just saw a ghost," Troy said as I turned toward him.

I was tempted to tell him what Jackie just revealed, but it wasn't my place to say anything. With a firm push away to the pain of her words, I did what I was paid to do. I acted as if nothing was wrong and slapped him on the shoulder as I reached his side. "Nope, everything is fine."

Jackie was already in the limo when we reached it. I slid in beside her, careful to give her space as she stared out the side window. We didn't have to pretend that everything was all right in front of Troy. As soon as we were seated and the limo stared to move, Troy was on the phone.

She sat beside me; her hands crossed gently in her lap over her black cargo pants. She wore a pale purple shirt today that was un-tucked, and she'd pulled her hair back into a ponytail at the nape of her neck. When the limo made a sharp turn to the right, she leaned into me slightly with the movement.

I reached over and took her hand in mine, our fingers laced together, and I kept it in her lap. The hint of a smile reached her lips, and she wrapped her other hand around mine.

If that was what I could do to comfort her, to hold her hand, to be there for her, I would do it. I would do anything for the woman beside me with the fragile heart and the strongest of shoulders.

As we arrived in town, there were crowds lining the street. We figured there would be a lot of press, but I didn't think there would be as many observers as there were.

"Holy cow, looks like the whole county is here to see you." She shook her head as she spoke, but it seemed to be more in wonder than anger or concern.

"Sorry you have to be a part of this." I watched her profile.

She squeezed my hand. "Actually, now that I know the movie, and I've seen some of how it all works, this is kind of exciting." She surprised me by grinning openly.

"Oh, okay then," I said stupidly, unsure about how to take the turn of her mood.

When the limo stopped, Troy opened the back door. Drew stood outside and held people back as I stepped out and held my hand out for Jackie. She slipped her hand into mine and climbed out an overwhelming number of camera flashes.

Without a thought, I put on one of my prize-winning smiles and held her close as we moved toward the building we rented for today's use. It was an office building that had a few vacant offices and would act as our wardrobe and makeup space; it would also house the actors between scenes. Today was really my day to work solo, but there were a few supporting actors who would assist on the scenes, like the clerk at the florist's shop.

All around us, people yelled my name. I realized with a happy surprise that they were calling out to Jackie, too. One woman pushed a pen and piece of paper toward her, asking her for an autograph. She stared at the woman as if she had two heads.

With a chuckle under my breath, I pulled Jackie away so that she wouldn't have to say anything to the woman, and we entered the building.

"How do you handle that all the time?" She pulled her hand away from mine, wiping her damp palms on her pants.

I followed the signs to the area we were using and nodded at a few people who stopped to stare at us. "You just get used to it."

"Not me. It reminds me of the time after the airport incident when all the press was hounding me. I couldn't walk out of the station without being mobbed. I hated it." She caught up as we entered the office suite we were renting.

I gave her a wry smile and followed her through the doors. My hopes that she would become accustomed to my life were fading, and I fought to keep the negativity from my thoughts.

Within minutes of arriving, we were wrapped up in a whirlwind of things to be done. Marie whisked me away and tsked again over the circles under my eyes, telling me I needed to get more sleep and to stop spending so much time with Jackie while I was working so hard. I bit my tongue so that I didn't say anything nasty to her.

And so, the week went by. Every morning for six more days, we got up and went to work early. Jackie stayed by my side, pretending to be my romantic interest, while keeping her guard high and staying as professional as she could.

In the evenings, we all gathered on the back patio or in the family room to talk about the day. Roseanne and Jackie developed a strong friendship and spent a lot of time laughing and telling stories about what they had seen during the day. I tried not to be jealous of their relationship, and at the same time, I found that I learned bits and pieces of her by watching her open up with Rose.

We kept our distance from each other at night when we were home, even though I longed to hold her every second of the day. I found myself watching her every move sometimes, in awe of how her face broke out in a smile just before she laughed aloud, and how when she was trying to act serious, she would clear her throat before she spoke.

There had been no other threats toward me, and no word about the fingerprints off the letters. I was glad that things had stopped, but I had a feeling we had not seen the last of trouble.

"I can't believe we have one more day to shoot and then we get a day off," Roseanne said as she slumped in a chair, "It's been a long week."

"Yeah, it will be nice to finally sleep in," Troy added as he flipped through the pages of an entertainment magazine.

"It would only be better if we had two whole days off," Roseanne added.

I saw Jackie yawn and stand to stretch. The shirt she wore rose high enough for me to see a sliver of her smooth stomach, and my groin tightened. "Speaking of sleep, I'm going to head up. I could use an extra hour."

Jackie was an early riser. Over the last few days, she was up way before I stumbled downstairs. Troy said that every morning when he came down, the coffee was made, and she was sitting at the table writing notes down. She never said what they were about and always slipped the notebook into her backpack when anyone was around.

We all said goodnight, and I watched her leave the room. All week, I had kept my distance only staying close to her in public. I craved the feel of her lips and the touch of her hands in a private, passionate setting. Every kiss we shared at the filming had been done to set the stage, and it filled me with a wanting so deep I could barely contain myself. She, on the other hand, didn't seem bothered by it in the slightest. She seemed to have gotten the acting part down pat.

"I'm heading up, too," I added and left the room about two minutes after she did. I could use the extra sleep. The filming was going well, but it was exhausting. Kayla and I were on set together in a few days. I dreaded the scene we were going to have to do where I pretended to be drunk and argued with her before we fell to the floor in a moment of pure lust. In the movie, Kayla played my wife; in real life, I pretended as if we were divorced.

I climbed the stairs two at a time, and when I rounded the corner at the top, I crashed into Jackie.

I grabbed her by the arms as she started to fall back, her hands grasped my shirt and pulled it out of the waistband in the front.

"I'm so sorry, Jackie. I didn't see you there." I helped her stand up straight, but I didn't release her from my grasp. In fact, I moved closer to her.

"No, that was my fault. I heard you coming up the steps. I should have moved out of the way faster. I'm sorry." Her hands rested on my stomach, my T-shirt still in her fist.

I took another step, and her hand pushed against the taunt muscles of my abs causing my groin to tighten again. I stared at her lips and felt the unstoppable urge to devour them.

For a week, I kept my distance. With her hand pressed against my body, and her face so close to mine, I could no longer do so. I swooped down on her, turning her so that she was pressed against the wall as I crushed my body to hers.

With a soft moan, she gave in to what I was asking for and kissed me back with all the passion I knew she had stored deep inside her. My hands were everywhere on her while hers moved slower but almost as much.

We tasted, touched, nipped, and licked. The only sounds in the hallway were of our heavy breathing and rustling of clothing.

Neither of us heard Troy reach the top step. "About damn time," he muttered as he walked past us, "Why don't ya'll choose a bedroom instead of using the hallway?" He walked past us as we both panted and watched his retreating back until it disappeared behind his bedroom door.

If Troy hadn't interrupted us, we could have easily lost control and made love right there in the hallway; at least, I know I could have. The look on her face said a different story. She moved her hands up to my chest and pushed just enough to get my attention and tell me I needed to back up.

I swallowed, trying to get my heart rate and breathing under control.

"I'm sorry, Ryan." She put her forehead on my chest and sighed. "That shouldn't have happened."

I slid my hand down the back of her head, smoothing her long, soft blond hair. "Yes, it should have, and a lot more should have, too." I paused and put my thumb under her chin to lift it. "It still can, you just have to say yes."

Mixed emotions splashed over her face. I knew she was torn, but I had to show her that we were meant to be together.

"No, Ryan. We can't." She pushed a little harder on my chest. "I'm sorry. I can't do this."

I opened my mouth to tell her, yes we could, but she shook her head and pushed away hard enough that she slid her body out from between me and the wall and rushed to her room.

"Jackie," I called out to her, but the only reply was the click of her door.

Damn it!

JACQUELYN

hat the hell got into me? I leaned back against the door, resting my head on its cold hard wood. If it wouldn't have made so much noise, I would have banged my head a few times to knock some sense into it. *What the hell was I thinking?*

Oh right, I wasn't! I wasn't using the logical side of my brain, I let my over-active hormones take control.

For the last week, we had reached a kind of truce. He kept his distance when we were home, never coming near me or touching me if he didn't have to. When we were out in public, things were a different story.

Everywhere we went, when he was not busy doing something else, he had his arm around me possessively. He placed kisses on my forehead, neck, cheek, and lips whenever he got a chance. Each time, my body wound even tighter, a child's toy primed to let loose. The surprise of slamming into him by the stairs just now had snapped the taut string and away I went.

I closed my eyes and felt my heart beating. I traced my swollen lips with my fingers, imagining Ryan doing it. I groaned and dropped my chin to my chest. I was in so much trouble.

I had to get this job done, had to get out of here before he affected me anymore than he already had. Every morning, I took a few minutes to think over what I had seen the day before. In the afternoons when I had a chance, I made a few phone calls to see what information I could find out. I was getting close and ruling people out, but I wasn't quite there yet.

If the damn forensic report would come back on the latent prints we pulled from the envelopes, I might have my suspect. I needed to figure this out. My sanity was balancing on a precarious edge, and I wasn't sure how much longer I could keep my balance.

I pulled my gun off my ankle and set it on my nightstand where I kept it while I slept. After getting ready for bed, I remembered why I'd had been heading downstairs in the first place. I glanced at the lounge pants and camisole that I wore. Ryan and Troy had gone to bed, maybe everyone else had, too.

I opened my door as carefully as I could. The hallway was dark and quiet. I glanced at Ryan's door, wondering what he was doing, and realized I shouldn't even ponder such a thought. I would make myself imagine things I had no right to conjure up.

On my tiptoes, I made my way down the steps and into the family room. The house was quiet, and all the lights were off. I stepped into the family room and moved to the chair I sat in earlier. My black backpack leaned against the side. I scooped it up.

It wasn't that I didn't trust those who lived in the house, I did. It was the ones who came and went who didn't live here that I wasn't so sure about. I made my way silently to the stairs and stared to climb. A light flashed up on the wall for just a fraction of a second, I stopped dead in my tracks.

Where did that light just come from? If it was from headlights coming up the driveway, it would have swooped over the walls and brightened the whole room, and not been just a single, brief flash.

It wasn't lightening. I could see the stars out in the night sky, with no sign of clouds; and again, that would have lit up the atrium brightly. The hairs on the back of my neck twitched as I moved slowly up to the second floor.

When I got to the landing, I let my backpack slide down my shoulder to the floor, and I put my back to the wall. This wall was only about two feet in length before it opened up to the bridge that crossed from one side of the house to the other.

I listened for a moment, finding that all was quiet inside. I tried to listen harder, but I didn't hear anything. I peeked my head around the corner and scanned the darkness out in front of the house. My Jeep was out there, along with three other cars, and the limo. All of them were supposed to be there. I searched carefully around the cars but saw no movement or additional light.

I could see the guard shack down below and a single light was on, but I couldn't see the guard inside. He might be sitting down or have stepped out to take a walk around the grounds. Maybe it was his flashlight I had seen. I searched the darkness one more time but saw nothing.

My shoulders were tense, and I shrugged them to relieve it. I picked up my backpack and made my way to the third floor. This time, I didn't sneak around the corner, but I did stop in the center of the balcony and examined the darkness intently.

The light I saw was probably the guard's flashlight and nothing more. I went to my room and climbed in bed.

After a restless night, I dressed in my normal cargos and polo shirt, grabbed my backpack, and made my way to the kitchen. With the coffee on, I sat down at the table and started reading through my notes again. I had to figure all this out.

I knew that Diane was off the list. She was in Europe filming a movie and had been for a several months. There was no reason to suspect her. Rebecca was able to help cross off a few more, but they were people who weren't at the top of my list in the first place.

This morning, I woke up with a renewed vow to figure this out and get out of here as fast as possible. I needed to do that for my own peace of mind. If I got out of this now, I could look back on my time with Ryan with warm feelings. I would know that, although I had feelings for him and he had some for me, I had done my job and kept him safe. Safer than even he knew.

"Wow," Roseanne's voice startled me, and I jumped in my seat. "Sorry, I can't believe you're always up so early, dressed, and working." She covered her mouth while she stretched and released a yawn.

"Crime doesn't stop just because you're sleeping." I closed my notebook and slipped it into my backpack. My quiet time was over. I glanced at my watch; it was almost six-thirty.

Rose gave me a lopsided grin before pouring coffee. I lifted my mug to my lips. What was left was cold, but I was used to drinking cold coffee. I chugged down what remained in my mug.

"What time did you get up?" she asked as she scooted a chair out from across the table.

"My alarm went off around four." I twisted my coffee mug in my hands, having nothing else to do.

"You set your alarm for four!" Her eyes bugged out. "In the morning? Are you nuts?"

I laughed, but before I could respond, Ryan entered the room. "She's a dedicated employee, Rose."

He didn't look at me. In fact, he didn't look at Roseanne either. He made a beeline for the coffee mugs and poured himself a large one. Good thing I just made a new pot before they got up.

"That she is, Ryan. That she is," Rose replied winking at me. Troy joined us as she finished.

"That she is what? And who are we talking about?" he asked as he flopped down in the chair next to Rose. Ryan would either have to sit next to me or on a stool at the counter.

"Ryan said she was a dedicated employee." Rose pointed to me as she answered him. Ryan turned with his mug up to his lips, our eyes met; he was the one to look away. Okay, not his normal behavior. Obviously, he was upset with me?

I stood,. "If you'll excuse me, I have a few things to do." I set my coffee mug in the sink and walked the long way around the kitchen to avoid Ryan. I snatched my backpack off the floor and left three people staring at my back.

I heard Troy speak as I turned the corner. "Something I said?" I heard Rose's faded laughter as I made my way down to the study that we used for work.

I dropped my backpack by the desk and stood in front of the window with my arms crossed. Was Ryan angry with me? The way he barely glanced at me in the kitchen and dismissed me so quickly shouldn't bother me. But it did.

I had to stop thinking about Ryan and focus on this investigation. He was turning me into a basket case.

Troy found me a few minutes later sitting at the desk reading over what I learned this morning in my last phone call. It wasn't much.

He plopped himself in a chair in the room, stretching out his long legs. "Sorry for interrupting last night." I felt a blush creep up my neck.

"It's all right. I'm actually glad you did." I dropped the pen I was holding onto the desk and reclined in the high-back leather chair with my fingers laced over my stomach.

"You might be, but he's not." I shrugged. Ryan's feelings were not my concern.

"Jackie, what's going on?" He turned his serious dark brown eyes on me while I fought not to fidget.

I played dumb. "What are you talking about, Troy?"

"I thought things were going well between you and Ryan. You guys are so damn good together that it actually makes me ill sometimes to be around you. Other times, I envy the hell out of you and only hope that I'll find someone who cares half as much about me as you do each other."

"Wow, Troy. I'm not sure what you are seeing, but there is nothing personal going on between Ryan and me." I was lying almost as well as some of the criminals I interviewed.

"Yeah, all right, Jackie. You can lie to yourself, and you might be able to lie to him, but you're not going to lie to me." He sat up and leaned his elbows on his knees. "When are you going to let go of what happened in your past and move forward?" My heart skipped a beat. Did he know exactly what had happened?

"What are you talking about?" My voice was just above a whisper.

"Do you think I don't know what happened to your parents and to Logan?" He clasped his hands together.

"How?" I croaked.

"You are not the only one who can investigate. I looked into it after you mentioned it. And no, I never told Ryan about it. I figured if you two ever got together, then you could tell him. I think it's time you do, and time that you let the past go and move forward."

What the hell? He had not only looked into my past, but now he was giving me relationship advice? Next, he was going to ask me if I wanted to talk about it and turn into a freaking shrink!

My jaw hurt from how hard I clenched it. I took an extremely deep breath while I counted to ten, and then released it.

"I appreciate you not telling him, I really do. But, Troy, if you know what happened, you also know that I can't allow anyone to get close to me."

His brown eyes cut deeply into mine. "Do you think we can't keep him safe?"

"I don't want anyone else to get hurt because of me, Troy. I couldn't handle it again."

He stood and walked to the front of the desk. "You have to trust that we can keep him safe. Give him a chance, Jackie. Give yourself a chance to love again."

Tears welled in my eyes, and I blinked furiously to clear them. One trickled out of the corner, and I swiped it away as quickly as it appeared.

"Just think about it." He turned slowly after I gave him a single nod.

Give yourself a chance to love again. *But at what cost?* I watched his wide shoulders as they cleared the doorway.

RYAN

I fell into a restless sleep with a deep, throbbing ache in my loins, and woke up to a razor-sharp chip on my shoulder.

In the bathroom, I stood with my palms flat against the granite leering into the mirror image, my subconscious warring with my attitude.

I am Ryan Palmer. *So what?*

I get what I want; nothing stops me. *Except her.*

I could walk down the street right now and have ten different women throw themselves at me. *But not one of them would measure up to her.*

I don't want her. *Keep telling yourself that, buddy. Someday you might believe it.*

I don't. She's just a woman, just some small-town cop, she's nothing special. *She's a better person then you will ever be. She's also the best thing you have ever had in your life, and you know it.*

I don't need her! *Like hell you don't.*

If that was true, then I would be in love with her, and I'm not. *Look closer at yourself, dude. You're head over heels.*

The last words echoed through my skull, and my head hung between my shoulders. Was I head over heels in love with Jacquelyn? Probably. But did that mean I had to act like an idiot and throw myself at her every second of the day? No. It didn't, and as of now, I wouldn't. I was done. If she wanted me, then she would have to come to me. If it wasn't meant to be, it wasn't meant to be.

I avoided Jackie in the kitchen, and when she walked out, I wanted to kick myself for being such an ass. She had gone to the far study, and I went into my private one. Troy joined me as I sat brooding out the back window.

After he sat down, I swiveled my chair to the side, examining him for a moment. His face looked too damn serious, and I knew him all too well. I turned back to the window.

"So, what's going on?" I heard the chair creak under his large frame.

There was no way I could pretend I didn't know what he was talking about, but I didn't want to discuss it. My subconscious mind was already having a field day at my expense. I didn't need him to do it, too. I shrugged in response.

He was persistent. "What happened last night?"

I spun my big leather chair around again and rested my chin on my fist. "You're not going to leave me alone, are you?"

"No, what happened?" At least he was blunt and honest.

"Nothing happened, and nothing ever will. I'm done trying to get her to open up." I lifted my head and let it fall back against the leather chair. "She's not interested in me, plain and simple."

"Bullshit! She is as much in love with you as you are with her. Every single one of us can see the way you two look at each other when the other one isn't watching." He shook his head.

"Then why does she fight it? I don't get it. Is she just playing hard to get?" I felt exasperated, and the tone of my voice echoed it.

A muscle in his jaw ticked for a moment as he contemplated me and his answer. "No, she's not playing hard to get. She told you about her fiancé dying right?"

I gave him a nod because I not only remembered, but I could still hear every word she spoke and the haunted look that had been in her eyes.

"There is a lot more to that story, Ryan, and it's not my right to tell you, but I will tell you that she feels responsible for his death." He stopped to let that sink in. "I think that is what holds her back. She just needs time and to know that we can keep you safe."

Was that all it was? That she needed to know I would be safe? I had known there was a deeper story there, but Troy was right, Jackie had to tell it to me herself. Would she trust me enough before this was all over?

Troy advised me that it was time to leave and we climbed into the limo without her. As the day loomed ahead of me, my brooding got worse. It was a good thing that today's filming was a dark scene. I felt dark.

We rehearsed the scene a few times, and Sheila and I were talking about another scene we would be filming soon when Jackie joined us. I peeked over at her in mid-sentence and then looked back. Her face radiated confidence. Her eyes were bright and shiny, and she looked more relaxed than she had in days. The smile she gave me pierced my heart, and I absently placed a kiss on the top of her head as she leaned into my side.

When Jackie walked up, there was another woman with her, and she introduced us to the author of the book this movie was based on.

"Wow, it's a pleasure to meet you." I shook her hand; it was strong and solid like Jackie's.

"The pleasure is all mine." She shook hands with Sheila, too, and we talked for a few minutes about how the screenplay differed from the book. She was looking forward to watching this particular scene. She said when she wrote it, she wanted people to be mad at Mitch. If the script was anything like her book, I think the people watching it would get the feeling she was aiming for.

Jackie stood quietly beside us listening to our conversation. When it was time to get back to filming, they walked off to the side and were deep in conversation.

My character today was on a quest of self-destruction. His lust was getting the best of him as he took a total stranger and pushed her up against the wall, intent on having his way with her. I had no problem with this scene, as I based it on what happened last night with Jackie. Pure adult need filled me as I kissed Tammy, the other actress in this scene, and pushed her hard against the brick wall with my body, all the while imagining it was Jackie.

The look on Jackie's face just minutes ago flashed through my mind. Something had happened. Had she finally figured out who was threatening me? Was she getting ready to say goodbye?

Oh, hell no! Not before I got a chance to show her how I really felt about her. There was no way. When the director called out, "It's a wrap," I charged her like a bull.

The actress had been against me during the filming, but it was Jackie's body I was now ravishing. I planted a kiss on her that would have burned the film if it had been on tape. She was utterly shocked, and I took full advantage of that fact.

I fought to control my emotions as I grabbed Jackie by the hand and headed over to the limo where Troy was waiting for us. I knew I was acting like a he-man pulling her around, but I had every intention of getting her back to the house and locking us in either my room or hers until we worked this out. I told Troy I'd get a ride home with Jackie, and he nodded, never missing a beat on his phone conversation.

As we approached Jackie's car, I had to release her hand so that she could grab her keys from her pocket. She fumbled with them, and they dropped to the ground. Over Jackie's shoulder as she bent to pick up her keys, I saw the limo driver close his door.

Jackie stood up, and I was about to inform her of my intentions when a blast rocked me off my feet and through the air to the ground, and everything went silent and black.

JACQUELYN

$\mathcal{I}$ sat in the chair and thought about my past, thought about the loss I had sustained, and the threat that hovered over my head since that awful day and every single day after.

Roseanne found me later, still lost in thought. "Hey, Jackie, we have to leave in a few minutes, are you coming with us?" My cellphone rang at the same time that she posed the question. I held up my finger to her as I picked up my phone.

"Hold on a second, Rebecca." I covered the phone with my hand. "No, you guys go ahead. I have to take this, and then I'll be right behind you."

I watched her leave and then put the phone back to my ear. "Hey, you have anything for me?"

"How are things? You sound stressed." I heard the dispatcher talking over her radio in the background as she asked.

"I'm all right. It's been a long week." I fought not to sigh as I heard the front door close. "I thought we worked long hours, but damn, these guys never seem to stop."

"It's sounds like it, but I think I have something that might make it a better day," she said in a singsong voice over the phone.

Was she going to give me something that would help clear the case?

Would I be free to leave now? Could I? I pushed all the questions out of my mind and told her to start talking.

An hour later, I pulled up to the parking area and made my way over to the tech trailer. When I stepped in, Markus was leaning over a computer. He lifted his head to see who came in. His eyes tightened, and I repressed a knowing smile.

"Hey, Markus," I said as I grabbed my headset and radio.

The only reply I got was a grunt. We'd see how much grunting he'd be doing later. I walked out of the trailer, hooked the radio up, and laced the headset cord through my shirt. My shirt wasn't tucked in today because I was wearing my full-sized Glock. With what I learned this morning, I wasn't taking any chances. While I listened to what was going on through my headset, I made my way back to my truck.

They were filming a scene outside a bar, and everyone was already there. I climbed in and made my way over to the location. We used a school parking lot to park our vehicles and house the few trailers and a food cart we needed because it was a weekend.

I saw the limo parked at the front entrance and pulled into the grassy area to the right of it. I left my backpack in my truck, got out, and started to make my way down to the shooting location.

I heard someone call my name and stopped to see my friend, and the author who wrote the book behind the movie, making her way toward me. I gave her a hug when she caught up and said, "I can't believe I get to watch this being filmed. You know how much I loved your book."

"You can have the filming if you'll let me have the hunk," she replied. We both laughed and started toward the set.

"So, I heard you're working undercover, what's the scoop?" she asked as we walked.

A girl about seventeen ran up to me and asked me for my autograph. I chuckled and pulled the pen out of her hand, signing my name on the small pad of paper she was holding. I handed the paper to my friend.

"Here, you sign this, too," I said. The girl looked at me closely. "She's the one who wrote the book this movie is based on." A huge smile filled the young girl's face, and she thanked us profusely. I smiled at her because, right now, I was in a good mood. The lab results came in, and I knew who had been sending the threats. That's why I probably took the moment to sign the girl's paper.

Tomorrow, I would talk to the suspects, yes more than one, and hopefully in a day or two, I would be on my way home and back to my real life. My signature wouldn't be worth anything by the end of the week.

"The scoop is, yes, I've been working undercover, but I think I just got it all figured out. Tomorrow we'll be able to make a few arrests."

We talked about a few more details as we made our way to the set location. I gently pushed my way through the group of onlookers, and smiled at the guys standing along the crowd line, holding people back. They let us under the rope right away and I scanned the area. I knew whom I needed to watch now, and they were nowhere in sight.

Ryan walked through his scene as we stood back and watched. As much as I missed doing my job, I did enjoy being here and observing all of this. I fought the melancholy that tried to take over my soul. It was better for both of us.

The practice run-through went well, and when they finished rehearsing, Ryan stood off to the side and talked to Sheila. I casually walked up to them. Ryan glanced at me and did a double take. A curious expression floated across his eyes when he took in my features. I gave him one of my loving girlfriend smiles that came just too damn easily, and slipped my arm around his waist to snuggle up and play the part.

Yes, I was playing a part. I wasn't enjoying it, and I sure wasn't looking at it like it would soon be over. He kissed my forehead, and I swear I didn't close my eyes and try to memorize the feel of it or anything.

"I can't wait to get home." Sheila gazed at me with a wistful look in her eye. "Watching you two makes me miss my husband so much. The love you two have for each other is so obvious. It reminds me of what I have waiting for me back at home. You two make sure you don't let that go."

I sure hope you have better than what we have, I wanted to say. As for love, I realized that if my police job ever fizzled out, I could look into acting. Apparently, I'm pretty good at it.

I pushed the thoughts away and introduced Sheila and Ryan to Stacy, the author. I listened while they chatted, but then we needed to step away to watch when they were ready to start filming.

Ryan was acting intoxicated and had a strange woman up against the building. I remembered that moment in the book. I was so angry at the character, Mitch, that I wanted to smack him for doing that.

Ryan got right into character, and as I watched him act out the scene with an actress I hadn't met yet, it reminded me of our aggressive tryst in the hallway last night. A shiver raced up and down my spine as I remembered the feel of his hands on my body. I would never know what it felt like to make love to him now. The temptation would be removed very soon.

My friend got a phone call and walked away just before the scene ended.

It only took nine takes for them to get it from different angles and how they wanted it. Ryan walked directly for me, his eyes growing more intense with each step. When he reached me, he didn't stop, didn't hesitate. He yanked me into his arms and smothered my mouth with a kiss so strong that my knees gave way, and I quivered at his touch.

He pulled away, his focus on my surprised expression. "I'm not giving up."

He grabbed my hand and pulled me to walk with him. I was at a loss for words, unable to form a single coherent thought as I glided on air beside him.

I heard someone joking with another crew member as we passed. "That was a hot scene, looks like those two are going to have a good afternoon."

If I wasn't so discombobulated, I might have blushed, but all I could do was continue beside Ryan and try to keep up with his purposeful steps.

We got back to the parking area and found Troy standing next to the limo talking on his phone. Ryan moved in that direction as I still attempted to gain control of my erratic heartbeat.

"Jackie, is your truck here?" Ryan asked as we got closer to Troy. I nodded, unable to find my voice.

He stopped a few feet from the limo and told Troy, "I'm driving home with Jackie."

Troy studied us for a moment and must have noticed the dazed look on my face and the way our hands locked tightly. He smirked and nodded, never missing a stride on his phone call.

Troy pulled open the limo door and raised his hand to the driver who was standing beside the front door. "Where is your car?"

I pointed with a shaking hand into the field, and he moved that way, pulling me behind him.

I tried to yank my hand out of his, but he'd locked his fingers around mine. "Wait, I need my hand for a moment, my car keys are in my pocket. I can't get them out."

I dug my heels in to get him to stop, my arm extended, and my fingers twisted in his. He relaxed his hand enough so that I could slip mine out. My fingers were numb, and as I tried to pull my key out of my pocket, it slipped out of my shaky grasp and fell to the ground. I bent at the waist to pick it up.

When I stood again, Ryan was contemplating me. His face was more determined than I had ever seen, and I wasn't sure if I should be excited or scared. He took a step closer and opened his mouth to say something, but I never heard the words that came out of his mouth.

Our world changed in that second. A blast so loud and powerful came from behind me that it blew both of us off our feet. I landed on the ground face first with a painful thud, but pain was good, pain meant you were alive. After the initial shock of being on the ground, I attempted to suck air into my lungs, but sharp pains surged through my torso from my back. I fought to take inventory of my body. My legs were there, though my knee ached, and I could see my arms and hands. Obviously, I still had my head, since I was seeing and thinking. I pulled myself up to my knees.

A secondary explosion from the same direction brought me back to the ground on my own accord, and I put my hands over my neck to protect it. I rolled to my side and sat up to see that the limo was gone. Only pieces of the frame remained and what little was left, was burning. A car that was parked in front of the limo was on fire, too; so that must have been the secondary explosion.

Ryan! Oh my God, where was Ryan? I flipped to my knees, searching the grassy field we just walked through. He was about fifteen feet away from me, lying prone on his back. I tried to stand and stumbled back to my knees. The pain subsided in my back enough that it allowed me to breathe almost normally.

He lifted his head as I began to crawl his way. "Ryan!" I reached him, grabbed him by the shoulder, touched his chest searching his torso for injuries, and then ran my hand over his arms and legs to examine them. He grunted and tried to sit up.

The panic of him being injured diminished only slightly as I sat on the ground trying to breathe and control the overwhelming urge to burst into tears that he was alive.

Hands grabbed my arms and jerked me off the ground. I spun around in fight mode to find my friend, the author, in front of me. She was talking, but I couldn't hear her, my ears were ringing. I shoved away from her as I watched people moving toward the limo over her shoulder. These weren't fire fighters or police officers, they were civilians. My need to protect the scene kicked in, and I rushed toward the crowd, telling them to get back. There were other cars in the area, and who knew if any others had explosives connected to them.

When I turned back around, I saw my friend holding Ryan back. Ryan was unsteady on his feet, and she had no trouble controlling him. My ears rang, and sounds were distorted, but I could see Ryan's mouth screaming Troy's name. My last view of Ryan was of him being dragged away by officers to safety.

I stared at the scene in front of me. There were people screaming and running. A few injured people were scattered around the area. My line of sight fell back on the black smoke billowing from the limo and rising into the sky as I remembered the smirk on Troy's face just before he climbed in.

My knees gave way as I realized that Ryan would have been in there, but he had all but demanded to ride home with me. I collapsed to the ground, and the sobs wracked my body. What would I have done if I had lost him like this? Like Logan?

RYAN

*M*y ears still rang like church bells when I was dropped back off at home. Several police officers were scattered around the property, and some of them had dogs with them. I figured Jackie probably had them making sure there weren't any bombs planted here. I was glad that one of us was thinking, because I certainly wasn't.

Over and over again, the memories of what happened played in my mind like I was hitting rewind on a DVD player. The intense pressure and sound of the explosion made me feel claustrophobic just from the memory. I got out of the patrol car and made my way absently into the house. I felt numb.

As I approached the front door, it opened, and Roseanne came running out. She threw her arms around me and we stood on the steps. She cried as we stood there. I probably would have, too, but I just couldn't feel any emotion.

Eventually, I went inside and took a long hot shower. Every time I closed my eyes, I saw the images of the smoke rising in a cloud over the limo in the cloudless sky. Pieces of debris scattered around me, and people were screaming, running, and crying.

Jackie came to me on her hands and knees. A look of panic and concern was all over her face as she grabbed my shoulders and examined me from head to toe. I stared at her, unable to do anything else. She turned her face from mine to look over at the limo that was burning. She sobbed once, and then she dropped her hands from my arms and hung her head into her palms.

Her friend came running up to her, reached down, and pulled her to her feet. Jackie pushed her away and ran toward the limo. I wanted to jump up and tell her to stop, but I was frozen on the ground. I realized that she wasn't going toward the burning limo, but was headed toward the crowd of people to tell them to back away.

I remembered that Jackie's friend was also a police officer in another district, and I stared at her as she spoke quickly into her phone, scanning the area, her eyes constantly going back to Jackie as she moved people away from the scene and to safety. It was only then that I remembered who was in the limo.

Troy. Oh my God. "Troy!" I yelled. I tried to stand up. Troy had been in there. I felt arms wrap around me, keeping me from running closer to something I would never want to see. Another officer came and helped her friend, but I didn't know who it was. All I knew was that I couldn't get to Troy.

They pulled me back against a brick building about five hundred yards from the vehicle, and I slumped to the ground staring at everything that was happening in front of me, seeing it, but not comprehending it at all. Fire trucks and ambulances came in droves. Police officers were everywhere and several of them had dogs that were walking around different things.

From time to time, I saw Jackie out in the crowd, and I wanted to go to her, but I knew she was working. This was what she did, so I stayed where I was and observed her when I could keep her in my view. Eventually, an officer came to get me and told me they were taking me home. I don't remember if I said anything or not.

I stood in the shower with the hot water streaming over my head, images racing through my mind. I washed my body four times trying to get the invisible smell of the death off my skin. Somehow, I didn't think I ever would.

I paced for a long time in my room and then along the atrium hallway. I didn't want to be alone. The house was too quiet, and I knew that

Roseanne was asleep. She told me she was taking a sleeping pill. I stood on the balcony and watched the two police officers patrolling around the house and speaking on their phones and radios.

Finally, I went down to the living room and poured myself a drink. Maybe if I had one, it would soothe my nerves enough to let me sleep. I found myself walking up the stairs again and stopped in front of Jackie's room. I reached down and turned the knob.

As the smell of her soft perfume hit me, I was drawn into the room further. I closed the door and went to sit in the wingback chair near the window. I would sit here and wait for her. The smell of her perfume drifting in the air around me made me feel less lonely.

I don't know how long I sat there, but when I saw a car pull up outside and Jackie climb out, I glanced at the clock and saw that it was after one in the morning. We had left for the set at seven a.m. the day before. She was going to be exhausted. I thought about getting up and going back to my room, but I just couldn't find the energy to move.

I must've held my glass for hours, never taking a drink. I heard her as she opened her door, and I didn't know if I should say something before she stepped in. She jumped when she saw me, and I watched as she regained her composure. Her clothes were filthy with streaks of black down the legs. The bottoms of her pant legs were totally black. She had on a sweatshirt that she hadn't been wearing earlier today, and I absently wondered where it came from.

"Sorry," I said softly as I studied her.

"What are you doing in here?" She didn't sound angry, just tired.

"Waiting for you." She stood in front of me, and I looked up at her briefly before I examined my glass. I swirled the whiskey around in the crystal, watching as it slid smoothly around the insides.

"Can you give me just a few minutes? I really need to take a shower, Ryan. We can talk when I'm done."

I could see the raw pain and exhaustion in her eyes to an extent that I didn't understand fully. "Do you want me to leave?"

"No, you're fine. Just give me a few minutes." She turned and I looked away to give her some privacy to gather her clothing. I heard her set something on the table next to the bed. I stared out the window, and when I heard her close the bathroom door, I turned to see she had set her gun and holster on the nightstand. I returned my focus to the window.

She was done much quicker than I expected. When she stepped out of the bathroom, steam poured out around her. Her hair was still wet and brushed back. Her light blue camisole hugged her chest and small waist. She came toward me and I watched the way her pale pink cotton pants rubbed against her legs. Any other time, it would have aroused me, but the pain of today made me recognize the facts and not react.

She knelt in front of me and took my hand. The moment she touched me, the tears I held back since the first explosion came. She took the glass out of my hand, and looked at her through blurry eyes.

When she turned back to me, I pulled her into my lap and held her tightly. The soft skin of her hand touched my face, and my tears fell silently. She wrapped her arms around me and held me as I cried for the loss of my friend, and the pain I caused so many people.

After a while, the tears dried up, and yet, we still sat there. Neither of us spoke as we held one another for hours and watched the sky start to brighten the horizon. I felt her yawn, and I knew that we both needed to sleep, but I couldn't gather the strength to get up and leave. "I don't want to be alone," I said quietly against her neck.

"Neither do I. Come on, let's go lay down." She got off my lap and pulled me up.

As I followed her over to the bed, I felt empty and exhausted. She pulled the sheets down and I climbed into her bed. She tucked me in as if I was a child, and then climbed right over the top of me and got under the covers. I was prepared to pull her to me when she opened her arms, and I moved to lay my head on her shoulder.

Those few moments from the chair to the bed made me feel so empty. As soon as I put my arm around her waist, the feeling dissipated. She ran her hand lightly through my short hair while gently rubbing my other arm with her hand. I pulled her close to me one more time, breathing in her clean scent.

I didn't think there was any way I would be able to sleep, but with her soft touches, I must have dozed off. When I opened my eyes again, the room was bright. I was now lying on my back with her nestled against my chest. Her soft hair cascaded over me, and my arm curved tightly around her back.

I felt a stirring in my body as she started to wake. I squeezed her hipbone gently, and I almost gasped when she snuggled deeper into my chest.

The feel of her soft hair against my chest made me reach out and start running my hand through it, allowing the silky strands to slide over my fingers. I was just pulling my hand through her long hair when the bedroom door opened.

Jackie snapped her head toward the door as I turned mine slower. Her quick movement caused our bodies to separate, but I held her hip tightly so she couldn't move completely away from me.

The look on Roseanne's face was priceless as she took in the scene of Jackie and I in bed together, but the better look was the one of utter shock on the guys face who stood behind her. The word "mine" ran through my head as I saw him look at her hotly.

Jackie moved away from me while she spoke. I detected a faint blush on her cheeks from where I was. A minute later, the door closed again, I slid over to pull her back to me. I wasn't surprised when she dismissed me. It had obviously hurt her when Jim, that was his name, saw me in bed with her. Not that I was worried, I was glad that the first time I saw him, it was with Jackie lying across my body.

She went to her closet and grabbed some clothes. I figured I better apologize for what happened. I owed it to her after what she did for me last night. "I'm sorry, Jackie. I didn't mean to get you in trouble with your boyfriend."

"It's fine, Ryan. He's not my boyfriend." She was staring at her clothes. I knew she didn't want to look at me.

"Well, you might want to tell him that, because it was pretty obvious he was pissed that we were in bed together." She had no clue what Jim felt for her. Though it was clear to me when I saw the way he looked at her.

"We were sleeping in the same bed. It's not like we had sex, and you're wrong about Jim." She was quick to dismiss my words.

"You're blind, Jacquelyn. That man is crazy about you." I walked away from her and stopped when I got to the door. "Yeah, we might not have had sex, but that doesn't mean that nothing happened." I stared at her a second longer and then walked out.

Something had happened, that was for sure. Something had been happening since the first moment I laid eyes on her in the airport. After yesterday, when she had crawled over to me to make sure I was all right, and then went to work helping everyone and yet still came back here exhausted, and held me through the night, I realized that things had changed with us.

I wasn't sorry about the change. I welcomed it. Yet, I also found myself afraid. What if I cared about her more, and she got hurt because of all of this? What if she was killed and it was my fault?

JACQUELYN

I was exhausted, and it took everything in me to keep my eyes open on the ride back to Ryan's house. Jimmy offered to drive me back, but I told him he had too much to do. I grabbed a ride with one of the uniform cops.

Before Ryan went home earlier, I sent several officers to his house with a couple of the bomb squad dogs to search the property. It came up clean, and I was grateful for that. One bomb in a day was enough. Well, two, but I wasn't going to think about the second one. I had someone take Ryan home once I knew it was safe. There were now two uniformed officers stationed at the house at least for tonight. I would get a hold of my friend's security company tomorrow and set up other guards for around the clock security while Ryan was at home and for when he traveled.

Right now, the only thing I could think about was climbing the stairs and taking a long hot shower. Steve dropped me off at the front door, and I spoke to Brandon who was stationed out front. He told me that Brad was out back, and they would be here until another two guys relieved them in the morning. I thanked him and drug myself into the house and up the stairs.

It was dark inside the house, and I assumed Ryan was asleep when I saw his door closed. I quietly opened the door to my room and slipped inside. A light on the other side of the room was on and as I turned, I saw Ryan in the chair next to the window. I jumped, I hadn't expected him to be here and I was so tired, I couldn't control the surprise.

"Sorry," he mumbled as he looked at me from across the room. He was wearing black and green pajama bottoms and no shirt. I noticed the hardball glass in his hand, and wondered what exactly he was drinking. I could probably benefit from one myself.

"What are you doing in here?" I asked as I moved closer. He looked like hell, plain and simple. There were dark circles under his eyes, and his face looked pale even in the soft glow of the light next to him. I figured I probably didn't look much better. In fact, I probably looked worse because my clothes were a mess from digging through debris at the scene.

"Waiting for you." He lifted his face, and when our eyes met, I saw a deep sadness in them that I understood all too well.

After telling him I needed a few minutes and assuring him he could stay, I turned away and gathered some clothes out of my dresser. I pulled my gun holster out of the back of my pants, set it next to the bed, and then headed for the bathroom. I turned and studied him as he sat in the chair. He was staring out the window to his right. His somber look tore at my soul. I closed the door and turned on the hot water.

Ten minutes later, I walked out of the bathroom. My hopes of a long hot shower were cut short with the image of Ryan sitting in my room. He was still staring out the window, the drinking glass held absently in his hand that rested on the arm of the chair. It appeared to have the same amount in it that it did when I went into the shower.

I moved toward him, and he turned to me. I knelt down on the ground in front of him so that I was between his knees. As I reached for his hand, I saw tears well up in his eyes. I took the glass out of his other hand and set it on the table next to the window. When I turned back to him, a single tear rolled down his cheek and broke my heart.

He pulled my arm toward him, and I got off my knees. I settled myself onto his lap and cradled his face into the crook of my neck. He held me tightly, and I felt his silent tears sliding down the skin of my chest into the edge of my camisole. My arms held him snugly, and I tried to comfort him in the only way I knew how.

I'm not sure how long we sat there. He didn't move from where he was, and I didn't either. It wasn't until I stifled a yawn that he finally spoke. "I don't want to be alone," he whispered.

I pulled my face back enough so that I could look at him; I placed my hand on his cheek, and he peered up at me. "Neither do I," I whispered. His eyes were red-rimmed and swollen from being tired and emotional. "Come on, let's go lay down," I said as I climbed out of his lap. I kept hold of his hand as we walked over to the bed.

I pulled the sheets back and he climbed in. Instead of walking around to the other side, I climbed up onto the bed and crawled over him. I snaked my way down under the covers and put my arm out to him. He moved toward me slowly, laying his head on my shoulder and putting his arm around my waist to pull me closer.

I wrapped my arm around him and felt his warm breath on my neck. My other hand rested on his arm that lay across my stomach. I gently stroked it, while I lifted my hand that I'd wrapped around him and ran it through his hair absently. Ryan squeezed me and I returned it. It was not that much longer before I heard his breathing even out and felt his tense body relax against mine.

When I knew for sure he was asleep, I turned my head and placed a single soft kiss on his forehead. I finally closed my eyes and fell into a hard sleep almost instantly.

Sometime during the day, we changed places. I no longer held him; when I awoke from a hazy sleep, he was holding me. I heard his heart beating under my ear as my head lay on his solid chest. His arm was wrapped securely around my back, his hand softly rubbed my hip where it rested.

I should have moved away, but the feeling of being held felt so good that I didn't want to. It was very rare for me to stay all night with a man. I didn't want to be close to anyone. The intimacy of waking in someone's bed was not something I wanted or could afford to do. I had learned that the hard way years ago. Yet today was different. It felt right to be here in Ryan's arms. It was probably because of everything that had happened yesterday. The need to feel someone close after death was a normal feeling.

I slid my hand over his stomach to his chest and heard him sigh. I knew this was way too intimate of a position for us to be in, but I couldn't move yet. He squeezed my hip and I unconsciously nuzzled his chest with my cheek.

His hand came to my head, and his fingers slid through my hair. It felt good, too good, and I was about to move when the bedroom door opened behind us. I lifted my head abruptly and looked at who walked in.

My hand was on Ryan's chest giving my body the leverage to turn around. His arm was still wrapped around me and immediately went to my waist to keep me from moving too far away as I sat up.

I was not shocked that Roseanne was at the door. The part that shocked me was seeing Jimmy standing behind her staring at me with a look of shock and anger on his face.

"Okay..." Roseanne said quietly. "Sorry, didn't mean to disturb you guys. Ummm...Jacquelyn, you have company." She looked away from us and down at the floor, obviously embarrassed.

She wasn't the only one. My cheeks grew pink, and I pushed off Ryan's chest and out of the hold that had grown tighter when we saw Jimmy at the door.

"Okay, people, it's not what you think," I said as I slid to the side of the bed, putting my feet on the floor. Jimmy stared at Ryan with menace in his eyes. He glared at me and raised his eyebrows. "Jimmy, give me a minute, alright? Can you wait for me downstairs? We will be down in a few minutes."

I was a grown woman, a single woman at that, and what I did was my business. I didn't need people judging me, especially not Jimmy. Roseanne lifted her head and nodded quickly, still pink in the face from walking in on what she thought was a romantic moment. I guess it did look rather romantic to her. She stepped back and started to leave the room. Jimmy's eyes narrowed as the door closed between us.

"Crap," I said as I looked down at the floor. I felt the bed shift, and Ryan slid up behind me, his arm wrapping around my waist. I put my hand down on his arm for a second and then pulled away.

"You need to get up and go get dressed. We have a lot to do today." I didn't look at him as I walked to my closet and stepped inside.

Ryan grunted but got out of bed. He startled me when he appeared at the doorway to the closet. "I'm sorry, Jackie. I didn't mean to get you in trouble with your boyfriend, again."

I shook my head. "It's fine, Ryan. He's not really my boyfriend." I didn't want to make eye contact with him right now, so I stared at the clothes in front of me, not really seeing them.

"Well, you might want to tell him that, because it was pretty obvious he was pissed that we were in bed together."

I focused on him then. "We were sleeping in the same bed. It's not like we had sex, and you're wrong about Jim."

"You're blind, Jacquelyn. That man is crazy about you." I watched him spin around and stalk toward the bedroom door. He stopped with his hand on the knob and looked at me over his shoulder. "Yeah, we might not have had sex, but that doesn't mean nothing happened." He turned and walked out.

I stood in the closet staring blindly at the closed door, his comment echoing through my mind. Not the comment about Jimmy, but the comment that something had happened between us. Each time the echo bounced in my mind, I felt with more certainty that he was right. Something had happened between us. I exhaled loudly and turned back to my clothes.

A few minutes later, I walked downstairs to find RJ and Jimmy sitting on the back patio with Roseanne. Lunch had just been served and both of them were filling their plates. Roseanne peeked up at me and I smiled to let her know I wasn't upset with her. She nodded once.

It was probably better to just forget about what happened upstairs, so I didn't look at Jimmy as I walked to the table. "RJ, I wasn't expecting you this soon. I didn't think I would hear from you until later today."

I pulled out a chair and heard footsteps behind me. I knew it was Ryan by the look that flashed across Jim's face. I ignored it and sat down. Ryan came over and sat beside me and I could feel the anger rolling off Jim from across the table. I looked up at him and tightened my eyes. He looked down at his plate.

"RJ, this is Ryan Palmer. Ryan this is RJ Miller, he is in charge of the bomb squad." I wasn't sure how Ryan would behave after yesterday, but he seemed to have gotten himself under control and held his hand out to RJ.

"Thank you for your help," Ryan said huskily to RJ as they shook hands.

"I'm sorry about your friend, Mr. Palmer. We are going to do everything we can to figure out who did this," RJ said quietly to him.

Ryan nodded and looked down at his plate. Normally, I knew he would have piled his plate full of food, but right now, he only reached for the coffee.

"So what did you find, RJ?" I asked when the silence began to fill with tension.

He seemed thankful that I crossed us over the awkward moment and took a bite of his sandwich. After he swallowed, he spoke, "We gathered quite a bit of debris from the field. After the initial examination, we discovered that the device on the limo was exactly the same as the one on your Jeep."

I winced. I hoped it didn't show on my face, but when I glanced at Jimmy, I figured it probably had. Ryan, who was lifting his coffee cup up to his mouth, froze and looked at me. I could see him out of the corner of my eyes.

"There was a bomb on your Jeep?" he asked. I inhaled deeply, holding it while I figured out how to answer that.

"I guess he didn't know about that one," RJ said with a look of apology on his face.

"Jacquelyn. You didn't tell me there was a bomb on your car." He put the coffee cup down hard on the table. "Why didn't you tell me?"

I looked at him. "Ryan, I…"

"Maybe if you hadn't gotten her into bed so quickly last night, she would have told you," Jim taunted from across the table. My head snapped toward him, my eyes squinting with anger.

"That was totally inappropriate, Jim," I said through gritted teeth.

I scowled at him another moment and then returned to consider Ryan. His face was pale again, and he was staring at Jim. I reached over and put my hand on his arm. "Ryan."

He blinked twice before he pushed his chair back and stood. He looked down at me, swallowed, and then turned and walked toward the house. I jumped up out of my chair and went after him. "Ryan, wait."

He spun around a foot from the back door. Pain radiated from his eyes. "Why didn't you tell me?" he asked tensely.

"After everything that happened yesterday, I was exhausted when I got home. You were so upset, and I didn't want to add anything else to that. I was going to tell you today." I stepped closer as I spoke. "I'm sorry, Ryan. I really was going to tell you today."

He took a step closer and glared down into my face, his eyes bright and intense. "You could have been killed, and it would have been my fault. Troy and the limo driver were killed because of me, and how many people were injured because of that damn bomb?" His voice rose as he spoke. I didn't blame him; he was angry and it was finally starting to hit him. "That damn bomb was meant for me and other people got hurt because of it!"

He got closer as he yelled, and he reached out and grabbed my shoulders tightly. It hurt, but I knew he wasn't doing it on purpose.

"Ryan, it's not your fault. There is a very sick person who is trying to hurt you, but just because the others got hurt, that's not your fault." I put my hands on his chest. I needed him to calm down.

"Of course, it's my fault!" he yelled, and I flinched when his fingers dug into my shoulders even more deeply.

"Let go of her," Jimmy's stern voice came from behind me. Ryan's face snapped up to face off with Jim, and I felt his fingers loosen.

As soon as he released me, I spun around to stand in front of Jimmy, my back to Ryan.

Jim was staring over my head at Ryan. "Jim, you need to leave," I said as I stared daggers at him.

Jim regarded me for a moment. His eyes were burning with his own anger. "Pretty hypocritical of you, huh, Quen?" I gasped at his words.

"What are you saying, Jim?" I stared at him hard, my heart beating loudly in my chest.

He flicked a glance at Ryan before he returned his attention back to me. "Don't you think you should take your own advice before you tell someone else to do it?"

My eyes tightened into slits, and I barely got the words out. "Get out, Jim. Get out right now."

"Come on, Jimmy, let's get going. I need to get back to the station." RJ stood beside Jim and pulled him by the arm.

Jimmy glared at me a few more seconds before RJ tugged on his arm again, and he finally turned away and headed toward the side of the house.

My shoulders slumped as I watched him walk away. "I'm sorry, Jackie. Look I'll call you later today when I know some more," RJ said as he followed Jim.

"Thanks, RJ." I hung my head and tried to relax the muscles in my neck that felt like steel knots.

Ryan put his hands on my shoulders. "Jackie, I'm so sorry." He pulled me to him. My back leaned against his chest while his mouth rested in my hair. I closed my eyes for a second and took a deep breath.

"It's okay, Ryan." I pulled out of his grasp and walked to the table, stopping when I stood next to Roseanne. With my hand on her shoulder I asked, "Are you all right?"

She nodded and picked up her napkin to wipe the tears from her face. "I'm sorry," she whispered.

"You have nothing to be sorry about, Roseanne." I squeezed her shoulder. She put her hand over mine for a second before allowing it to slide off.

Ryan looked almost as bad as he did last night. I knew that none of us were doing well, but I had things I needed to get done. I squeezed her shoulder one more time and then stepped away from the table.

"I'll be in the study. I have some phone calls to make." I didn't look at Ryan as I walked past him. I was afraid of what I would see there if I did.

RYAN

I got dressed in my room and waited until I heard Jackie's bedroom door close before I followed her down to the patio.

Roseanne, Jimmy, and another man I recognized as a police officer from the scene last night were sitting at the table eating lunch. Well, the men were. Roseanne was pushing food around on her plate, and Jackie was just sitting down.

I purposely sat next to Jackie and made eye contact with Jim as I did. Oh yeah, he was not happy with me. Jackie started talking, and I looked at her with a brief smile.

I had no appetite as I spoke with the officer, so I poured myself some coffee and just inspected my empty plate.

I listened to Jackie and RJ talk and felt my heart skip a beat when he said there was also a bomb on her truck.

What? My heart stuttered in my chest and it hurt to breathe. "There was a bomb on your Jeep?" I put my mug down with a bang and scowled at Jackie.

RJ said something from the other side of the table, but I didn't look at him, I was staring a hole in the side of Jackie's head.

"Jacquelyn, you didn't tell me there was a bomb on your car. Why didn't you tell me?"

She looked at me with an expression I didn't understand. "Ryan, I..."

When Jim spoke from the other side of the table, I wanted to reach over and hit him in the face. Before I could respond to him, Jackie hissed at him from beside me.

I was still staring at Jim when I felt her hand on my arm. The world around me was buzzing. "Ryan."

I couldn't sit here anymore. I glanced at Jackie and abruptly stood so fast the world spun around me. I wanted to say something, but I couldn't get the words out. The thought of a bomb being on her vehicle was earth shattering. What if she had gotten into it? What if we had gotten into it? We would both be dead like Troy and the limo driver.

Jackie got up from her chair and called out to me. I spun around feeling like I was about to snap. "Why didn't you tell me?"

I didn't even realize that I grabbed her by the shoulders as I lost my shit, or that I might be hurting her. God knew that the last thing I wanted was for something to happen to her.

When she touched me and tried to calm me, I couldn't help but snap at her. "Of course, it's my fault!" The pain flashed across her features just before I heard Jim tell me to let her go.

At the sound of his voice, I immediately knew I had been hurting her, and I loosened my grip. Jackie spun around on Jim and told him to leave.

He stared at Jackie when he said, "Pretty hypocritical of you, huh, Quen?"

I felt the tension radiating from her as she glared at him.

RJ came up to Jim's side and talked him into leaving. I watched as the two of them walked away.

Her head hung down and I knew it was my fault. "Jackie, I'm so sorry." I grasped her arms and pulled her back to rest against me. I kissed her gently on the top of her head and kept my mouth there so that I could breathe in her fresh scent.

She spoke quietly to me and then walked to Roseanne. I watched as she spoke with her, and then our eyes met across the patio. There was more pain in her eyes now then there had been last night, and I wondered how much of that was my fault.

I wanted to pull her into my arms and tell her I was sorry. I wanted to hold her and kiss her and make that pain go away, but I let her walk past me. I was the cause of all this pain. I already knew that, and I couldn't drag her deeper into it.

I walked over to the table and sat down beside Roseanne. We were quiet for a long time. She looked down at the cellphone that was lying on the table. The little green light blinked in the corner telling her she had a message.

"Troy's funeral is on Thursday," she said after she read the message. We looked at each other, and I watched as tears slid down her face again. I fought hard to keep mine at bay, but eventually, I lost the battle, and we both sat there, food forgotten, while we both relived our memories of Troy.

JACQUELYN

I walked away from Ryan and Roseanne and went to the study. It wasn't until I sat down that the tears coursed down my face, and I allowed myself to start shaking.

How dare Jimmy say that to me! He had no right to do that. This whole thing was not the same as what had happened to me.

After I calmed down, I realized that Ryan had been right, and Jimmy was obviously jealous of what he had seen with us. His behavior today was because of that jealousy. I'd let him calm down and hope that when we had the chance to talk again, we could fix this.

I thought back to what Ryan said on the patio. He was blaming himself for Troy's death. I couldn't blame him for that. Most people went through the blame game when they lost someone. They often thought that it should have been them and not the other person. It would take a while before he could accept that it was his friend and that he still had a full life to live.

Wasn't I just like Ryan? Hadn't I blamed myself for the senseless death of my parents and Logan? Of course, I had. I still did!

I looked out the window and watched Ryan and Roseanne sitting quietly at on the patio. As I surveyed them, I realized that I would do everything I could to help Ryan know that he had a life to live and that this incident wasn't his fault. The first thing I could do was to make sure no one else got hurt.

I picked up the phone and called my friend, Jay, who owned the security company. After explaining what I needed, he told me that he would call me back shortly and tell me what he could give me. I made a few more phone calls and talked to Beth about setting up a press conference to talk about the incident.

I made arrangements for two black Chevy Tahoe's to be delivered to the house and called the director who was resting after being hit by flying debris during the explosion. It wasn't a bad injury, but there had been no good ones.

Jay called me back, just as I finished my conversation with the director, and told me that he would have four armed guards at the house twenty-four hours a day; they would arrive a little after four. He stated that he had some of his tech guys coming to the house around the same time to put in a visual security system, and he would have it manned at all times. He was able to round up four more guards who would travel with Ryan or be in place at his destinations when he needed them. They would all stay here at the house between shifts.

He explained that he even got in contact with his affiliate company in New York where Troy's funeral was being held and had secured several guards to escort Ryan there and be present at the service. I knew that Jay's local guys wouldn't be able to do that because it was across state lines.

I told him how much I appreciated everything he set up so quickly. We chatted for a few minutes about how business was and then we said our goodbyes. As I set the phone down, I looked up to find Ryan leaning on the doorjamb, his arms crossed over his chest. We visually explored each other for a moment.

"How are you doing?" I asked him. He looked better than the last time I saw him. His face wasn't as pale, but his eyes still looked drawn and haunted.

He shrugged. "You hungry? You've been in here for hours."

I glanced down at my watch and saw that it was already mid-afternoon. "Yeah, actually, I'm starved. I've been trying to line up extra security and get a new system in here. I have people showing up here in a few minutes."

I got up from behind the desk and made my way toward him. He pushed off the doorjamb and stood in the doorway blocking it. I slowed to a stop in front of him and lifted my chin to examine his face. His arms were still crossed, and it made his shoulders look hard and wide. I reached out and touched him without even thinking.

The pain in his eyes lessened the longer he held my gaze, and in that moment, I couldn't help but wish that he would pull me into his arms. I realized that I was more than capable of making that move myself, so I pulled his arm down.

The other one immediately dropped to his side. I stepped into him and slid my arms around his waist, resting my cheek on his chest. For a moment, I thought I'd done the wrong thing, but his arms finally circled me, and he held on tightly.

We stood like that for a few minutes, just holding one another. When my stomach growled, I chuckled and started to pull away. "Guess I'm hungrier than I thought." I gave him a lopsided grin while I still had my hands on his waist.

One of his hands came to my cheek, and I pushed my face into his palm. He needed no further help with the next step as he slid his hand behind my neck and pulled my face toward his. There was no question in my mind that I wanted him to kiss me. I needed to feel him.

As our lips grew closer, his eyes surveyed my face, slowly traveling over my features. As his line of focus came to my mouth, I couldn't help but lick my lips. I heard his soft moan as he closed the space and touched his lips to mine.

It was tender and soft, a slow exploration as my lips parted, and his tongue met mine. My hands slid up his arms to his shoulders and I wrapped one around his neck while my other hand slid into his hair and held him close.

I heard footsteps coming to the door just as we started to pull apart. "Oh!" Roseanne exclaimed as she stepped inside and saw us.

Ryan and I both chuckled. How many times had she caught us in this position? Ryan turned, still holding me around the waist with one arm.

"I'm sorry, I keep interrupting you two." She blushed again.

I laughed. "It's okay, Roseanne. Did you need something?"

"Yeah, you have several people who just showed up here, said they were sent by a security company on your request."

I glanced at my left wrist where my large black watch sat. "They are right on time. Thank you." I began to pull away from Ryan.

"Tell them she will be right there. I need to speak with her for a moment." Ryan held me at his side.

"Yeah, speak...hmmm, I like the way you talk." She laughed and walked out of the room. I chuckled as she left and looked up at him with a raised eyebrow.

"Sorry, I just needed an excuse to do this again," he whispered as he closed the space between us and kissed me one more time just as gently and loving as the last time.

I sighed when I pulled away. "How about you find something for us to eat? I need to go get these guys set up first."

He kissed me one more time before we walked out to the atrium arm in arm. Ryan was about to leave, and I stopped him.

"Tony! Wow, man it has been ages!" I went to him and pulled him into a huge hug as he gave me a wide father-like smile.

"Jackie, you look great. Moving up in the world, I see." He leaned his head back to look up.

I laughed. "Just an undercover job. I'll be going back to my desk soon." As I said the words, I wondered if that was what I really wanted to do. I shook it off quickly as Tony introduced me to the guys who would be staying here. I made sure that Ryan meet each of them and that they understood he was the one they were protecting, not me.

Once the conversation centered back to what I needed from them, Ryan excused himself and said he was going to get some food ready for us. I smiled but noticed he didn't return it as he went toward the kitchen. Tony and I started discussing what I needed them to do with the security cameras, dismissing Ryan's attitude without another thought.

About thirty minutes later, I entered the kitchen to find Ryan staring out the back window. He heard me enter and got to his feet, moving toward me. I was startled by how fast he pulled me into his arms, crushing my lips with his. I loved every minute of it, but I didn't understand it.

After a very long seductive kiss that made me think about how high the countertop was in comparison to how my legs would wrap around his waist, we parted. Both of us were a bit breathless as we rested our foreheads together. I was about to ask him what was wrong when he started laughing.

"Come on, your stomach is growling." I hadn't even noticed it until he said something. He pulled me over to the table.

While we ate our sandwiches, I told him about the security system and how it would all be installed. I explained how many guards would be here on a daily basis, and what would happen when he traveled to New York for the funeral. When pain flashed across his face, I moved the conversation away from Troy.

He told me the director put filming on hold for two weeks, and he would let us know what would change with the new schedule when we got closer.

I didn't tell him that in two weeks, I would no longer be here. In fact, I would probably be gone before the funeral.

We discussed the press conference for the next morning that would take place at the production site. He didn't seem very happy about the location, and I knew he wasn't ready to go back there yet.

"Ryan, you don't have to go. I can do the press conference on my own. I already have Roseanne working on it with your agent." I put my hand on top of his. He flipped his hand over and squeezed my fingers.

It was horrifying and amazing that so much tragedy had happened in the last twenty-four hours, yet I felt a sense of happiness as I focused on him. Was that wrong? Life was short; I knew that too well. So was it wrong to make the most of it?

"No. Troy was my best friend. I need to do it, but I want you right there with me, along with Roseanne and the rest of my crew." I nodded at him and squeezed his hand before I got up and put our plates in the sink.

"I need to go check on Tony and the guys." I watched him for a moment. He was staring out the window again. I came back to him and stepped behind him, putting my arms around his neck. I leaned down and kissed his temple.

"Ryan, I'll be right beside you. I promise I won't leave you alone." I said it quietly next to his ear.

"I'll talk to you later." I left feeling guilty that he might think I meant longer than the press conference. As I rounded the corner into the hallway,

I thought I heard Ryan say something, but as I peered over my shoulder, I saw he was staring at the table.

I found Tony and checked on everything that was happening. Word had gotten out about where Ryan was living, and we had confirmation from the main gate that traffic had picked up quite a bit around the entrance. I asked Tony if they could put some other guys down there to help and he said he'd be happy to do that.

Tony and I caught up as the guys worked around us. We had worked together for years until he retired and went into private security. He looked great, and I was enjoying the light conversation and the memories after all the stress from the day before.

It wasn't until a bat flew down at my head that I realized the sun had set. I glanced at my watch and saw that it was almost eight o'clock. "Oh man, Tony. You better get out of here, or Stella is gonna have your head." He laughed because we both knew his wife was a sweetheart, but she loved her time with her husband.

"Oh, don't worry. She knows where I am, and she told me to take as long as I needed to get this done right. She loves his movies, so she doesn't want anything to happen to him." We shared a laugh.

I glanced up at the house and saw a silhouette up on the third floor. Ryan was watching us. I motioned for him to come down, and he hesitated but finally made his way toward the stairs.

When he walked out the front door, he hesitated again before coming to my side. Tony was just finishing up a story about his wife and one of her latest adventures and I was enjoying the humor as Ryan joined us.

I wrapped my arm around him tentatively and he made it known that he didn't mind and pulled me securely against him.

Tony flicked his eyes between the two of us, a warm smile on his lips, before he shared another story about his crazy, but loving, wife. I lifted my head from Ryan's shoulder where I was resting it and saw a genuine smile on his lips.

"You will need to autograph something for Stella. She loves you," I said with great humor.

"When we get back to filming, Tony, why don't you bring your wife to the set?" He gave Tony one of his thousand-watt smiles, and I realized this one was real. In the few moments that he had been standing outside with us, he seemed more relaxed. This was the real Ryan. Not the man who was all concerned with what others thought about him, but the man who could be himself and just relax and unwind, even in the aftermath of tragedy. I put my head back on his shoulder, and he leaned down and kissed the top of my hair.

"Hey, Ryan." We all turned toward the door as Roseanne yelled out. "Beth is on the phone."

"Will you excuse me? I need to go talk to her." Ryan gave me a gentle smile before he left my side.

Ryan walked into the house, and I followed his every move with my hungry eyes. When I turned back to Tony, he was watching me closely with a knowing look on his face.

Trying to avoid what he was going to say, I suggested something. "Hey, you think these guys could finish this up without you being here to hawk eye over them? Why don't we go out back and have a beer?"

"I'm sure they would love for me to leave them alone, and I could use a cold beer." I put my hand on his shoulder as we walked into the house.

With two cold beers, we sat out back, and I kicked my feet up onto another chair, my head leaning back while I searched the sky.

"So what's up with Ryan?" he asked me.

I rolled my head to the right to look at him. "I have no idea," I said and laughed.

"Well it looks like something good. You know, it's nice to see you smile again," he said it jokingly, but I knew he was serious.

I shook my head dramatically. "Don't know what you're talking about, Tony. I'm always smiling." I did know what he was talking about, but I didn't want to dampen the mood.

"Yeah, right. I thought you were seeing Jimmy. I never saw you smile like that around him." He took a swig of his beer, and I watched his Adam's apple bob while he swallowed.

"Yeah, well…" I blew out a heavy breath and looked down at my beer bottle. I started peeling the label. "I guess things are over with Jimmy. I think he wanted more than I could give him."

"You need to stop worrying about what you can give other people and give yourself something. You know you deserve to be happy, Jackie," he said softly.

I shrugged.

He took another sip of his beer. "Does Ryan know about what happened?"

"What? No!" I shook my head quickly. "Well, he knows that I lost my parents and Logan, but he doesn't know how or why. And there is no reason to tell him. That was a long time ago, Tony. I would prefer to forget it."

"You can't just pretend like it never happened, Jack. That is the reason you can't get close to anyone. You need to forgive yourself and move on."

I took a drink from my bottle and then peeled more of my label off. "I wish it was that easy," I said softly. We got quiet for a minute. "You know as well as I do that until the contract is off, I can't get close to anyone."

"It might be easier than you think. Look at the resources he has here. He can keep himself safe." He watched me intently.

I glared at him for a moment. "He might have great resources, but look at what happened to Troy, and that had nothing to do with me." I stopped and thought about it. An odd feeling rose in the pit of my stomach, and I tried to squash it.

"Once this case is over and the filming is done, Ryan will be off to some other place and some other film. He'll have a proper woman on his arm, and I'll be just a memory." I took a big swig of my beer.

He laughed. "Yeah, I doubt that. I saw how he looked at you outside."

"Whatever!" I laughed at him and turned my neck when I heard foot-steps coming out the door.

"Jackie, you have a phone call." Ryan approached us. I stood and went toward the house. I turned back just as I got to the door. Ryan was watching me, and with no lights on out here, I couldn't see his eyes, but I could feel the heat of them.

RYAN

I took the seat that she had just vacated. "How long have you known her?" I asked Tony as I made myself comfortable.

"Jackie? Oh, I've known her since she first started with Rosewood Township about twelve years ago. I trained her to be great like she is now." He chuckled, and I smirked in the dark. "She's a good person, been through a lot."

I had heard the tail end of their conversation as I stood by the patio door. The way she said it to Tony, she expected me to drop her like last week's leftovers into the trash. I decided to pretend I hadn't heard that and find a way to prove her wrong.

"Like what?" I asked hoping he would tell me.

He studied me for a long time. "I can't tell you the particulars. You're going to have to wait for her to do that. Everyone has their own sad story, and it should only be told by them to the people they trust." He took a drink from his beer bottle. "What I will tell you is, she had a tragic loss in her past, and she blames herself for it."

"Why would she blame herself?" I wanted to know more, but he had already told me he wasn't going to give me details.

"That again is something you will have to ask her. I'll tell you this, Ryan. I haven't seen her smile at anyone the way she smiles at you in a very long time. It's been about six years since she looked at anyone that way. She's an incredible woman and she seems tougher than nails, but she has emotional scarring that can be tough to get through. If she means anything to you, go slow and be careful, but be ready to fight for her. She's worth it, but I don't want to see that smile disappear from her face again." The last sentence was said with a fatherly strictness to it.

I understood what he was saying. He wanted to protect her, and he wanted to see her happy, too. It was the same thing I wanted now, but I wasn't sure I could do that for her. Jackie was right that all my resources hadn't been enough to save my best friend.

We chatted a few minutes longer, and then he excused himself to check on the guys. I wandered back inside and went to the study to find Jackie, but the room was empty. I checked around the bottom floor but couldn't find her, so I climbed up the stairs. Maybe she had gone to bed already. When I got to the landing, I heard music coming from her room. I stopped in the hall near her door and saw it was partially open.

With one finger, I pushed it a bit wider. She stood in front of the window looking out. Soft piano music filled the room from her laptop set on the table next to her. "Jacquelyn?"

She spun at the sound of my voice. She was wearing the same thing she had worn to bed last night, the blue camisole and pale pink pants. The pain that squeezed my chest all day vanished as I soaked up her image. Yes, Troy was dead, but I was alive, and so was Jackie. I stepped into the room.

She regarded me as I took three steps. Her face heated as she explored the length of my body with her eyes. It was like her hands were caressing me instead of her gaze, and I felt my body flood with heat.

When she met my stare, a look of determination filled the blue depths. What was she thinking?

She came to me, but instead of stopping in front, she walked past and closed the door. I waited, not sure what to do, afraid that if I moved, it would spook her.

The door clicked softly, and she moved to stand behind me, sliding her hands around my waist. I put one hand on her arm as it encircled me. Her cheek leaned against my back, and my heart began to gallop.

She placed her lips on my back lightly. I pulled her hands off my waist and all but dragged her around in front of me. She stood with her mouth slightly parted, and her eyes glittered with passion and vitality. The skin on her face was flush as she stood on her toes and brought her face closer to mine. I leaned the last inch and took her mouth with mine.

There was nothing soft about this kiss. It was hot, and wanting, promising passionate things to come. Both of her hands wrapped around my neck and held me close.

I gasped and groaned in the same breath as she nipped at my bottom lip. My hands grew hungrier as did my mouth, and I ravished her with a new energy. Gone were the thoughts of losing her; she had come to me, and now was my time to show her how much I cared about her.

I scooped her in my arms and carried her to the bed. I laid her as carefully as I could without letting her go. I wasn't going to give her a chance to back out now. With my body half sprawled over her, I allowed my hands to wander along the side of her body.

She arched into me as I caressed her breasts and moaned gently deep within her throat as I touched her. Her hands rubbed their way down my back and tugged on my shirt. I took my hand away only long enough to help her pull it over my head and returned my hand to her hip, pulling her against me so that she would see how much she affected me.

I gazed down into her face, memorizing every detail of her beauty. Our eyes met, and all the feelings I had for her rushed to the surface.

"Jackie," I started to speak, but she put her fingertips over my lips to shush me.

She whispered, "No words, Ryan. Make love to me, show me."

And I did.

For hours, we shared an intimacy that I had never imagined I could have with another person. No words were ever needed to tell each other what we wanted, or how to please. Our bodies spoke to one another all on their own.

We fell asleep late that night, sated and content, our legs, bodies, and arms tangled together. I had never felt so much for any person in my life. I knew that I loved her more than I could have ever imagined loving another person.

She did not have to speak the words either. I saw it in her gaze, tasted it on the salty tears she briefly shed, felt it from every inch of her body.

I slept dreamlessly that night and awoke to a beautiful sunrise streaming in through her window. A ray of sunlight highlighted her blond hair as it fell over my chest. Golden, rich, soft, her hair looked like an extension of the sunbeam, and I suddenly felt like I had been touched from above. Had Troy sent the sunbeam to me to say he approved? I'd like to think so.

A soft foot moved up my leg an inch or two, and I felt her coming out of her deep slumber. A moment of panic filled me as I wondered if she would regret what we did once she saw the light of day.

A humming nose came from her throat as she stretched like a cat. Her body became more taut than it usually was and a grin spread over her face as she blinked a few times to clear the sleep from her eyes.

She raised her arms over her head as she woke her muscles up, and she allowed her hand to fall on my cheek as I watched her. There was no regret in her face as she continued to grin.

"Good morning, handsome." Her voice was deep and sultry and made my groin go to attention immediately.

"Good morning, beautiful," I responded, and her eyes crinkled around the sides as her smile grew wider. She rubbed my jaw line, and I absently wondered what she thought of the stubble on my face.

Her short manicured nails scraped over the whiskers causing my body to twitch in all the right places. "If you keep that up, you aren't getting out of bed anytime soon."

She raised her eyebrows playfully, "My thoughts exactly."

That was all the invitation I needed to twist in the bed so that she was now under me, and I kissed her until both our heads spun. Like last night, our loving was gentle and unrushed. It spoke the words that our lips did not, and we lay happily spent on the mattress when we were done.

I felt her lift her arm up, my head rested on her shoulder this time. "Oh wow, it's after nine. We need to get up."

"Not yet," I mumbled into her neck and kissed the soft skin.

She laughed. "We have people coming in a little while; we need to get up and get dressed."

The words she spoke brought back the horrible memories of the last two days and I felt as if cold water had been thrown on me.

I sat up and pushed a pillow against the wooden headboard to lean against it. "Who's coming over?"

She sat up on one of her elbows, pulling the sheet over her chest. "I called a meeting with some of your team."

I wondered why she would do that, and out of the blue remembered the look on her face when she had joined me on the set before the horrific incident. "Did you find out who was threatening me? Who killed Troy?"

Suddenly, I realized that I didn't want to know, because if she knew, then the chances that she would leave me grew tenfold.

She was regarding me with a closed expression, was she thinking the same thing?

"Yes, I did." After she released the words, I looked away from her, trying not to let the panic I felt show on my face.

"Let's get dressed, and then I'll explain." Her voice no longer held a sweet loving tone. It had changed to her professional business voice, and I hated it at that moment.

I flipped the sheet back and climbed out of bed, grabbing my jeans and pulling them on.

"Ryan." I saw her sit up, but I didn't turn to her, I just held my hand up.

"I'll meet you downstairs." I grabbed my T-shirt and shoes off the floor and left the bedroom without another word.

Why I fled without allowing her to speak, even I couldn't understand. I just knew that I had to get away before I started begging her to stay.

The fear that she would be gone from my life filled me to the point that my muscles tensed, and my stomach rolled.

I got dressed and made my way downstairs all the while trying to push the fear of losing her from my mind and my heart.

Roseanne was sitting in the kitchen staring out the window. Dark clouds rolled in, and I stared at them wondering if they were an omen of things to come.

I no longer cared who threatened me. I wanted to know who killed Troy and had tried to kill Jackie and me. Why had they escalated from notes and bad pranks to deadly events? Could someone have gotten so drastic that quickly? Or were they different?

"Morning, Ryan." Rose turned to me when she heard me.

I pulled a coffee mug down. "Morning, Rose." I poured the coffee and sat down across from her, returning my contemplation to the stormy clouds moving in from the horizon.

"Did you know about the meeting today?" I asked her as the clouds swirled outside the window.

"Yeah, Jackie asked me to get in touch with several people and bring them in." I peered over at her, but she was staring at the newspaper in front of her.

"You're not going to tell me anything, are you?" I glared at her, but she never lifted her head, shaking it side to side instead.

I grunted just as Jackie walked into the room. The sweet gentle woman I made love to and held in my arms all night was gone. In her place was the closed off, professional police officer I had hired to do a job, one that she had evidently completed.

The coffee suddenly tasted bitter on my tongue, and I set down my mug.

She got her own coffee cup out and poured herself some. Drew walked into the room rubbing his eyes, obviously having just rolled out of bed. His shirt was wrinkled as if he'd picked up yesterday's throw away and pulled it back on.

I heard the front door close as Jackie walked over to the table. "Why don't we take this to the family room?" Roseanne peeked up at her, folded the paper, and stood, following behind Jackie as she left the room.

I heard a yawn come from behind me and turned to see Drew closing his mouth while he tried to pour his coffee into his cup. A few drops spilled over the edge, but he didn't seem to notice.

He left the room without a word. My shoulders were rigid with tension as I sat there trying to find the courage to walk into the other room. The front door opened and closed again.

I slammed my eyes shut, clenching them as I tried to inhale enough air to help me relax. I rolled my shoulders and stood, moving to the family room.

When I entered, I was surprised to find quite a few people. Of course, Jackie, Roseanne, and Drew were there. But Jackie wasn't the only police officer; Jim was there too, along with a woman I didn't know, though she looked familiar.

Jim was in slacks and a button-up shirt, while the woman was in full uniform. Did Jackie have them here because someone was going to be arrested?

Jim and I glared at one another, and I wondered if he had ever slept with Jackie. The thought of him touching her pissed me off; I clenched my jaw and walked further into the room.

In one of the armchairs, Markus watched everyone closely and looked uncomfortable as hell. So did he have something to do with this? I gave him the same glare I gave Jim, and he looked away from me.

Marie sat on the couch attempting to look comfortable, but she did not achieve the look. *Not Marie!* She couldn't have anything to do with this. I gaped at her, but she wouldn't meet my eyes.

I sat down slowly; beyond surprised that Marie could have anything to do with this, until I started to remember her chastising me for spending so much time with Jackie. But why? What did she have to gain from this?

Jackie was talking with Jim and the other woman quietly over in the corner. I heard the woman's radio crackle to life, and she put her hand on a knob turning the volume down without missing a beat in the conversation she was having.

When someone else walked into the room, I was shocked to see her here. She searched the room, and her eyes landed on me. A huge smile spread over her face as she all but ran to me. I stood up as she got closer, confused as to why she was in my house.

She threw her arms around my neck, and I put my hands on her hips to push her away. I searched out Jackie, she watched carefully, but she wasn't looking at me, she was watching Markus and Marie react.

I scrutinized both of them for a few seconds. Marie hung her head lower, and Markus rolled his eyes and got even more uncomfortable.

"Ryan, I'm so glad you wanted me back!" Monique squeaked loudly in my ear as she continued to crush herself against me.

"Excuse me?" I said and grabbed her by the arms to physically remove her from my neck.

"I got your message. I knew things wouldn't work with that other woman."

I gaped at her. "What the hell are you talking about?" I turned to stare at Jackie. "What the hell is she talking about?"

Jackie stepped closer to the couch. "Ryan, I'd like you to meet, Lucinda, but you probably know her as Monique. Markus knows her as LaLa, his little sister."

I glared at Markus, while Jackie continued to talk.

"And of course, Marie knows her as her daughter." She crossed her arms over her chest while I digested her words.

I pushed Monique away from me and spun on Marie. "Marie, what's going on?"

She shook her head, staring at her hands as she held a wadded up tissue in them.

"Marie?"

She finally lifted her head, and while it was obvious that she was frightened, she also had a defiant look set into her hazel eyes. "I just wanted you to be with Monique. She is the one who is right for you, not that," she threw her chin in Jackie's direction, "that blue collar working girl."

Anger bubbled under my skin. I encompassed them all with a look. "You were all in on it?"

They all had the decency to look away, but Monique came back to me to plead.

"Ryan, I love you. We were meant to be together. Why did you call me if you didn't want me?"

I shoved her away. "I didn't call you!"

"He's right; he didn't call you. Drew did," Jackie answered when I couldn't give her an answer.

Monique's resentful look shot knives at Jackie, and she made a move toward her, but Jim stepped in front of her and took her by the arm. The female officer stepped around her and placed her hands in cuffs.

Jim moved toward Markus and motioned for him to stand up. Markus mumbled something under his breath but did what he was told. Jackie went around the back of the couch and took Marie by the arm, forcing her to her feet. Jackie pulled a pair of handcuffs from her pocket and slipped them on Marie as I stood there in shock.

I had never even thought that Monique would do something like this, or Marie for that matter. I followed behind them as they marched the three out of the house.

Just before they put them into the two police cars that were parked out front, I found my voice.

"Wait!" They all stopped and turned to me. "Are they the ones responsible for killing Troy?" My voice cracked on the last two words.

A voice piped up from a man I hadn't even realized was there. Everyone turned their attention to the side of the driveway where a police SUV was parked. RJ stood there.

"No, they had nothing to do with it," he said as he looked me straight in the eye. "But, I know who did." He looked away then and focused on Jackie.

"Jackie, we need to talk." RJ's voice was dead serious.

I followed his line of vision and saw Jackie's face pale at his words.

Her voice was deadpan as she barely whispered, "No, please tell me no."

JACQUELYN

The phone call was from Rebecca, and we spent a few minutes talking about what was going to happen the next day. I would expose the three people involved with Ryan's threats. Then, my part of this undercover investigation would be over.

After tomorrow morning, I'll have fulfilled my part of the investigation, and would be free to go home and back to my life and my job. What kind of a life would it be now without Ryan in it? The thought depressed me, and instead of joining Ryan and Tony outback, I made my way to my room.

I changed out of my clothes and into my pajamas and stood at the window looking out at the officers who were patrolling the grounds.

I wasn't sure if these same three people were involved in the explosion. Markus had enough technology knowledge that he could probably figure it out. There were enough websites that explained how to make a car bomb.

A niggling doubt sat in the back of my mind. What if it wasn't them, but someone else was trying to get to Ryan? Could I walk away from him knowing that he could still be in danger?

A tremor raced down my spine like an electrical shock, making me weak. What if they tried to get to him as they had my parents and Logan? I would never be able to stop them. This whole farce of me being his girl-friend might have put his life in more jeopardy than it was before, and that would be my fault.

Ryan stepped into my room and called my name. I spun to confront him, to tell him he couldn't be here with me, that there would never be anything between us. The moment I met his gaze, those thoughts vanished and the only ones that filled my mind were ones of holding him, loving him, just one time before this whole thing was over.

I crossed the room and bypassed him to close the door. My heart tripped over itself as it beat hard and fast in my chest. I took in his wide shoulders and his thin waist, and my arms wrapped around it without further thought. I rested my cheek on his back, the sound of his heart so powerful that I wanted to weep for what I might have done to him.

He snagged my hand from his waist and pulled me around so that I faced him. I didn't want to think about death, or pain, or being alone. I only wanted to feel. To feel Ryan and the love I had for him. Yes, I knew I loved him.

He carried me to the bed, a scene to rival any movie that depicted such an event. When he went to speak, I hushed him. I could not bear to hear him express his feelings, not now. Not when I knew I was leaving tomorrow.

Tonight, I wanted to love him and have him love me in the simplest and most intimate way.

And I was.

I still carried the heady feeling of a happy woman the next morning, and for just a little while longer, I wanted to bask in that glow and feel his love one last time.

The mood changed completely when I spoke of the meeting. Ryan appeared to close up, and while it hurt deep inside my heart, I knew that it was for the best.

I showered and dressed, replaying the moments of our glorious night together in my mind. At one point, I wanted to cry as the water ran over my head, but I didn't. I forced myself to push the memories into the back of my mind and pull forward what I needed to do today.

We barely acknowledged each other downstairs, and I met Jimmy and Rebecca in the atrium as they arrived right on time.

Rebecca gave me a hug and inspected every inch of the house that she could see, her jaw hung slack as we entered the family room. Jim gave me an abrupt nod of the head. I knew it was hard for him to be here, but I trusted him and knew that, while he might not like Ryan or my feelings for him, he was a professional, like me.

We stood off to the side and chatted for a few minutes until everyone arrived. When Ryan entered the room, a butterfly took flight in my stomach. This was why he had brought me here, and now I was about to wrap it up.

His eyes scanned the room, taking in the occupants. Curiosity, anger, and confusion moved over his features, but none as strongly as the one that plastered his eyes wide open when Monique rushed into the room and threw herself at him.

He was stunned and pleaded with me with his eyes to rescue him. I moved forward to make the introductions.

The day that all hell broke loose, Becca called me to report that the forensic report had come back on the envelopes. Not only were Markus's fingerprints on it, but Marie's and Monique's, too. She did some digging around into their backgrounds and found that all three of them had been arrested for a similar stalking event back in Nevada where they were from.

Marie wanted her kids to have what they wanted and stopped at nothing to help them get it. At this moment, officers were seizing the computers from inside the tech trailer, and they would be forensically examined for further evidence.

Jimmy was here so that after they brought them to the station, he could question them one at a time and then file the charges. I had to give him credit for stepping up to the plate, even though this was on a more personal level.

I tried to avoid Ryan's wounded gaze as I took Marie into custody and we shepherded them out to the waiting patrol car. My job here was done. I should feel happy, but with each step toward Rebecca's patrol car, I felt my resolve dropping and the urge to run back to Ryan and beg him to let me stay.

"Wait." My heart thudded in my chest as I turned to look at him. "Are they the ones who killed Troy, too?"

It was a logical question, and one I wish I could give him a straight answer to. I hadn't been prepared to have RJ respond though.

"No, they had nothing to do with it." My thudding heart skipped a beat when he turned to me. "But I know who did." I felt my heart falter again. Would it stop beating, because as I stared into RJ's face, I knew.

"Jackie, we need to talk."

"No, please tell me no." Please! I wanted to shout! Make it not true. My worst nightmare had come to life, again.

Rebecca put Monique in the car and took Marie from my still hands. RJ and I continued to stare at one another, my legs began to shake harder the longer we did.

I didn't understand the words that Becca murmured to me as she climbed into her car and left behind Jimmy's vehicle. I only knew that because of my actions years ago, I had brought more death to people I cared about. My heart tore in two as RJ approached and took my arm.

"Let's go inside." He pulled my numb body along beside him. Ryan stepped out of the way to allow us to pass, his face full of confusion, his eyes asking for answers to questions he would never truly understand.

When we got back to the family room, RJ let go of my arm. I sank down into a chair. Roseanne and Drew were still in the room and recognized the tension for what it was. They got quiet and sat still. Only RJ seemed un-phased by what he was about to reveal as Ryan found a chair across from me and fell into it.

"So who was it?" Ryan asked as he looked between RJ and me. I couldn't look him in the eye, but I watched him out of corner of my eye.

"Jackie." RJ waited until I lifted my face to him. "It was the same. I'm sorry."

I shook my head. "It couldn't be. You have to be wrong."

He returned the shake of the head. "I'm sorry. I checked it twice and had someone else check it, too. The wiring harness was the signature, and they are exact replicates of the other ones."

"What other ones?" Ryan demanded.

RJ faced him. "The ones that killed her parents and her fiancé six years ago." I cringed as he spoke.

"What?" Ryan asked. I flicked a quick glance at him, and his face was ashen.

"You never told him, Jackie?" RJ asked me, and I shook my head afraid to meet either of their eyes.

"Well, I think he has a right to know now." I didn't deny that as I sunk further into the chair and tried to hide.

"Ten years ago, Jackie got involved in a case that involved the mob. She put two and two together, in a roundabout way, and we were able to put one of the mafia heads behind bars for life." He paused to give Ryan a chance to absorb what he said.

"The problem is that Ciminera was so pissed, he put a contract out on Jackie. He promised to take out any person whom she loved, and he didn't care if his associates took her out either."

I hung my head as tears filled my eyes. I had brought this on Ryan. Troy's death was my fault, just like Logan's and my mother's and father's.

"A year after he was incarcerated, Jackie was going to her parents' house for Christmas Eve dinner. She had been stuck on a case, and Logan got there before her. Just as she pulled onto their street, the house exploded and killed everyone right before her eyes."

Roseanne gasped, and Drew threw out an explicative, but it was Ryan's response I waited for. Thunder growled outside the walls of the house.

Ryan said nothing, and I lifted my head. He stared at me, so hard that I thought he was looking right through me. After a long time, he looked at the floor and then stood up and turned to leave.

"Ryan," I called out in a hoarse voice. I couldn't let him leave without saying something, anything!

He stopped, his tense back facing me. "I can't talk to you right now." He left the room without another word or glance back.

The room was silent after he left. I sat forward to lean on my elbows. My long hair fell around my face, hiding my despair from everyone but me. RJ put his hand on my shoulder and squatted down beside me.

"I'm so sorry, Quen." I sobbed at the use of the nickname Logan and my parents had used on me. Since the day they died, I could not handle someone else calling me by that name. But hearing it now was fitting. It was Quen who had gotten four people whom she cared about killed. It was Quen they were punishing and would be forever.

"Thanks, RJ," I spoke softly. "Do you know any more about who actually placed the bombs and how?"

"I don't know who yet, but I think it was done here at the house." I lifted my head up fast.

"What?" I croaked.

"When the dogs were checking the outside of the house, they found some wires in the driveway. Just small pieces mostly, like someone was in a hurry. They probably did it at night and missed the little pieces that fell into the stone of on driveway. We collected that and we are having it checked for DNA."

The memory of a burst of light in the stairway the night before the explosion filled my mind. I told RJ about it, and we concluded that was probably when it had happened.

I thanked RJ for coming and walked him out. When I closed the door, I rested my heated skin against the cold wood.

"You should have told me." I spun around, startled by Ryan's voice.

"I'm sorry, Ryan. I didn't think about it at first."

His jaw tightened along with his eyes. "You didn't think about it? You didn't think about the fact that you had a contract on your life that could have killed my whole team!"

I flinched at his words. He was right. I should have told him at the beginning. If I had, he could have decided if he wanted to play this dangerous game or not.

"Because of you, Troy is dead!" A stab went through my heart, and it split in two. I knew this was coming. "Get out of my house. Your job here is finished."

"Ryan, wait." I moved to reach out to him, not to beg him to let me stay. I knew that would never happen, but to calm him.

He slapped my hand away. "Get out, Detective Liveon!" He spun around and stalked down the hallway.

I watched him disappear and knew that was the last time I would see him. I climbed the stairs, my feet feeling like lead weights.

Less than an hour later, I carried my bags down the stairs. Drew met me on the bottom floor and took one of my suitcases from me.

We were silent as we headed toward my car. I lifted the back hatch just as Drew spoke.

"He's upset right now. He needs someone to blame. He'll get over it." He put the suitcase in the back. "Rose and I don't blame you." He met my emotional gaze, and I gave him one quick nod.

He stepped away from my truck while I put the other bag inside along with my backpack. As I reached up to grab the hatch, my eyes went to the atrium, and I found Ryan standing on the balcony watching me. I couldn't see his face, but I could just imagine the pain and anger that was on there.

I slammed the hatch and climbed into my truck. With a quick twist of my wrist, I turned the key in the ignition and drove out of the driveway, never looking back. How could I, my eyes were filled with so many tears it was hard to see what was right in front of me.

RYAN

I towered above her, inspecting her every move as Drew helped her put her stuff in the Jeep. I was furious with her; hurt beyond belief that she had not thought it was important to share with us the deadly contract she had over her head.

Drew walked away, and she lifted her arms to close the tailgate. Our gazes locked. So many emotions flitted over her face. Just as my mind began to war with my heart, she looked away and got inside her vehicle.

I watched the SUV drive down to the gate and out of my life. It was for the best. It didn't matter that I loved her, it only mattered that she held back a very important fact. A fact that had caused the death of my best friend. I went to my room and closed the door on what I had shared with Jackie.

"I can't believe we finished the film in record time. Even with the two-week unscheduled hiatus, we finished a week early!" Roseanne exclaimed happily as she dropped into the seat next to me in the limo.

Drew sat across from us. He was the acting head of security ever since

Troy's funeral. Troy. I hadn't thought much about him during the last few weeks of filming.

His funeral was devastating for all of us. While we stood in the cemetery, I wondered if Jackie would show, but deep down, I knew she wouldn't. After the way I treated her, I knew she would never want to face me again.

When we returned to filming, the director told us that he was dedicating the film to Troy; it was a bittersweet moment for us all. Everyone got back to the film with a vengeance, especially me. I needed to get this film over with and move on. I already spoke to a realtor about selling the house and figured I'd go back to Los Angeles until I found another place. Now that the film was over, I could do just that.

I leaned my head back against the seat. During the last few months, I went about my life, doing my job and being social when needed. It was the moments when I was alone that I dwelled on the face of the woman I fell in love with and missed everyday more than I ever could have imagined I would.

"You have that look on your face again, Ryan. Are you thinking about her?" Rose squeezed my knee reassuringly.

Normally, I would deny it, but it seemed fitting that I think about her now that the film was finished, and I was moving on. It would get easier when I didn't have the constant reminders of her memories in the house.

"Yeah." I gave Rose a lopsided smile. "Yeah, I guess I was."

"You know that after she handled the case with Markus, Marie, and Monique, she took some time off."

I shook my head. "No, I didn't know that. How did you?"

"We've emailed a few times. She's staying with friends down south right now." This was the first news I heard of her since she left, and I soaked up every word.

"She asks about you," she said softly.

I nodded absently. She probably wanted to know if I was still angry with her. In a way, I was. However, somewhere along the line, I realized it wasn't exactly her fault. I was the one who had forced her to do the job, and hadn't really cared what she had wanted. If I had known about the contract, would it have changed my mind? I'd come to the conclusion that it probably wouldn't have. I had been obsessed with her, and I would have been cavalier about the threat.

I think my anger now stemmed from the fact that she hadn't trusted me enough with the information. Maybe it wasn't really anger, but more disappointment. She might have had feelings for me, but she hadn't cared enough to tell me the darkest and most important thing about her life.

"You should call her, Ryan." I turned to look out the window.

"No, Rose, it's over. I'm not going to call her." We drove the rest of the way in silence.

Nine months later, it was time to release the movie. I was hip deep in another film, with two more starting right after this one finished. I'd taken two weeks off so that I could help promote the new film.

Tonight was the premiere, and I sat in the limo with Roseanne by my side as we drove to the theater. As usual, I sat in silence, dwelling on memories that were better left dead, yet not being able to since I was back in the area. I had left the day after filming was over and vowed never to return. Of course, the higher ups decided this is where we would release the film, so here I was.

I was aware that Rose had given Jacqueline tickets to see the debut, but I had no idea if she would come. Nor did I know how I would feel about it if she did.

"Are you going to talk to her if she's there?" Roseanne broke through my thoughts. She always knew when I had Jackie on my mind.

"I won't be a prick if that's what you're thinking." I peered at her sitting on the other side of the leather seat.

She snorted. "I didn't think you would." She grew quiet for a few moments. "You know, it must be very lonely for her."

I sighed. "Why do you say that, Rose?"

"How would you feel if you knew you could never love again, or someone would kill that person? I can't imagine how hard life would be never being able to get close to people."

I stared out the window and thought about what Roseanne had said. She was right. Jackie had been thrown into a life sentence, and she wasn't even in prison. It didn't matter though. It had been too long, and that part of my life was over. I had moved on, although there had yet to be another woman in my life.

Something that everyone, including Beth, was shocked about. My playboy life was over. I wanted a serious relationship that included a family and only one woman. Deep inside, I knew that I wanted Jackie, but I also knew I could never have her.

A few minutes later, we pulled up to the red carpet. "Put on that gorgeous smile," Rose said as I reached for the door handle. Just like that, I put on my movie star smile and greeted my screaming fans.

I scanned the hordes of people, not looking at them, but searching for her. I could tell myself that it was over, but I still wanted to see her, if only for a moment.

I signed a few autographs before making my way toward the theater's doors. Inside, I was able to drop the superstar smile down a notch, but kept an eager and happy look on my face.

I glanced around the inside area but didn't see her. However, I did see RJ, the bomb squad guy, and a female standing next to him. She turned, and I recognized her as the officer who came to take Marie and the others away on that fateful day.

Without telling my feet to do it, I moved toward them, stopping along the way to shake hands and receive pats on the back from people. I made eye contact with RJ, and he broke out in a friendly grin as he saw me approaching. Just before I reached him, I got snagged by someone and had to turn to answer a few questions.

When I turned around, I bumped right into someone. I looked down and saw the stunned look in Jackie's eyes. I froze.

I forgot how beautiful her eyes were, how gorgeous every part of her was. She took my breath away.

"Jackie," Roseanne broke through our stare and threw her arms around Jacquelyn in a long-lost friend hug that immediately made me jealous. I stepped back to give them more room and shook hands with RJ. He introduced me to Rebecca, Jackie's friend, who was in her own right a beautiful woman, but my mind dismissed her immediately and I turned to stare at the woman talking animatedly to Rose.

"I'm so glad you came!" Rose hugged her again. "Oh, sorry, I don't want to mess up your dress, you look absolutely amazing." With Rose's words, I took in Jackie's appearance. Her dress was a soft emerald green silk. It glowed against her tanned arms and chest. My groin tightened as I observed the material slide over her breasts as she moved.

"Ryan, doesn't she look gorgeous?" Rose brought me back to the room, which was good, because I had traveled back in time to a place I shouldn't be visiting.

Jackie turned and gave me a shy smile, but her lips quivered. Was she nervous? "You do look beautiful, Jacquelyn."

So what if my voice shook like her lips were. I wasn't nervous. I was freaking terrified!

Not scared that I was seeing her but a nervous wreck because the moment I let my eyes embrace her face, I fell immediately back in love with her all over again.

"Thank you, Ryan. You look handsome as usual," she replied.

The lights dimmed in the reception area, telling us that we needed to find our seats. Just before I reached for Rose's arm to lead her in, RJ pulled his cellphone out.

"Jackie, I need to take this." She nodded at him as he pushed through the crowd to get someplace quiet. Jackie turned to her friend and took a quick look up at me.

"Let me take you to your seat," I suggested and held my arm out to her.

Rose leaned up and whispered into my ear, "By the way, she's sitting right next to you. Sorry I forgot to tell you." She turned from me before I could speak and walked next to Rebecca to show her the way.

Jackie took my arm, and I felt the touch of her hand zing through me from head to toe. I wrapped my hand around hers as it rested in the crook of my arm, and we entered the theater.

Sneaky little Rose had set this up. How was I going to sit next to her and make it out in one piece?

We found our seats and turned quite a few heads as we did. Murmurs drifted around us when people saw us together again. Let them think what they want. I didn't care.

My whole crew was there and sat around us; all of them smiled and said hello to Jackie. She left a seat open next to her for RJ, and I sat down beside her. Suddenly, I felt like a high school boy on a first date. My hands started sweating and I wiped them on my tuxedo pants.

Jackie sat up straight, crossing her right leg over her knee, and I sucked in a breath as I remembered the soft feel of her skin rubbing against mine that one night a very long time ago.

The director stood up and picked up a microphone. He took a few minutes to talk about the production, sharing a few laughs about the funnier moments, and even some of the more stressful ones we had endured. He finished his speech by talking about Troy.

Jackie and I both tensed. I didn't have to touch her to know. I felt the tension surround us.

RJ found us just as the lights were going out. He whispered something to Jackie, and she shushed him. I heard him raise his voice saying, "Jackie, you're going to want to hear this."

"When this is over, I want to watch this." She turned back as pictures filled the screen. They weren't part of the film. The first few minutes were just for us. They were moments in time that had been forever stopped by the click of a shutter or captured on film, and they were all of Troy.

I heard Jackie suck in a sharp breath, and we both stared at the screen. There were ones of him on the phone, looking intent. A few of him flirting with members of the crew, and then there were the ones where he stood beside me.

In the last few pictures, Jackie was by my side. I stared at the photographs. In every single one, Jackie and I were lost in each other, and Troy was watching from the side, a smile on his lips as though he approved of us being together.

My eyes filled with moisture, and I heard Jackie sniff beside me. Did she see the same thing? I reached for her hand, our fingers laced completely, and we held on as we both shared silent tears for the man who had been our friend.

When the final picture faded from the screen, Jackie leaned her head on my shoulder, and I kissed the top of her soft hair while I tried to regain my composure.

The movie began a moment later, and we were all pulled into the paranormal world of *Garda* and the story of love lost and found again amongst the guardian angels in the realm.

JACQUELYN

*I*t hadn't been the leaving him that was the hardest. It was the reason why he sent me away that hurt like hell. I told myself that it didn't matter because I was planning on leaving anyway. Maybe the anger he felt would allow him to get over me faster and move on with his life. I could only hope one of us was doing that.

On the day of Troy's funeral, I stood at a far distance and watched. Being in a cemetery was agonizing enough. But watching Ryan mourn from a distance had torn my heart to pieces. When everyone left and the casket was covered with dirt, I stood in front of it.

The stem of a single white rose rolled between my fingers as I prayed that Troy would forgive me. As if the answer were no, I somehow pricked myself on a thorn from the long green stem. I set the flower of innocence on the mound of dirt and studied my finger. A bead of blood appeared. I knew then that his blood would forever be on my hands.

I tried to go back to work, but my cases held no interest for me. Before, they were everything in my life; now I simply saw them as work, and I didn't have the energy to do it.

It didn't help that I knew Ryan was still in the area. I avoided the places where they were filming like the plague, and instead, spent my nights stalking entertainment shows and web sites for any news about him.

There rarely was, and the only photographs that appeared were of him alone or with Roseanne.

I ended up taking another leave of absence, but this one was for my own mental health benefit. I traveled for a while and spent some time with friends and family in Florida. I walked the beach at sunrise or sunset and remembered the beauty of seeing them from behind the glass walls of the atrium. There was a longing deep inside that would never be fulfilled.

Jim and I finally talked when I returned, and he understood that I wasn't able to be in a relationship with him, now or ever. We remained friends, but it was fragile at best.

I sat on my couch and stared at an envelope I received in the mail today. Inside, it contained three tickets to the opening of the movie. I was torn, wanting to be there and afraid that it would cause a scene. It had been well over a year, but I feared that Ryan would always look at me as the woman who killed his best friend.

Roseanne and I stayed in touch, and she filled me in on tidbits of what Ryan was doing, but after a few emails, I told her to stop. I couldn't take knowing that his life was going so well, while mine was stuck and would never go anywhere. She did her best not to mention Ryan, but since he was such a big part of her life, she always did, and the pain would slice through my heart.

Don't get me wrong, I was happy for him. I wanted him to have a wonderful life; but secretly, deep inside, I wanted to be a part of that life. I wanted Ryan.

It was Becca who talked me into going to the premiere. She and RJ had been dating for a while, and I knew that if I went, I would invite them to attend with me. Rose even said she would have a limo sent to pick us up, but I told her that wasn't necessary.

Even on the afternoon of the event, I struggled with whether I should go or not. Again, Becca talked me into it, saying that maybe Ryan had forgiven me, and we could renew a friendship or something. It felt wrong to hope for even a small thread of reconciliation, but eventually, I succumbed to my friend's begging and said I would go. Besides, I longed to see him in person one more time.

They picked me up, and I fidgeted the whole way there. Would he ignore me? Would he glare at me or say something horrible in front of everyone? My nerves were frayed by the time we arrived, and I went to the ladies' room to compose myself.

As I rejoined RJ and Rebecca, Becca pointed her chin to a direction behind me. I turned around just as Ryan did, and we crashed into each other.

My knees shook as I focused on his face. It didn't look angry; it looked surprised and for some reason fascinated.

The pictures on the internet didn't do him justice as I gazed up into his twinkling blue eyes and tried to breathe.

Rose broke the awkward moment by throwing her arms around me and giggling. Leave it to her to set everything up. She probably planned on us bumping into each other, just like she planned on us sitting next to one another.

When Ryan wrapped his hand over mine, emotions tingled through my body like the electrical charge of a Taser. I walked with pride beside him and ignored the looks others directed at us as we took our seats.

I ended up right beside him, and my awareness of him was almost overwhelming. I knew that there was a dedication to Troy at the start of the film, and I shook as I dreaded what Ryan would do as we watched it together.

I never imagined he would hold my hand. Or that he would kiss my head as I leaned on him for just a moment at the end. Troy looked so wonderful in those pictures, and toward the end, when I was beside Ryan in a few of the photos, I couldn't help but notice the pleased look upon his lips.

He had wanted us to be together so badly. If only we could.

The movie was excellent, and Ryan held my hand the entire time. Our fingers laced tightly, and every once in a while, his thumb skirted over my knuckles and the back of my hand. I felt the tight squeeze when we watched the scene of him drunk up against the wall with the stranger. So much had happened in those twenty-four hours.

When it was over, we sat and watched all the credits roll. It was something that few people ever did, but I guess at opening night, it was important to pay respect to every single one of those names up on that screen. If it wasn't for them, you wouldn't have the movie you just experienced.

Ryan let go of my hand when the lights came back on and the chatter started immediately. He shook hands and hugged people as he made his way into the walkway. Roseanne joined us and we talked about the movie as we followed slowly behind him into the reception area.

"Are you guys going to the party?" Roseanne asked as we got out of the thick row of people leaving the theater.

"I don't think so—" I started to say, but RJ interrupted me.

"Oh, yes you are. We can't miss the party!" He grinned at Becca, who gave him a funny look. She knew I didn't want to go to the after party. He pulled her away for a moment and whispered in her ear.

When she came back, she grinned at Roseanne and said, "Yeah, we'll be going to the party." Rose and I shared a brief confused look but ignored the funny behavior away.

Rose asked us to ride in the limo with her. My heart constricted in my throat, making it hard to breathe.

"Sure," RJ said from behind me. Becca whispered in my ear that I would be just fine. I wanted to smack her.

Rose led us to a side door where the limos were waiting. We all piled in and waited for Ryan to join us. My hands shook, and my mouth was dry. When the driver opened the door for him, Rose jumped seats, leaving the one next to me the only available seat for him to take without climbing over everyone. I glared at her, and she tried to suppress a grin, but failed.

Ryan sank into the seat and stared at me with a slack jaw. "I didn't know you were coming with us," he said more casually than his tense body language spoke. Instantly, I knew it was the wrong thing to do.

"I'm sorry, Ryan," I said. I was about to go on, but his stare stopped me.

"What are you sorry about?" he whispered.

This was my moment and probably the only time I would be able to apologize for not telling him about my past. After tonight, I would have no reason to see him ever again.

"Everything," I breathed out. "I'm sorry that I didn't tell you up front. I should have, then you could have decided for yourself if you still wanted me there."

"Why didn't you?" I couldn't tell what he was thinking or feeling. He had pulled his acting mask over his features. My voice shook as I answered him.

"I was afraid."

He turned in his seat to see me better. "And now?"

"Now?" I knew my eyes were wide.

"Yes, now." He plucked my shaking hand off my lap and slid closer to me.

I shook my head, unsure of what he was asking.

"Do you love me, Jackie?" His blue eyes bore into mine, and I saw just the briefest moment of uncertainty cross his features.

"Yes," I whispered, "Yes, I do, but I can't put your life in jeopardy just because I love you."

Ryan was about to speak, but RJ interrupted, and I suddenly remembered we had an audience watching us. Heat rose up the column of my neck as I blushed.

"And I think this is where I come in." RJ grinned.

Ryan sounded slightly perturbed that we had been interrupted, but he asked, "How do you come into any of this?" Ryan looked between the two of us, and I raised my eyebrows and shrugged, unsure of where this was going.

He sat up on the edge of his seat. "Remember the phone call I had to take just before the movie?"

We both nodded at him. I glanced at Becca, and she was biting her lip to keep from smiling. I could see it in her eyes. I peered over at Rose, but Rose looked mystified.

"Well, it seems that they finally figured out who made the bombs. They took him into custody about three hours before they called me. When the ATF agents went to the prison to talk to Ciminera about it, he had a heart attack."

My jaw dropped. I had to hear the words. "He's dead?"

RJ grinned. "Poor bastard didn't make it." I closed my eyes fighting the emotion I was feeling.

"So what does that mean?" Ryan asked RJ.

RJ laughed. "What that means, Ryan, is that the contract on Jackie is over. It dies with the one who issued it. It was a personal vendetta, and that person is now dead."

A tear slipped down my cheek, and Ryan slowly turned back to me. "It's over? No more death threats?"

I nodded as more tears cascaded down my cheeks. It was over. I was free to love again and have a life. But would Ryan have me?

He cupped my cheek and wiped away a few of my tears with his thumb. He lifted my chin, so that he could look straight into my eyes. Everyone in the limo stayed silent as we all waited to see what Ryan would say.

"I have a job proposition for you." His lips twitched.

A job proposition? Um, that was the last thing I had expected to come out of his mouth. "What?"

He smirked down at me. "Actually, it's a two-part proposition." He stroked my cheek again. "I want you to be the head of my security team."

I almost laughed because I had not expected that. "You what?"

"I know you would work very hard to keep me safe, but that's not all." He paused and I saw all the emotion begin to bloom in his gaze, "I want you to marry me, Jacquelyn." As I gazed into his eyes and saw the love pouring out toward me, all the broken pieces of my heart and soul started to stitch themselves back together.

"If you don't say yes and hurry the hell up and kiss him, I'm going to!" Becca stated from her seat.

Everyone burst into laughter, and Ryan moved his lips closer to mine. "You have about one second to answer those questions."

Instead of tears of pain, ones of joy filled my eyes and spilled over as I leaned in the last fraction of an inch and said, "Yes!" just before I kissed him.

He kissed me briefly and pulled back. "Yes, to which question?" he asked. He searched my face with concern.

"Yes, to both." I watched his concern float away, and I pulled him close to me and kissed him like he was my life, my breath, and my future.

And he was.

The End

ABOUT THE AUTHOR

Stacy Eaton is a USA Today Best Selling author and began her writing career in October of 2010. Stacy took an early retirement from law enforcement after over fifteen years of service in 2016, with her last three years in investigations and crime scene investigation to write full time.

Stacy resides in southeastern Pennsylvania with her husband, who works in law enforcement, and her teen daughter. She also has a son who is currently serving in the United States Navy and has two grandchildren.

Be sure to visit www.stacyeaton.com for updates and more information on her books.

Sign up for all the latest information on Stacy's Newsletter!

ALSO BY STACY EATON

Paranormal Romance:

My Blood Runs Blue, Book 1

The Pulse of Blue Blood , Book 2 (Short Story)

Blue Blood for Life, Book 3

Mixing the Blue Blood, Book 4

Blue Bloods Final Destiny, Book 5 (Spring 2020)

Garda ~ Welcome to the Realm

Domestic Violence – Crime - Suspense:

Whether I'll Live or Die**

Barbara's Plea

You're Not Alone**

Romantic Suspense·

Liven ~ No Evil

Second Shield

Distorted Loyalty**

Six Days of Memories

Second Shield II: The Return

Contemporary Romance:

Tempt Me Too**

Finding the Strength

Finding Love on Christmas Vacation

Heart of the Family Series

Mistletoe & Cocoa Kisses, Book 1

Roses & Champagne Kisses, Book 2

Orchids & Hurricane Kisses, Book 3

Carnations & Hot Toddy Kisses, Book 4 (Oct 2019)

Heal Me Series

Cured, Book 1

Revived, Book 2

Mended, Book 3

Rescued, Book 4

The Celebration Series

Tangled in Tinsel, Book 1

Tears to Cheers, Book 2

Heathens to Hearts, Book 3

Rainbows Bring Riches, Book 4

Sweet as Sugar, Book 5

Making Mom Mad, Book 6

Sparklers or Spankings, Book 7

Raffles to Rattles, Book 8

Flirting with Fireworks, Book 9

Working under Wheels, Book 10

Masquerading at Midnight, Book 11

Blessings & Beans, Book 12

Velvet & Vows, Book 13

The Sometimes Series:

Sometimes You Win, Book 1**

Sometimes You Lose, Book 2**

Sometimes You Play The Game, Book 3**

Pleasure Your Fantasies Series

Mistletoe Fantasies, Book 1

Whispered Fantasies, Book 2

Secret Fantasies, Book 3 (Nov 2019)

The Twisted Love Series

with Amy Manemann Co-Author

Love Lorn, Book 1 (Manemann)**

Love Torn, Book 2 (Eaton)**

Love Inked, Book 3

Love Drowned, Book 4

Love Carved, Book 5 (Fall 2019)

Love Trapped, Book 6 (2020)

Love Crossed, Book 7 (2020)

Love Twisted, Book 8 (2020)

Love Lies, Book 9 (2020)

Rise Again Warrior Series

Mission: Believe, Book 1 (Nov 2019)

** These books are also available on Audio